WEIRD WOMEN, WIRED WOMEN

Also by Kit Reed

WEIRD WOMEN, WIRED WOMEN

Kit Reed

Wesleyan University Press

Published by University Press of New England

Hanover and London

Wesleyan University Press
Published by University Press of New England,
Hanover, NH 03755
© 1998 by Kit Reed
All rights reserved
Printed in the United States of America
5 4 3 2 1
CIP data appear at the end of the book

Of the stories in this collection, most first appeared in *The Magazine of Fantasy and Science Fiction*; others appeared in *Omni, Asimov's SF* and *The Missouri Review*. "Winter" was anthologized in *The Norton Anthology of Contemporary Fiction*. Three are previously unpublished, and seven have never before been collected.

To the memory of my mother,
Lillian Hyde Craig,
who would have been proud.
And horrified.
And proud.

CONTENTS

FOREWORD

by Connie Willis

I read my first Kit Reed story when I was thirteen. I had just discovered science fiction and was working my way through every book in the library with a rocket-ship-and-atom logo on its spine when I picked up a copy of *The Year's Best Fantasy and Science Fiction, Second Series*. In it was a story called "The Wait," and it scared the spit out of me.

This was in the days when I was oblivious to the authors who wrote the stories (or possibly even to the fact that stories *had* authors), so I was unaware that it was a Kit Reed story. It was only later, when I had become an author myself and was asked, "Who's your favorite author?" and had gotten sick of saying, "There was this *great* story about a girl and her mother, and this town where they didn't believe in doctors . . . ," that I went back and rummaged through all the *Year's Best* collections and found out "The Wait" had been written by Kit Reed.

I also found, to my surprise and delight, that a good many of my other favorites—"Automatic Tiger" and "The New You" and "The Food Farm" —had also been written by Kit Reed.

From then on, of course, I looked for every Kit Reed story I could find, and read anything with her name on it. And jumped at the chance to write this foreword because it would give me the excuse to read everything all over again and maybe even find a story I hadn't read before.

I did. It was "Frontiers," which I had somehow missed the first time around. And reading it, reading "Last Fridays" and "Chicken Soup" for the second time and "The Wait" for the umpteenth, I realized something. All Kit Reed stories scare the spit out of you.

This is not just because Kit Reed is a master of horror, which she unquestionably is. She is frequently compared to Shirley Jackson, though she also calls to mind Hitchcock with her gift for taking the most benign and everyday things—puppies, balls of colored yarn, mother love—and revealing their dark undersides.

But there is more than horror here. Even when she is writing about werewolves, there is helplessness and regret as well as monstrousness, and the end of "The Wait" is serene as well as chilling.

And when Kit Reed writes in other veins—the sharp satire of "Like My Dress," or the Gracie Allenesque farce of "Cynosure," or the almost elegiac "Pilots of the Purple Twilight"—she still scares the spit of me.

It's because she sees things no one else does. She looks at the same things we all do—doting mothers and facelifts and furniture polish ads—and sees something new and strange. And disturbingly familiar.

She watches the Miss America pageant and sees, "On Behalf of the Product." Her mother comes to visit, and she composes, "The Mothers of Shark Island." "Empty Nest" is like no other empty-nest-syndrome story ever written, and when she looks at fat girls and rock-and-roll idols and teenage crushes, she sees entirely different dangers than would have occurred to the rest of us. We were worried about the harmful effects of Nelly's believing that Tommy Fango could actually *love* her. It never occurred to us that Nelly's fantasy was anything other than wish fulfillment. Or that the fulfilling of those wishes could have such terrible side effects.

But it isn't just that she sees something new in werewolves and liposuction and teenagers who believe they're adopted because they can't *possibly* be related to these people who *claim* to be their parents. It's also that she has a rare gift for constructing fantastic, metaphorical platforms from which to show us what she sees—the Food Farm, the Chateau d'If, the Hall of Faces, the compound where the wives wait endlessly for their missing men—making the subconscious visible and the intangible concrete. And an even rarer gift for taking totally familiar settings—kitchens and closets and sleepy Southern towns—and slowly, imperceptibly, changing them into something else.

What Reed most reminds me of is not Shirley Jackson or Hitchcock, but Philip K. Dick's "We Can Remember It for You Wholesale," a story in which the floor keeps falling out from under you to reveal another reality underneath, and another under that.

Only in a Kit Reed story, there isn't any floor below the floor below the floor. There is only the abyss.

In "The New You," a dumpy, insecure woman who wishes she could be svelte, beautiful, sophisticated, everything her husband ever wanted, answers a magazine ad and gets exactly that. In most people's hands, this would be a little fable about society's love of the false and the trivial, but for Kit Reed, that's only the surface. There are other surfaces below that, other floors. And basements and subbasements. And surprise after surprise.

What you think the story is about at first is almost invariably wrong. "Ah," you think, as you begin a story like "The Bride of Bigfoot." "This is a story about the repression of women and their need to be free." And, as you listen to the husband, it seems also to be about beasts both inside and outside the home, and you think, "Ah, an indictment of men and their notion of women as property." Those things are certainly there, but you'd better not relax and settle into statements and sympathies because it's all much more complicated than that, and more problematic.

Kit Reed's true genius lies in her ability to see straight through to the center of things. It's this clear-eyed ability to get below the surface and down to the reality—more than her flair for detail and dialogue, her quirky insights, her fantastical stage settings—that makes Kit Reed stories unique. She sees straight through to the truth. And understands just how complicated that truth is.

The love the mothers on Shark Island have for their children is both destructive and noble. The things women do to themselves in the Hall of Faces are sometimes worse than anything society does to them. You can both want and dread someone's return, and freedom and death, victimization and complicity, love and hate, are sometimes inextricably intertwined.

In "Songs of War," my favorite piece in this collection (I don't count "The Wait" because it's clear to me that, even after all these years and all those readings, I'll never have anything approaching critical detachment regarding it), Kit Reed uses her full arsenal of gifts to explore the women's movement. In anyone else's hands this story of women going to war for their rights and a better world would have become a polemic. Or an indictment.

But this is Kit Reed. Not only does she bring it vividly to life by envisioning it as an actual war, with smoke on the horizon and rebel encampments and gunfire, she also explores the subtleties of not altogether noble motives, reasons that are sometimes rationalizations, ambivalent yearnings for the impossible—a world where everyone is fulfilled and no one gets stuck with KP duty.

But she doesn't stop there, and this is not just about the women's movement. "Songs of War" is also about the mixed motives and muddy aspirations of all enlistees in all causes, the disillusionments and dreadful side effects and inevitable outcomes of all wars.

Kit Reed's subject matter is always the human condition, in all its complexity and absurdity. And, in *Weird Women, Wired Women*, she shows it to you in a way that will make you laugh, make you nervous, make you think. And leave you wanting more.

You'll also want to read her wonderful novels, *Tiger Rag* and *Fort Privilege* and *The Ballad of T. Rantula*, and her utterly original suspense novels (written under the name of Kit Craig), *Gone* and *Twice Burned*. And especially her short stories. They're also collected in *Thief of Lives* and *Other Stories and: The Attack of the Giant Baby* and *The Revenge of the Senior Citizens*. I particularly recommend "Mister da V" and "Final Tribute" and my absolute favorite Kit Reed story, "Great Escape Tours, Inc." And "The Vine" and "Judas Bomb" and "Attack of the Giant Baby."

I guarantee every one of them will surprise you, unsettle you, show you things you never thought of. And scare the spit out of you.

WHERE I'M COMING FROM

In adult life I have been in the hospital five times, all related to the fact that I've had three children. Biology may not be destiny, but it is unarguably a pain in the ass.

If you are a woman people expect certain things.

When I was little, people expected every woman to have a man. Fairy tales, movies, magazines, the way other people's parents regarded you made this clear. In the gauzy, hope-chest world that flourished in the dawn of the media explosion, every woman's daughter was born looking forward to her wedding. She worried about bad breath and other more "offensive" odors and used every conceivable product to make herself nice for him. When she found him! The search was the central activity of her life.

They met, they fell in love; when they went out together they would be gorgeous, he strong and handsome, she draped on his arm like a beautiful scarf. Marriages were happy endings and little girls didn't think much about what came after.

I found out what happened to a woman who lost her man after my father was declared missing in action, presumed lost in World War II. Overnight my mother and I were disenfranchised, unpeople in a society that marched two by two. Nobody said anything directly but it was somehow our fault; through some act of personal carelessness, we personally had lost our man. A tentative person at best, sweet and uncertain, my mother responded with a combination of toughness ("We have to do this alone") and terrifying vulnerability. She was the only person I had left, the one person I had that I knew I could count on; I was the only thing about her world that she could hope to control. She loved me but, One Woman Alone, she *worried*; would I fall short in some way and embarrass us all?

The resulting tension and ambiguity drive much of my work, perhaps most obviously "Chicken Soup," a horror story about the ultimate mother. An editor had asked me to "write about the thing that frightens you most."

And the sense of loss that propelled us, my mother and I, informs "Pilots of the Purple Twilight," in which women keep a perpetual vigil for

xiii

men at war who may or may not be interested in coming back to them. This is territory I explore further, and at length, in the novel *Little Sisters of the Apocalypse*.

Brought up to be the quintessential Southern lady, my newly widowed mother moved us several times, drove great distances, masterminded house renovations and car repair even as she tried to build me according to her own mother's antebellum expectations. She had been trained to live in a world that did not exist.

"Ladies" didn't work. "Ladies" didn't interrupt, never contradicted and were never "disagreeable." "Ladies" assumed older people were wiser simply because they were older. A knot of contradictions, she worried endlessly about appearances: "what will people *think?*"

My mother's relentless gentility, compounded by the social expectations of the Fifties, threw me into an automatic posture of rebellion. Educated by nuns, academics who had been spared the exigencies of housekeeping and child-rearing, I came up believing I could do anything I wanted. I decided—well before my college classmates noticed there was something going on—that you were what you did, not who you married; that if you tried you probably could have it all: the career, the marriage, the kids, what was the big deal? I would in my time get married and stay married, have two sons and a daughter and in fact fight my share of dirt backwash but for me, *housewife* was already a dirty word.

I went from college into the newspaper business, and when my last story had cleared the city desk, sat down uneasily at a card table at "bridge club" with other women just out of college. Expecting to keep their jobs only until they got married, they were deeply concerned with china and silver patterns, wedding showers and the social pecking order in our middlesized Florida city, where I was a crusty *old maid* at twenty-two.

If satire is the instrument of rebellion, I was loaded for bear.

Push reality a little bit in fiction and you underscore what the society is telling you about itself. Push it a little harder to make your point and you find that most editors are afraid of any thing that diverges from what they take to be real life. When you're a little bit weird, it makes conventional editors unhappy.

As I taught myself to write through trial and error and peppered magazines with my unconventional short stories, one group of editors did accept me—precisely because the stories were a little weird. Maybe people who edit speculative fiction are by nature experimental readers and editorial visionaries, or maybe from the beginning S-F editors understood that my stories of domestic terrors were set in a terrain as alien as the surface of any forbidden planet. The periodicals include *The Magazine of Fantasy and Science Fiction* (Anthony Boucher bought my first story in 1958 and just today Gordon Van Gelder bought the newest), *Asimov's SF, Omni, Missouri Review*. The two dozen anthologies where the stories appear include the *Norton Anthology of American Literature*.

You go where they'll take you. When the dark strain that goes through all my fiction runs too close to the surface the work finds a home under the aegis of S-F. Put science to one side here, unless you count anthropology.

Speculative fiction is the accurate term for what I do. Standing back from some thirty-plus years of work, I think that what I do in this particular group of—not feminist but certainly "womanist"—stories, by which I mean stories centered on women, is probably social criticism. At the time I thought I was making sense of things by writing about them.

What is interesting to me now is how many of these stories devolve on feminist concerns, and that my work went in this direction well before women in the Sixties threw out their hair spray and took a long look at their lives.

At twenty-three I wrote my first published short story, *The Wait*, which appeared in the *Magazine of Fantasy and Science Fiction* as the Fifties ran down. If Shirley Jackson's *The Lottery* is science fiction, then so is *The Wait*. A high school girl is used as a pawn by an insecure mother intent on fitting into a new society. A friend with an insider's knowledge of psychiatric establishments said, "You're very brave to write about your mother like that."

Wuow, is that what I was doing?

If so, then what has followed over the last three decades-plus is a fairly accurate representation of my attitudes in what I think of as prefeminist, feminist and postfeminist (as in postmodern) times. I can't stand back far enough to mark the spikes on the graph of the national feminist consciousness, but my sense is that I came early to the feast, sat at a reserved distance from the table and stayed long enough to see the dinner guests start squabbling among themselves, another story I need to write some day.

Most of us write better about what we hate and fear than about what we love, and it would appear that at some level I have always been afraid of my sisters' expectations, from the day in high school when I understood that I would never fit in with the girl gang to the moment when I pushed back from the bridge table with the sense that I'd blundered into a territory where I did not belong. If it was somehow my fault that I'd "lost" my father, was it my fault that I couldn't fit in? I wondered; I still do.

The stories I wrote in the late '50s and early '60s ("Empty Nest," "Cyno-sure," "The New You") are about women defined by their roles—the mother who loves her young no matter how hideous, the housewife who will do anything to protect her hardwood floors, the woman who will do anything to keep her man. In ads in the magazines and commercials on TV in those days the woman's face was pretty and wholesome, but wait. Was her upper lip always filmed with the sweat of anxiety, or was it only mine?

In the early Seventies my friends' lives caught up with the women's movement; women who had been living according to their mothers'—or was it their partners'—expectations were in full rebellion by that time. So, fine, and welcome. What took you so long? Career was an issue; so was the place where feminists stood in relation to other feminists. Lives changed. Marriages started to blow apart and in the lexicon of extrapolation it seemed logical for antagonists of both sexes to take to the streets with guns and clubs.

Other people went to consciousness-raising groups. I wrote "Songs of War."

Most of us have emerged in one piece into a world in which One Woman Alone not only survives but triumphs—too late for my mother, but not too late for the rest of us.

In spite of which, not that much has changed. The woman in print ads and TV commercials may wear jeans, but she's still pushing that mop or brandishing that bottle of lemon-scented dishwashing liquid while he wipes. Women still worry over pleasing the one they love and they worry about their looks; *plus ça change.*

If image figures in early Kit Reed stories like "The Food Farm" and "In Behalf of the Product," it also figures in the late. Someone I know had her face lifted twenty years too soon and I responded with "The Hall of New Faces." The perennial fashion parade inspired "Like My Dress," and I should report that like the committed and successful professional women who are among my best friends I happily shop 'til I drop and wonder what would happen if I let a surgeon cut my face up just a little bit. We don't only become what we behold. We who are writers behold what we have become.

And motherhood?

If we behold what we become, we also become what we behold. In some of our best moments, my friends and I used to sit around discussing our mothers. We vowed that we'd do anything to keep from being like that. When I look around I see that we are close to our adult sons and daughters. In fact, although my grown kids delight in telling me just what about their childhood—moments when I lost it, eggplant Parmesan, certain cakes—was *weird*, we're pretty good friends. Still, I saw myself in "The Weremother" and I recognize myself in "The Mothers of Shark Island." I don't have to stand back to see this, nor do I need a psychiatrically sophisticated friend to point out exactly who those women are poised on the cliff outside the Chateau D'If, wondering what heinous crime against society put them there. One of them is me.

Middletown,   *August 1997*
Connecticut

WEIRD WOMEN, WIRED WOMEN

THE WAIT

Penetrating a windshield blotched with decalcomanias of every tourist attraction from Luray Caverns to Silver Springs, Miriam read the road sign.

"It's Babylon, Georgia, Momma. Can't we stop?"

"Sure, sweetie. Anything you want to do." The little round, brindle woman took off her sunglasses. "After all, it's your trip."

"I know, Momma, I know. All I want is a popsicle, not the Grand Tour."

"Don't be fresh."

They were on their way home again, after Miriam's graduation trip through the South. (Momma had planned it for years, and had taken two months off, right in the middle of the summer, too, and they'd left right after high school commencement ceremonies. "Mr. Margulies said I could have the whole summer, because I've been with him and Mr. Kent for so long," she had said. "Isn't it wonderful to be going somewhere together, dear?" Miriam had sighed, thinking of her crowd meeting in drugstores and in movies and eating melted ice cream in the park all through the good, hot summer. "Yes," she'd said.)

Today they'd gotten off 301 somehow, and had driven dusty Georgia miles without seeing another car or another person, except for a Negro driving a tractor down the softening asphalt road, and two kids walking into a seemingly deserted country store. Now they drove slowly into a town, empty because it was two o'clock and the sun was shimmering in the streets. They *had* to stop, Miriam knew, on the pretext of wanting something cold to drink. They had to reassure themselves that there were other people in the town, in Georgia, in the world.

In the sleeping square, a man lay. He raised himself on his elbows when he saw the car, and beckoned to Miriam, grinning.

"Momma, see *that* place? Would you mind if I worked in a place like *that* ?" They drove past the drugstore, a chrome palace with big front windows.

"Oh, Miriam, don't start that again. How many times do I have to tell you, I don't want you working in a drugstore when we get back." Her mother made a pass at a parking place, drove once again around the square. "What do you think I sent you to high school for? I want you to go to Katie Gibbs this summer, and get a good job in the fall. What kind of boy friends do you think you can meet jerking sodas? You know, I don't want you to work for the rest of your life. All you have to do is get a good job, and you'll meet some nice boy, maybe from your office, and get married and never have to work again." She parked the car and got out, fanning herself. They stood under the trees, arguing.

"Momma, even if I *did* want to meet your nice people, I wouldn't have a thing to wear." The girl settled into the groove of the old argument. "I want some pretty clothes and I want to get a car. I know a place where you only have to pay forty dollars a month, I'll be getting thirty-five a week at the drugstore—"

"And spending it all on yourself, I suppose. How many times do I have to explain, nice people don't work in places like that. Here I've supported you, fed you, dressed you, ever since your father died, and now, when I want you to have a *nice* future, you want to throw it out of the window for a couple of fancy dresses." Her lips quivered. "Here I am practically dead on my feet, giving you a nice trip, and a chance to learn typing and short-hand and have a nice future—"

"Oh, Momma." The girl kicked at the sidewalk and sighed. She said the thing that would stop the argument. "I'm sorry. I'll like it, I guess, when I get started."

Round, soft, jiggling and determined, her mother moved ahead of her, trotting in too-high heels, skirting the square. "The main thing, sweetie, is to be a good girl. If boys see you behind a soda fountain, they're liable to get the wrong idea. They may think they can get away with something, and try to take advantage . . ."

In the square across the street, lying on a pallet in the sun, a young boy watched them. He called out.

". . . Don't pay any attention to him," the mother said. ". . . and if boys know you're a *good* girl, one day you'll meet one who will want to marry you. Maybe a big businessman, or a banker, if you have a good steno job. But if he thinks he can take advantage," her eyes were suddenly crafty, "he'll never marry you. You just pay attention. Don't ever let boys get away with anything. Like when you're on a date, do you ever—"

"Oh, Momma," Miriam cried, insulted.

"I'm sorry, sweetie, but I do so want you to be a *good* girl. Are you listening to me, Miriam?"

"Momma, that lady seems to be calling me. The one lying over there in the park. What do you suppose she wants?"

"I don't know. Well, don't just stand there. She looks like a nice woman. Go over and see if you can help her. Guess she's sunbathing, but it *does* look funny, almost like she's in bed. Ask her, Mirry. Go *on* !"

"Will you move me into the shade?" The woman, obviously one of the leading matrons of the town, was lying on a thin mattress. The shadow of the tree she was under had shifted with the sun, leaving her in the heat.

Awkwardly, Miriam tugged at the ends of the thin mattress, got it into the shade.

"And my water and medicine bottle too, please?"

"Yes ma'am. Is there anything the matter, ma'am?"

"Well." The woman ticked the familiar recital off on her fingers: "It started with cramps and—you know—lady trouble. Thing is, now my head burns all the time and I've got a pain in my left side, not burning, you know, but just sort of tingling."

"Oh, that's too bad."

"Well, has your mother there ever had that kind of trouble? What did the doctor prescribe? What would *you* do for my kind of trouble? Do you know anybody who's had anything like it? That pain, it starts up around my ribs, and goes down, sort of zigzag . . ."

Miriam bolted.

"Momma, I've changed my mind. I don't want a popsicle. Let's get you out of here, please. Momma?"

"If you don't mind, sweetie, I want a coke." Her mother dropped on a bench. "I don't feel so good. My head . . ."

They went into the drugstore. Behind the chrome and plate glass, it was like every drugstore they'd seen in every small town along the East Coast, cool and dim and a little dingy in the back. They sat at one of the small round wooden tables and a dispirited waitress brought them their order.

"What did Stanny and Bernice say when you told them you were going on a big tour?" Miriam's mother slurped at her Coke, breathing hard.

"Oh, they thought it was all right."

"Well, I certainly hope you tell them all about it when we get back. It's not every young girl gets a chance to see all the historical monuments. I bet Bernice has never been to Manassas."

"I guess not, Momma."

"I guess Stanny and that Mrs. Fyle will be pretty impressed when you get back and tell 'em where all we've been. I bet that Mrs. Fyle could never get Toby to go anywhere with her. Of course, they've never been as close as we've been."

"I guess not, Momma." The girl sucked and sucked at the bottom half of her popsicle, to keep it from dripping on her dress.

In the back of the store, a young woman in dirty white shorts held onto her little son's hand and talked to the waitress. The baby, about two, sat on the floor in gray, dusty diapers.

"Your birthday's coming pretty soon, isn't it?" She dropped the baby's hand.

"Yeah. Oh, you ought to see my white dress. Golly, Anne, hope I won't have to Wait too long. Anne, what was it like?"

The young woman looked away from her with the veiled face of the married, who do not talk about such things.

"Myla went last week, and she only had to stay for a couple of days. Don't tell anybody, because of course she's going to marry Harry next week, but she wishes she could see Him again . . ."

The young woman moved a foot, accidentally hit the baby. He snuffled and she helped him onto her lap, gurgling at him. In the front of the store, Miriam heard the baby and jumped. "Momma, come *on*. We'll never get to Richmond by night. We've already lost our way twice!" Her mother, dabbling her straw in the ice the bottom of her paper cup, roused herself. They dropped two nickels on the counter and left.

They skirted the square again, ignoring the three people who lay on the grass motioning and calling to them with a sudden urgency. Miriam got into the car.

"Momma, come *on* ! Momma!" Her mother was still standing at the door by the driver's seat, hanging onto the handle. Miriam slid across the front seat to open the door for her. She gave the handle an impatient twist and then started as she saw her mother's upper body and face slip past the window in a slow fall to the pavement. "Oh, I *knew* we never should have come!" It was an agonized, vexed groan. Red-faced and furious, she got out of the car, ran around to help her mother.

On their pallets in the park, the sick people perked up. Men and women were coming from everywhere. Cars pulled up and stopped and more people came. Kneeling on the pavement, Miriam managed to tug her mother into a prone position. She fanned her and talked to her, and when she saw she wasn't going to wake up or move, she looked at the faces above her in sudden terror.

"Oh please help me. We're alone here. She'll be all right, I think, once we get her inside. She's never fainted before. Please, someone get a doctor." Then, frantically, "I just want to get out of here."

"Why, honey, you don't need to do that. Don't you worry." A shambling, balding, pleasant man in his forties knelt beside her and put his hand on her shoulder. "We'll have her diagnosed and started on a cure in no time. Can you tell me what's been her trouble?"

"Not so far, Doctor."

"I'm not a doctor, honey."

"Not so far," she said dazedly, "except she's been awfully hot."

(Two women in the background nodded at each other knowingly.) "I thought it was the weather, but I guess it's fever." (The crowd was waiting.) "And she has an open place on her foot—got it while we were sightseeing in Tallahassee."

"Well honey, maybe we'd better look at it." The shoe came off and when it did, the men and women moved even closer, clucking and whispering about the wet, raw sore.

"If we could just get back to Queens," Miriam said. "If we could just get home, I know everything would be all right."

"Why, we'll have her diagnosed before you know it." The shambling man got up from his knees. "Anybody here had anything like this recently?" The men and women conferred in whispers.

"Well," one man said, "Harry Parkins's daughter had a fever like that, turned out to be pneumonia, but she never had nothin' like that on her foot. I reckon she ought to have antibiotics for that fever."

"Why, I had somethin' like that on my arm." A woman amputee was talking. "Wouldn't go away and wouldn't go away. Said I woulda died if they hadn't of done this." She waved the stump.

"We don't want to do anything like that yet. Might not even be the same thing," the bald man said. "Anybody else?"

"Might be tetanus."

"Could be typhoid, but I don't think so."

"Bet it's some sort of staphylococcus infection."

"Well," the bald man said, "since we don't seem to be able to prescribe just now, guess we'd better put her on the square. Call your friends when you get home tonight, folks, and see if any of them know about it; if not, we'll just have to depend on tourists."

"All right, Herman."

"B'bye, Herman."

"See ya, Herman."

"G'bye."

5

"The mother, who had come to during the dialog and listened with terrified fascination, gulped a potion and a glass of water the druggist had brought from across the street. From the furniture store came the messenger boy with a thin mattress. Someone else brought a couple of sheets, and the remainder of the crowd carried her into the square and put her down not far from the woman who had the lady trouble.

When Miriam last saw her mother, she was talking drowsily to the woman, almost ready to let the drug take her completely.

Frightened but glad to be away from the smell of sickness, Miriam followed Herman Clark down a side street. "You can come home with me, honey," he said. "I've got a daughter just about your age, and you'll be well taken care of until that mother of yours gets well." Miriam smiled, reassured, used to following her elders. "Guess you're wondering about our little system," Clark said, hustling her into his car. "What with specialization and all, doctors got so they were knowin' so little, askin' so much, chargin' so much. Here in Babylon, we found we don't really need 'em. Practically everybody in this town has been sick one way or another, and what with the way women like to talk about their operations, we've learned a lot about treatment. We don't need doctors any more. We just benefit by other people's experience."

"Experience?" None of this was real, Miriam was sure, but Clark had the authoritative air of a long-time parent, and she knew parents were always right.

"Why, yes. If you had chicken pox, and were out where everybody in town could see you, pretty soon somebody'd come along who had had it. They'd tell you what you had, and tell you what they did to get rid of it. Wouldn't even have to pay a doctor to write the prescription. Why, I used Silas Lapham's old nerve tonic on my wife when she had her bad spell. She's fine now; didn't cost us a cent except for the tonic. This way, if you're sick we put you in the square and you stay there until somebody happens by who's had your symptoms; then you just try his cure. Usually works fine. If not, somebody else'll be by. 'Course we can't let any of the sick folks leave the square until they're well; don't want anybody else catchin' it."

"How long will it take?"

"Well, we'll try some of the stuff Maysie Campbell used—and Gilyard Pinckney's penicillin prescription. If that doesn't work we may have to wait until a tourist happens through."

"But what makes the tourists ask and suggest?"

"Have to. It's the law. You come on home with me, honey, and we'll try to get your mother well."

Miriam met Clark's wife and Clark's family. For the first week she wouldn't unpack her suitcases. She was sure they'd be leaving soon, if she could just hold out. They tried Asa Whitleaf's tonic on her mother and doctored her foot with the salve Harmon Johnson gave his youngest when she had boils. They gave her Gilyard Pinckney's penicillin prescription.

"She doesn't seem much better," Miriam said to Clark one day. "Maybe if I could get her to Richmond or Atlanta to the hospital—"

"We couldn't let her out of Babylon until she's well, honey. Might carry it to other cities. Besides, if we cure her she won't send county health nurses back, trying to change our methods. And it might be bad for her to travel. You'll get to like it here, hon."

That night Miriam unpacked. Monday she got a job clerking in the dime store.

"You're the new one, huh?" The girl behind the jewelry counter moved over to her, friendly, interested. "You Waited yet? No, I guess not. You look too young yet."

"No, I've never waited on people. This is my first job," Miriam said confidentially.

"I didn't mean *that* kind of wait," the girl said with some scorn. Then, seemingly irrelevantly, "You're from a pretty big town, I hear. Probably already laid with boys and everything. Won't have to Wait."

"What do you mean? I never have. Never! I'm a *good* girl!" Almost sobbing, Miriam ran back to the manager's office. She was put in the candy department, several counters away. That night she stayed up late with a road map and a flashlight, figuring, figuring.

The next day the NO VISITORS sign was taken down from the tree in the park and Miriam went to see her mother.

"I feel terrible, sweetie, you having to work in the dime store while I'm out here under these nice trees. Now you just remember all I told you, and don't let any of these town boys get fresh with you. Just because you have to work in the dime store doesn't mean you aren't a nice girl and as soon as I can, I'm going to get you out of that job. Oh, I *wish* I was up and around."

"Poor Momma." Miriam smoothed the sheets and put a pile of movie magazines down by her mother's pillow. "How can you stand lying out here all day?"

"It isn't so bad, really. And y'know, that Whitleaf woman seems to know a little something about my trouble. I haven't really felt right since you were nine."

"Momma, I think we ought to get out of here. Things aren't right—"

"People certainly are being nice. Why, two of the ladies brought me some broth this morning."

Miriam felt like grabbing her mother and shaking her until she was willing to pick up her bedclothes and run with her. She kissed her good-bye and went back to the dime store. Over their lunch, two of the counter girls were talking.

"I go next week. I want to marry Harry Phibbs soon, so I sure hope I won't be there too long. Sometimes it's three years."

"Oh, you're pretty, Donna. You won't have too long to Wait."

"I'm kind of scared. Wonder what it'll be like."

"Yeah, wonder what it's like. I envy you."

Chilled for some reason, Miriam hurried past them to her counter and began carefully rearranging marshmallow candies in the counter display.

That night she walked to the edge of the town, along the road she and her mother had come in on. Ahead in the road she saw two gaunt men standing, just where the dusty sign marked the city limits. She was afraid to go near them and almost ran back to town, frightened, thinking. She loitered outside the bus station for some time, wondering how much a ticket out of the place would cost her. But of course she couldn't desert her mother. She was investigating the family car, still parked by the square, when Tommy Clark came up to her. "Time to go home, isn't it?" he asked, and they walked together back to his father's house.

"Momma, did you know it's almost impossible to get out of this town?" Miriam was at her mother's side a week later.

"Don't get upset, sweetie. I know it's tough on you, having to work in the dime store, but that won't be forever. Why don't you look around for a little nicer job, dear?"

"Momma, I don't mean that. I want to go home! Look, I've got an idea. I'll get the car keys from your bag here and tonight, just before they move you all into the courthouse to sleep, we'll run for the car and get away."

"Dear," her mother sighed gently. "You know I can't move."

"Oh Mother, can't you *try*?"

"When I'm a little stronger, dear, then maybe we'll try. The Pinckney woman is coming tomorrow with her daughter's herb tea. That should pep me up a lot. Listen, why don't you arrange to be down here? She has the best-looking son!—Miriam, you come right back here and kiss me goodbye."

8

Tommy Clark had started meeting Miriam for lunch. They'd taken in one movie together, walking home hand in hand in an incredible pink dusk. On the second date Tommy had tried to kiss her but she'd said, "Oh Tommy, I don't know the Babylon rules," because she knew it wasn't good to kiss a boy she didn't know very well. Handing Tommy half her peanut-butter sandwich, Miriam said, "Can we go to the ball game tonight? The American Legion's playing."

"Not tonight, kid. It's Margy's turn to go."

"What do you mean, turn to go?"

"Oh." Tommy blushed. "You know."

That afternoon right after she finished work, Tommy picked her up and they went to the party given for Herman Clark's oldest daughter. Radiant, Margy was dressed in white. It was her eighteenth birthday. At the end of the party, just when it began to get dark, Margy and her mother left the house. "I'll bring some stuff out in the truck tomorrow morning, honey," Clark said. "Take care of yourself." "Goodbye." "B'bye." "Happy Waitin', Margy!"

"Tommy, where is Margy going?" Something about the party and some-thing in Margy's eyes frightened Miriam.

"Oh, you know. Where they all go. But don't worry." Tommy took her hand. "She'll be back soon. She's pretty."

In the park the next day Miriam whispered in her mother's ear, "Momma, it's been almost a month now. Please, please, we *have* to go! Won't you please try to go with me?" She knelt next to her, talking ur-gently. "The car's been taken. I went back to check it over last night and it was gone. But I sort of think, if we could get out on the highway, we could get a ride. Momma, we've got to get out of here." Her mother sighed a lit-tle, and stretched. "You always said you never wanted me to be a bad girl, didn't you, Momma?"

The older woman's eyes narrowed. "You aren't letting that Clark boy take advantage—"

"No, Momma. No. That's not it at all. I just think I've heard something horrible. I don't even want to talk about it. It's some sort of law. Oh, Momma, please. I'm scared."

"Now, sweetie, you know there's nothing to worry about. Pour me a lit-tle water, won't you, dear? You know, I think they're going to cure me yet. Helva Smythe and Margaret Box have been coming in to see me every day, and they've brought some penicillin pills in hot milk that I think are really doing me some good."

"But Momma, I'm scared."

"Now dear, I've seen you going past with that nice Clark boy. The

9

Clarks are a good family and you're lucky to be staying with them. You just play your cards right and remember: be a good girl."

"Momma, we've got to get out."

"You just calm down, young lady. Now go back and be nice to that Tommy Clark. Helva Smythe says he's going to own his daddy's business some day. You might bring him out here to see me tomorrow."

"Momma!"

"I've decided. They're making me better, and we're going to stay here until I'm well. People may not pay you much attention in a big city, but you're really somebody in a small town." She smoothed her blankets complacently and settled down to sleep.

That night Miriam sat with Tommy Clark in his front porch swing. They'd started talking a lot to each other, about everything. ". . . so I guess I'll have to go into the business," Tommy was saying. "I'd kind of like to go to Wesleyan or Clemson or something, but Dad says I'll be better off right here, in business with him. Why won't they ever let us do what we want to do?"

"I don't know, Tommy. Mine wants me to go to Katherine Gibbs— that's a secretarial school in New York—and get a typing job this fall."

"You won't like that much, will you?"

"Uh-uh. Except now I'm kind of anxious to get back up there—you know, get out of this town."

"You don't like it here?" Tommy's face clouded. "You don't like me?"

"Oh Tommy, I like you fine. But I'm pretty grown up now, and I'd like to get back to New York and start in on a job. Why I got out of high school last month."

"No kidding. You only look about fifteen."

"Aw, I do not. I'll be eighteen next week—oh, I didn't want to tell you. I don't want your folks to have to do anything about my birthday. Promise you won't tell them."

"You'll be eighteen, huh. Ready for the Wait yourself. Boy, I sure wish *I* didn't know you!"

"Tommy! What do you mean? Don't you like me?"

"That's just the point, I *do* like you. A lot. If I were a stranger, I could break your Wait."

"Wait? What kind of wait?"

"Oh"—he blushed—"you know."

A week later, after a frustrating visit with her mother in the park, Miriam came home to the Clarks' and dragged herself up to her room. Even her mother had forgotten her birthday. She wanted to fling herself

on her pillow and sob until supper. She dropped on the bed, got up uneasily. A white, filmy, full-skirted dress hung on the closet door. She was
frightened. Herman Clark and his wife bustled into the room, wishing her
happy birthday. "The dress is for you." "You shouldn't have," she cried.
Clark's wife shooed him out and helped Miriam dress. She started downstairs with the yards of white chiffon whispering and billowing about her
ankles.

Nobody else at her birthday party was particularly dressed up. Some of
the older women in the neighborhood watched Tommy help Miriam cut
the cake, moist-eyed. "She hardly seems old enough—" "Doubt if she'll
have long to Wait." "Pretty little thing, wonder if Tommy likes her." "Bet
Herman Clark's son wishes *he* didn't know her," they said. Uneasily,
Miriam talked to them all, tried to laugh, choked down a little ice cream
and cake.

"G'bye, kid," Tommy said, and squeezed her hand. It was just beginning to get dark out.

"Where are you going, Tommy?"

"Nowhere, silly. I'll see you in a couple of weeks. May want to talk to
you about something, if things turn out."

The men had slipped, one by one, from the room. Shadows were getting
longer but nobody in the birthday-party room had thought to turn on the
lights. The women gathered around Miriam. Mrs. Clark, eyes shining,
came close to her. "And here's the best birthday present of all," she said,
holding out a big ball of brilliant blue string. Miriam looked at her, not understanding. She tried to stammer a thank you. "Now dear, come with me."
Clark's wife and Helva Smythe caught her by the arms and gently led her
out of the house, down the gray street. "I'm going to see if we can get you
staked out near Margy," she said. They started off into the August twilight.

When they came to the field, Miriam first thought the women were still
busy at a late harvest, but she saw that the maidens, scores of them, were
just sitting on little boxes at intervals in the seemingly endless field. There
were people in the bushes at the field's edge—Miriam saw them. Every
once in a while one of the men would start off, following one of the bril-
liantly colored strings toward the woman who sat at the end of it, in a white
dress, waiting. Frightened, Miriam turned to Mrs. Clark. "Why am I here?
Why? Mrs. Clark, explain!"

"Poor child's a little nervous. I guess we all were, when it happened to
us," Clark's wife said to Helva Smythe and Helva nodded. "It's all right,

dear, you just stand here at the edge and watch for a little while, until you get used to the idea. Remember, the man must be a stranger. We'll be out with the truck with food for you and Margy during visitors' time Sunday. That's right. And when you go out there, try to stake out near Margy. It'll make the Wait nicer for you."

"*What* wait?"

"The Wait of the Virgins, dear. Goodbye."

Dazed, Miriam stood at the edge of the great domed field, watching the little world crisscrossed by hundreds of colored cords. She moved a little closer, trying to hide her cord under her skirts, trying not to look like one of them. Two men started toward her, one handsome, one unshaven and hideous, but when they saw she had not yet entered the field they dropped back, waiting. Sitting near her, she saw one of the dime-store clerks, who had quit her job two weeks back and suddenly disappeared. She was fidgeting nervously, casting her eyes at a young man ranging the edge of the field. As Miriam watched, the young man strode up her cord, without speaking threw money into her lap. Smiling, the dime-store girl stood up, and the two went off into the bushes. The girl nearest Miriam, a harelip with incredibly ugly skin, looked up from the half-finished sweater she was knitting.

"Well, there goes another one," she said to Miriam. "Pretty ones always go first. I reckon one day there won't be any pretty ones here, and then I'll go." She shook out her yarn. "This is my fortieth sweater." Not understanding, Miriam shrank away from the ugly girl. "I'd even be glad for old Fats there," she was saying. She pointed to a lewd-eyed old man hovering near. "Trouble is, even old Fats goes for the pretty ones. Heh! You ought to see it, when he goes up to one of them high-school queens. Heh! Law says they can't say no!" Choking with curiosity, stiff, trembling, Miriam edged up to the girl.

"Where . . . where do they go?"

The harelip looked at her suspiciously. Her white dress, tattered and white no longer, stank. "Why, you really don't know, do you?" She pointed to a place near them, where the bushes swayed. "To lay with them. It's the law."

"Momma! Mommamoommamomma!" With her dress whipping at her legs, Miriam ran into the square. It was well before the time when the sick were taken to sleep in the hall of the courthouse.

"Why, dear, how pretty you look!" the mother said. Then, archly, "They always say, wear white when you want a man to propose."

"Momma, we've got to get out of here." Miriam was crying for breath.

"I thought we went all over that."

"Momma, you always said you wanted me to be a good girl. Not ever to let any man take advan—"

"Why, dear, of course I did."

"Momma, don't you see! You've got to help me—we've got to get out of here, or somebody *I don't even know* . . . Oh, Momma, please. I'll help you walk. I saw you practicing the other day, with Mrs. Pinckney helping you."

"Now, dear, you just sit down here and explain to me. Be calm."

"Momma, *listen*! There's something every girl here has to do when she's eighteen. You know how they don't use doctors here, for anything?" Embarrassed, she hesitated. "Well, you remember when Violet got married, and she went to Dr. Dix for a checkup?"

"Yes, dear—now calm down, and tell Momma."

"Well, it's sort of a *checkup*, don't you see, only it's like graduating from high school too, and it's how they . . . see whether you're any good."

"What on earth are you trying to tell me?"

"Momma, you have to go to this field, and sit there, and sit there until a man throws money in your lap. *Then you have to go into the bushes and lie with a stranger!*" Hysterical, Miriam got to her feet, started tugging at the mattress.

"You just calm down. Calm down!"

"But Mother, I want to do like you told me. I want to be good!"

Vaguely, her mother started talking. "You said you were dating that nice Clark boy? His father is a real-estate salesman. Good business, dear. Just think, you might not even have to work—"

"Oh, Momma!"

"And when I get well I could come live with you. They're very good to me here—it's the first time I've found people who really *cared* what was wrong with me. And if you were married to that nice, solid boy, who seems to have such a *good* job with his father, why we could have a lovely house together, the three of us."

"Momma, we've got to get *out* of here. I can't do it. I just *can't*." The girl had thrown herself on the grass again.

Furious, her mother lashed out at her. "Miriam. Miriam Elise Holland. I've fed you and dressed you and paid for you and taken care of you ever since your father died. And you've always been selfish, selfish, selfish. Can't you ever do anything for me? First I want you to go to secretarial school, to get a nice opening, and meet nice people, and you don't want to do that. Then you get a chance to settle in a good town, with a *nice* family, but you don't even want that. You only think about yourself. Here I have a chance to get well at last, and settle down in a really nice town, where good families live, and see you married to the right kind of boy." Rising on her elbows, she glared at the girl. "Can't you ever do anything for *me*?"

"Momma, Momma, you don't *understand*!"

"I've known about the Wait since the first week we came here." The woman leaned back on her pillow. "Now pour me a glass of water and go back and do whatever Mrs. Clark tells you."

"Mother!"

Sobbing, stumbling, Miriam ran out of the square. First she started toward the edge of town, running. She got to the edge of the highway, where the road signs were, and saw the two shabby, shambling men, apparently in quiet evening conversation by the street post. She doubled back and started across a neatly plowed field. Behind her, she saw the Pinckney boys. In front of her, the Campbells and the Dodges started across the field. When she turned toward town, trembling, they walked past her, ignoring her, on some business of her own. It was getting dark.

She wandered the fields for most of the night. Each one was blocked by a Campbell or a Smythe or a Pinckney; the big men carried rifles and flashlights, and called out cheerfully to each other when they met, and talked about a wild fox hunt. She crept into the Clarks' place when it was just beginning to get light out, and locked herself in her room. No one in the family paid attention to her storming and crying as she paced the length and width of the room.

That night, still in the bedraggled, torn white dress, Miriam came out of the bedroom and down the stairs. She stopped in front of the hall mirror to put on lipstick and repair her hair. She tugged at the raveled sleeves of the white chiffon top. She started for the place where the virgins Wait. At the field's edge Miriam stopped, shuddered as she saw the man called old Fats watching her. A few yards away she saw another man, young, lithe, with bright hair, waiting. She sighed as she watched one woman, with a tall, loose boy in jeans, leave the field and start for the woods.

She tied her string to a stake at the edge of the great domed field. Threading her way among the many bright-colored strings, past waiting girls in white, she came to a stop in a likely-looking place and took her seat.

—1958

THE NEW YOU

"Now—The New You," the ad said. It was a two-page spread in one of the glossier fashion magazines, and it was accompanied by a shadowed, grainy art shot that hinted at the possibility of a miraculous transformation which hovered at every woman's fingertips.

Raptly, Martha Merriam hunched over the magazine, tugging at her violet-sprigged housedress so that it almost covered her plump knees. She contemplated the photograph, the list of promises framed in elegant italics, unaware as she did so that her mouth was working, gnawing a strand of dirty, dun-colored hair.

In her more wistful, rebellious moments, Martha Merriam forgot her dumpy body and imagined herself the svelte, impeccable Marnie, taller by six inches and lighter by forty pounds. When a suaver, better-dressed woman cut her at a luncheon or her husband left her alone at parties she would retreat into dialogs with Marnie. Marnie knew just the right, devastating thing to say to chic, overconfident women, and Marnie was expert in all the wiles that keep a man at home. In the person of Marnie, Martha could pretend.

"Watch the Old You Melt Away," Martha read, and as she mouthed the words for the second time Marnie strained inside her, waiting for release. Martha straightened imperceptibly, patting her doughy throat with a stubby hand, and as her eyes found the hooker—the price tag for the New You in small print in the lower right-hand corner—longing consumed her, and Marnie took over.

"We could use a New You," Marnie said.

"But three thousand dollars." Martha nibbled at the strand of hair.

"You have those stocks."

"But those were Howard's wedding present to me—part of his *business*."

"He won't mind . . ." Marnie twisted and became one with the photograph.

"But a hundred shares . . ." The hank of hair was sodden now, and Martha was chewing faster.

"He won't mind when he sees us," Marnie said.

And Martha, eyes aglow, got up and went to the telephone almost without realizing what she was doing, and got her broker on the line.

The New You arrived two weeks later, as advertised, and when it came Martha was too excited to touch it, alone in the house as she was, with this impossibly beautiful future.

In mid-afternoon, when she had looked at the coffin-shaped crate from every possible angle and smoothed the rough, splintered edges of the wood, she nerved herself to pull the ripcord the company had provided—and let her future begin. She jumped back with a squeak as the hard crate sides fell away to reveal a black and richly molded box. Trembling, she twiddled the gold-plated clasp with the rosebud emblem and opened the lid.

For a moment, all she saw was an instruction booklet, centered on top of fold upon fold of purple tissue paper, but as she looked closer she saw that the paper was massed to protect a mysterious, promising form which lay beneath.

IMPORTANT: READ THIS BEFORE PROCEEDING,
the booklet warned. Distracted, she threw it aside, reflecting as she did so that the last time she had seen paper folded in this way was around long-stemmed American Beauties, a dozen roses Howard had sent her a dozen years before.

The last piece of paper came way in her fingers, revealing the figure beneath, and Martha gasped. It was a long-stemmed American Beauty—everything she had hoped for. She recognized her own expression in its face, but it was a superb, glamorous version of her face, and at the same time it was Marnie, Helen, Cleopatra—more than she had dared anticipate. It was the new her. Quivering with impatience to get into it, she bent over it without another thought for the instruction book and plunged her arms to the elbows in the rustling, rising swirl of purple tissue paper. The sudden aura of perfume, the movement of the paper, a sense of mounting excitement overcame her and the last thing she remembered was clasping the figure's silken hands into her own stubby fingers and holding them to her bosom as the two figures, new and old, tossed on a rushing purple sea. Then the moiling sheets of purple kaleidoscoped and engulfed her and she lost consciousness.

She was awakened by a squashy thud. She lay in the midst of the purple tissue, stretching luxuriously, thinking that she ought to get up to see what the thud had been. She raised one knee, in the beginning of a move to get to her feet, and then stopped, delighted by the golden sleekness of the knee. She stretched the leg she knew must be just beyond that perfect knee and then hugged shoulders as lithe and smooth as those of a jungle cat, expanding in a gradual awareness of what had happened. Then, remembering that the new her was quite naked and that Howard would be home any minute, she pulled herself together in one fluid glide of muscles and got to her feet. With the air of a queen, she lifted one foot delicately and stepped out of the box.

She remembered the line from the advertisement, "Watch the Old You Melt Away," and she smiled languidly as she flowed away from the box. Yawning, she reached in the closet, picked up her old quilted wrapper and discarded it for the silk kimono Howard had brought her from Japan. It had fitted her ten years before and then it had gotten too small. She looped the sash twice around her middle and then—still not too good to be an orderly housewife—she began folding the tissue paper that seemed to have exploded all over the room. As she came to the side where the old her had first touched the gold-plated rosebud, she swooped up a whole armful of tissue in a gesture of exuberance—and dropped it with a little scream. Her toe had hit something. Not wanting to look, she poked at the remaining pieces of paper with a gilded toenail. Her foot connected with something soft. She made herself look down. And stifled a moan.

The old her had not melted away. It was still there, dowdy as ever in its violet-sprigged housedress. Its drab hair trailed like seaweed and its hips seemed to spread where it lay, settling on the rug.

"But you promised!" the new, sleek Martha yelped. With a sudden sinking feeling, she rooted around in the rest of the purple tissue until she found the castoff instruction book.

"Care must be exercised in effecting the transfer," the book warned in urgent italics. Then it went on with a number of complicated technical directions about transfer and grounding, which Martha didn't understand. When she had grasped the new her's hands she had plunged right into the transfer without a thought for the body she was leaving behind. And it had to be dematerialized at the time of transfer, no later. It was pointless to send botched jobs back to the company, the booklet warned. The company would send them back. Apparently, the new Martha was stuck with the old her.

"Oh . . ." There was a little moan from the figure on the floor. And the old Martha sat up and looked dully around the room.

"You—" the new Martha looked at it in growing hatred. "You leave me alone," she said. She was about to lunge at it in a fit of irritation when there was a sound in the driveway. "Oh-oh. Howard." Without another thought, she pushed the lumpy, unresisting old her into the hall closet, locked it in and pocketed the key.

Then, pulling the robe around her, she went to the door. "Howard, darling," she began.

He recognized her and he didn't recognize her. He stood just inside the doorway with the look of a child who has just been given his own soda fountain, listening as she explained (leaving out certain details: the sale of his stock, the matter of the old her) in vibrant, intimate tones.

"Martha, darling," he said at last, pulling her toward him.

"Call me Marnie, dear. Hm?" She purred, and nestled against his chest.

Of course the change involved a new wardrobe and new things for Howard too, as Marnie had read in a dozen glamour magazines how important an accessory a well-dressed man could be. The Merriams were swept up in a round of parties and were admitted, for the first time, to the city's most glittering homes. Howard's business flourished and Marnie, surrounded by admirers, Marnie, far more attractive than the most fashionable of her rivals, thrived. There were parties, meetings, theater dates, luncheon engagements and a number of attractive men. And what with one thing and another, Marnie didn't have much time for piddling around the house. The black box from the New You Company lay where she had left it, and the old her was still stacked (like an old vacuum cleaner, as Marnie saw it, outmoded and unused) in the closet in the hall.

In the second week of her new life, Marnie began to notice things. The tissue paper around the New You box was disarrayed, and the instruction book was gone. Once, when she had stepped out of the bedroom for a moment, she thought she saw a shadow moving in the hall. "Oh, it's you," Howard said with an ambiguous look when she returned to their room. "For a minute I thought . . ." He sounded almost wistful.

And there were crumbs—little trails of them—and empty food containers left in odd corners of the house.

Disturbed by the dirt which had begun to collect, Marnie refused two luncheon dates and a cocktail invitation and spent one of her rare afternoons at home. In slippers and the quilted house coat she had discarded the first day of her transformation, she began to clean the house. She was outraged to find a damp trail leading from the kitchen to the hall closet. With a rug-cleaning preparation she began scrubbing at the hall carpet, and she straightened her back, indignant, when she reached a particularly sordid little mixture of crumbs right at the closet door. Fumbling in her pocket, she brought out the key and applied herself to the lock.

"You," she said disgustedly. She had almost forgotten.

"Yes—yes ma'am," the old her said humbly, almost completely cowed. The dumpy, violet-sprigged Martha was sitting in one corner of the closet, a milk carton in one hand and a box of marshmallow cookies open in her lap.

"Why can't you just . . . Why can't you . . ." Marnie snorted in disgust. There was chocolate at the corners of the creature's mouth, and it had gained another five pounds.

"A body has to live," the old her said humbly, trying to wipe away the chocolate. "You forgot—I had a key to the closet too."

"If you're going to be wandering around," Marnie said, tapping one fingernail on a flawless tooth, "you might as well be of some use. Come on," she said, pulling at the old her. "We're going to clear out the old maid's room. Move!"

The old Martha came to its feet and shambled behind Marnie, making little sounds of obedience.

The experiment was a flop. The creature ate constantly and had a number of (to Marnie) disgusting habits, and when Marnie invited some of Howard's more attractive business contacts in for dinner, it refused to wear a maid's cap and apron, and made a terrible mess of serving the soup. When she called it down at table, Howard protested mildly, but Marnie was too engrossed in conversation with a Latin type who dealt in platinum to notice. Nor did she notice, in the days that followed, that Howard was putting on weight. She was slimmer than she had been in the first day of her new life and she stalked the house impatiently, nervous and well groomed as a high-bred horse. Howard seemed unusually quiet and withdrawn and Marnie laid it to the effect of having the Old Her around, flat-footed and quiet in its violet-sprigged dress. When she caught it feeding Howard fudge cake at the kitchen table the very day she found he could no longer button his tuxedo, she knew the Old Her had to go.

She had a Dispos-al installed in her kitchen sink and began a quiet investigation into the properties of various poisons, in hopes of finding a permanent way of getting rid of it. But when she brought a supply of sharp-edged instruments into the house the violet-sprigged Martha seemed to sense what she was planning. It stood in front of her, wringing its hands humbly until she noticed it.

"Well?" Marnie said, perhaps more sharply than she had intended.

"I—just wanted to say you can't get ride of me that way," it offered, almost apologetically." What way?" Marnie asked, trying to cover, and then, with a little gesture of indifference, she raised one eyebrow. "OK, smarty, why not?"

"Killing's against the law," the creature said patiently.

"This would hardly be killing," Marnie said in her most biting tones. "It's like giving your old clothes to the rag man or the Goodwill or burning them. Getting rid of old clothes has never been murder."

"Not murder," the old her said, and it produced the instruction book. Patiently, it guided Marnie's eyes over the well-thumbed pages to a paragraph marked in chocolate. "Suicide."

Desperate, she gave it a thousand dollars and a ticket to California.

And for a few days, the gay life went on as it had before. The Merriams were entertained or entertaining day and night now, and Howard hardly had time to notice that the quiet old Martha was missing. Marnie's new autochef made her dinner parties the talk of the city's smarter social set, and she found herself the center of an inexhaustible crowd of attentive, handsome young men in tuxedos. While Howard had abandoned the old her at parties, she saw little more of him now because the good-looking young men adored her too much to leave her alone. She was welcome in the very best places and there wasn't a woman in town who dared exclude her from her invitation list. Marnie went everywhere.

If she was dissatisfied, it was only because Howard seemed lumpier and less attractive than usual, and the bumps and wrinkles in his evening clothes made him something less than the perfect accessory. She slipped away from him early in the evening each time they went out together and she looked for him again only in the small hours, when it was time to go home.

But for all that she still loved him, and it came as something of a blow when she discovered that it was no longer she who avoided him at parties—he was avoiding her. She first noticed it after an evening of dinner and dancing. She had been having a fascinating conversation with someone in consolidated metals and it seemed to her the right touch, the final fillip, for the evening would be for the gentleman in question to see her standing next to Howard in the soft light, serene, beautiful, the doting wife.

"You must meet my husband," she murmured, stroking the metal magnate's lapel.

"Have you seen Howard?" she asked a friend nearby, and something in the way the friend shook his head and turned away from her made her uneasy.

Several minutes later the metal magnate had taken his sleeve and

Marnie was still looking for Howard. She found him at last, on a balcony, and she could have sworn that she saw him wave to a dark figure which touched its hands to its lips and disappeared into the bushes just as she closed the balcony door.

"It's not very flattering, you know," she said, coiling around his arm.

"Mmmmm?" He hardly looked at her.

"Having to track you down like this," she said, fitting against him.

"Mmmmmm?"

She started to go on, but instead led him through the apartment and down to the front door. Even in the cab, she couldn't shake his reverie. She tucked his coat tails into a cab with a solicitous little frown. And she brooded. There had been something disturbingly familiar about that figure on the balcony.

The next morning Marnie was up at an unaccustomed hour, dressing with exquisite care. She had been summoned to a morning coffee with Edna Hotchkiss-Baines. For the first time, she had been invited to help with the Widows' and Orphans' Bazaar. ("I've found somebody wonderful to help with the planning," the chichi Edna had confided. "You'll never guess who.")

Superb in an outfit that could withstand even Edna's scrutiny, Marnie presented herself at the Hotchkiss-Baines door and followed the butler into the Hotchkiss-Baines breakfast room.

Edna Hotchkiss-Baines barely greeted her. She was engrossed in conversation with a squat, unassuming figure that slumped across the table from her, shoes slit to accommodate feet that were spreading now, violet-sprigged dress growing a little tight.

Face afire, Marnie fell back. She took a chair without speaking and leveled a look of hatred at the woman who held the town's most fashionable social leader enthralled—the dowdy, frumpy, lumpy, old her.

It was only the beginning. Apparently the creature had cashed in the California ticket and used the fare and the thousand dollars to rent a small flat and buy a modest wardrobe. Now, to Marnie's helpless fury, it seemed to be going everywhere. It appeared at cocktail parties in a series of matronly crepe dresses ranging in color from taupe to dove gray. It sat on the most important committees and appeared at the most elegant dinners. No matter how exclusive the guest list or how festive the company, no matter how high Marnie's hopes that it had not been included, somebody had always invited it. It appeared behind her in clothing-store mirrors when she was trying on new frocks and looked over her shoulder in restaurants when she dined with one of her devastating young men. It haunted her steps, looking just enough like her to make everyone uncomfortable, enough like everything Marnie hated to embarrass her.

Then one night she found Howard kissing it at a party.

At home a few hours later, he confronted her. "Marnie, I want a divorce."

"Howard." She made clutching motions. "Is there . . ."

He sounded grave. "My dear, there's someone else. Well, it isn't exactly someone else."

"You don't mean . . . Howard, you can't be serious."

"I'm in love with the girl I married," he said. "A quiet girl, a grey-and-brown girl."

"That—" Her fashionable body was trembling. Her gemlike eyes were aflame. "That frumpy . . ."

"A home girl . . ." He was getting rhapsodic now. "Like the girl I married so many years ago."

"After all that money—the transformation—the new body—" Marnie's voice rose with every word. "—the CHANGE?"

"I never asked you to change, Marnie." He smiled mistily. "You were so . . ."

"You'd drop me for that piece of suet?" She was getting shrill. "How could I face my *friends*?"

"You deserve somebody better looking," he said with a little sigh. "Somebody tall and slim. I'll just pack and go . . ."

"All right, Howard." She managed a noble tone. "But not just yet." She was thinking fast. "There has to be a Decent Waiting Period . . ."

A period that would give her time to handle this.

"If you wish, my dear." He had changed into his favorite flannel bathrobe. In times past, the old Martha had sat next to him on the couch in front of the television, she in her quilted house coat, he in his faithful robe. He stroked its lapels. "I just want you to realize that my mind is made up—we'll all be happier . . ."

"Of course," she said, and a hundred plans went through her mind. "Of course."

She sat alone for the rest of the night, drumming opalescent nails on her dressing-table, tapping one slender foot.

And by morning, she had it. Something Howard had said had sent her mind churning. "You deserve somebody better looking."

"He's right," she said aloud. "I do."

And by the time it had begun to get light she had conceived of a way to get rid of the persistent embarrassment of the old her and the—*homier* elements of Howard at one stroke. As soon as Howard left for the office she began a series of long-distance inquiries, and once she had satisfied her curiosity she called a number of friends and floated several discreet loans in the course of drinks over lunch.

There was a crate in the living room just two weeks later. "Howard," Marnie said, beckoning. "I have a surprise for you . . ."

He was just coming in, with the old Martha, from a date. They liked to sit in the kitchen over cocoa and talk. At a look from Marnie, the old Martha settled in a chair. It couldn't take its eyes off the coffin-shaped box. Howard stepped forward, brows wrinkling furrily. "What's this?" he asked, and then without waiting for her to answer, he murmured, "Didn't we have one of these around a few months ago?" and pulled the cord attached to the corner of the crate. It fell open—perhaps a little too easily—and the lid of the smooth ebony box sprang up under his fingers almost before he had touched the rosebud catch. The tissue paper was green this time, and if there had been an instruction book nestled on top, it was gone now.

Both the new Marnie and the old her watched raptly as Howard, oblivious of them both, broke through the layers of tissue paper and with a spontaneous sound of pleasure grasped the figure in the box.

Both the new and the old woman watched as the papers began to swirl and rise, and they sat transfixed until there was a thud and the papers settled again.

When it was over, Marnie turned to the old her with a malicious grin. "Satisfied?" she asked. And then, eyes gleaming, she waited for the new Howard to rise from the box.

He came forth like a new Adam, ignoring both of them, and went to his own room for clothes.

While he was gone the old Howard, a little frayed at the corners, almost buried under a fall of tissue, stirred and tried to rise.

"That's yours," Marnie said, giving the old her a dig in the ribs. "Better help it up." And then she presented herself, facing the doorway, waiting with arms spread for the new Howard to reappear. After a few moments he came, godlike in one of Howard's pinstriped business suits.

"Darling," Marnie murmured, mentally canceling the dinner at the Hotchkiss-Bainses' and a Westport party with a new man.

"Darling," the new Howard said. And he swept past her to the old Martha, still scrabbling around in the tissue paper on the floor. Gently, with the air of a prince who has discovered his Cinderella, he helped her to her feet.

"Shall we go?"

Marnie watched, open-mouthed.

They did.

On the floor, the old Howard had gotten turned on its stomach somehow, and was floundering like a displaced fish. Marnie watched, taut with rage, too stricken to speak. The old Howard flapped a few times, made it to its knees and then slipped on the tissue paper again. Hardly looking at it, Marnie smoothed the coif she had prepared for the Hotchkiss-Baines dinner that night. There was always the dinner—and there was the party in Westport. Dispassionately, she moved forward and kicked a piece of tissue out of the way. She drew herself up, supple, beautiful, and she seemed to find new strength. The old Howard flapped again.

"Oh, get *up*," she said, and poked it with her toe. She was completely composed now. "Get up—*darling*," she spat.

—1962

CYNOSURE

"Now Polly Ann, Mrs. Brainerd might not like children, so I want you to go into the bedroom with Puff and Ambrose till we find out."

Polly Ann pulled her ruffles down over her ten-year-old paunch and picked up the cat, sausage curls bobbing as she went. "Yes Mama." She closed the bedroom door behind her and opened it again with a juicy, preadolescent giggle. "Ambrose made a puddle on the rug."

The three-note door chime sounded: Bong BONG Bong.

Norma motioned frantically. "Never *mind.*"

"All *ri*-ight." The door closed on Polly Ann.

Then, giving her aqua faille pouf pillows a pat and running her hand over the limed oak television set, Norma Thayer, housewife, went to answer the door.

She had been working at being a housewife for years. She cleaned and cooked and went to PTA and bought every single new appliance advertised and just now she was a little sensitive about the whole thing because clean as she would, her husband had just left her and there wasn't even an Other Woman to take the blame. Norma would have to be extra careful about herself from now on, being divorced as she was—especially now, when she and Polly Ann were getting started in a new neighborhood. They had a good start, really, because their new house in the development looked almost exactly like all the others in the block, except for being pink, and her furniture was the same shape and style as all the other furniture in all the other living rooms, right down to the Formica dinette set visible in the dining area; she knew because she had gone around in the dark one night and looked. But at the same time, she and Polly Ann didn't have a Daddy to come home at five o'clock like all the other houses did, and even though she and Polly Ann marked their house with wrought-iron numbers and put their garbage out in pastel plastic cans, even though they had centered their best lamp in the picture window and the kitchen was every bit as cute as the brochure said it was, the lack of a Daddy to put out the garbage and pot around in the yard on Saturdays and Sundays just like everybody else had put Norma at a distinct disadvantage.

Norma knew just as well as anybody on the block that a house was still a house without a Daddy, and things might even run smoother in the long run without all those cigarette butts and dirty pajamas to pick up, but she was something of a pioneer because she was the first in the neighborhood to actually prove it out.

Now her next-door neighbor was paying her first visit and Norma's housewifely heart began to swell. If all went well, Mrs. Brainerd would look at the sectional couch and the rug of salt-and-pepper cotton tweed (backed with rubber foam) and see that Daddy or no, Norma was just as good as any of the housewives in the magazines, and that her dish-towels were just as clean as any in the neighborhood. Then Mrs. Brainerd would offer her a recipe and invite her to the next day's morning coffee hour which, if she recollected properly, would be held at Mrs. Dowdy's, the lime split-level in the next block.

Patting the front of her Swirl housedress, she opened the door.

"Hello, Mrs. Brainerd."

"Hello," Mrs. Brainerd said. "Call me Clarice." She rubbed her hand along the lintel. "Woodwork looks real nice."

"Xerox," Norma said with a proud little smile, and let her in. "Brassit on the doorknob," Mrs. Brainerd said.

"Works like a dream. I made some coffee," Norma said. "And a cake . . ."

"Never touch cake," Mrs. Brainerd said.

"No greasy feel . . ."

"Metrecookies," Mrs. Brainerd said, and her jaw was white and firm. "And no sugar for me. Sucaryl."

"If you'll just sit down here." Norma patted the contour chair.

"Thanks, no." Mrs. Brainerd smoothed *her* Swirl housedress and followed Norma into the kitchen.

She was small, slender, lipsticked and perfumed, and she was made of steel. Norma noticed with a guilty pang that Mrs. Brainerd fastened the neck of her housedress with a Sweetheart pin.

"Something special," Mrs. Brainerd said, noticing her looking at it. "Got it with labels from the Right Kind of Margarine." She brushed past Norma, not even looking at the darling little dining area. "Hmm. Stains even bleach can't reach," she went on, peering into the sink.

Norma flushed. "I know. I scrubbed and scrubbed. I even used straight liquid bleach." She hung her head.

"Well." Clarice Brainerd reached into the pocket of her flowered skirt and came up with a shaker can. "Here," she said. She said it with a beautiful smile.

Norma recognized the brand. "Oh," she said, almost weeping with gratitude.

Clarice Brainerd had already turned to go. "And the can is decorated, so you'd be proud to have it in your living room."

"I know," Norma said, deeply moved. "I'll get two."

Her neighbor was at the back door now. Norma reached out, supplicating. "You're not leaving are you, before you even taste my cake . . ."

"You just try that cleanser," Clarice said. "And I'll be back."

"The morning coffee. I thought you might want me to come to the . . ."

"Maybe next time," her neighbor said, trying to be kind. "You know, you might have to entertain them here one day, and . . ." She looked significantly at the sink. "Just use that," she said reassuringly. "And I'll be back."

"I will." Norma bit her lip, torn between hope and despair. "Oh, I will."

"Cake," said Polly Ann just as the back door closed on Mrs. Brainerd's mechanically articulated smile. She came into the kitchen with Puff the kitten and Ambrose the beagle, trailing dust and hairs behind. "I think Ambrose might be sick." She got herself some grape juice, spilling as she poured. A purple stain began to spread on the sink.

Norma reached out with the cleanser, wanting desperately to ward off the stain.

"He just did it again in the living room," Polly Ann said. Norma's breath was wrenched from her in a sob. "Oh, *no*." Putting the cleanser in the little coaster she kept for just that purpose, she headed for the living room with sponge and Glamorene.

The next time Mrs. Brainerd came she stayed for a scant thirty seconds. She stood in the doorway, sniffing the air. Ambrose had Done It again—twice.

"It really does get out stains even bleach can't reach," Norma said, flourishing the cleanser can.

"Everyone knows that," Clarice Brainerd said, passing it off. Then she sniffed. "This will do wonders for your musty rooms," she said, handing Norma a can of aerosol deodorant, and then turned without even coming in and closed the door.

Norma spent four days getting ready for the day she invited Mrs. Brainerd to look into the stove. ("I'm having a little trouble with the bottoms of the open shelves," she confided on the phone. She had just spent days making sure they were immaculate. "I just wondered if you could tell me what to use," she said seductively, thinking that when Clarice Brainerd saw that Norma was worried about dirt in an oven that was cleaner than any oven on the block, she would be awed and dismayed, and she would have to invite Norma to the next day's morning coffee hour.)

At the last minute, Norma had to shoo Polly Ann out of the living room. "I was just making a dress for Ambrose," Polly Ann said, putting on her Mary Janes and picking up her cloth and pins.

Vacuuming frantically, Norma stampeded her down the hall and into her room. "Never *mind*."

"Arient did the job all right," Mrs. Brainerd said, sniffing the air without even pausing to say hello. "The *rest* of us have been using it for years."

"I know," Norma said apologetically.

In the kitchen, she spent a long time with her head in the oven. "I don't think you have too much trouble," she said grudgingly. "In fact it looks real nice. But I would take a pin and clear out those gas jets." Her voice was muffled because of the oven, and for a second Norma had to fight back wild temptation to push her the rest of the way in, and turn up the gas.

Then Clarice said, "It looks real nice. And thanks, I will have some of your cake."

"No greasy feel," Norma said, weak with gratitude. "You'll really sit down for a minute? You'll really have some coffee and sit down?"

"Only for a minute."

Norma got out her best California pottery—the set with the rooster pattern—and within five minutes, she and Mrs. Brainerd were sitting primly in the living room. The organdy curtains billowed and the windows and woodwork shone brightly and for a moment Norma almost imagined that she and Mrs. Brainerd were being photographed in behalf of some product, in *her* living room, and their picture—in full color—would appear in the very next issue of her favorite magazine.

"I would so love to do flower arrangements," Norma said, made bold by her success.

Mrs. Brainerd wasn't listening.

"Maybe join the Garden Club?"

Mrs. Brainerd was looking down. At the rug.

"Or maybe the Music League . . ." Norma looked down, where Mrs. Brainerd was looking, and her voice trailed off.

"Cat hairs," said Mrs. Brainerd. "Loose threads."

"Oh, I *tried* . . ." Norma clapped her hand to her mouth with a muffled wail.

"And scuff marks, on the hall floor . . ." Mrs. Brainerd was shaking her head. "Now I don't mean to be mean, but if you were to entertain the coffee group, with the house looking like this . . ."

"My daughter was sewing," Norma said faintly. "She *knew* I was having company, but she came in here. It's a little hard," she said, trying to smile engagingly. "When you have kids . . ."

Mrs. Brainerd was on her feet. "The rest of us manage."

Norma managed to keep the sob out of her voice. ". . . and pets . . ."

"The coffee hours," Norma said, maundering. "The garden club . . ."

But Mrs. Brainerd was already gone.

Norma snuffled. "She didn't even mention a *product* to try."

"I made Ambrose a baby carriage," Polly Ann said, dragging Ambrose through in a box. "Is that lady gone?"

"Gone," Norma said, looking at the way the box had scarred her hardwood floor. "She may be gone forever," she said, and began to cry. "Oh Polly Ann, what can we do? We may have to move to a less desirable residential district."

"Ambrose tipped over Puff's sandbox and got You Know What all over the floor." Polly Ann went outside.

Crumbs, hairs, threads, dust all seemed to converge on Norma then, eddying and swirling, threatening, plunging her into blackest despair. She sank to the couch, too overwhelmed to cry and it was then, looking down, that she spied the magazine protruding from under the rug, and things began to change.

 END HOUSEHOLD DRUDGERY,

the advertisement said,

YOUR HOUSE CAN BE THE CYNOSURE OF YOUR NEIGHBORHOOD.

Norma wasn't sure what cynosure meant but there was a picture of a spotless and shining lady sitting in the middle of a spotless and shining living room, with an immaculate kitchen just visible through a door beyond. Trembling with hope, she cut out the accompanying coupon, noting without a qualm that she would have to liquidate the rest of her savings to afford the product, or machine, or whatever it was. Satisfaction was guaranteed and if she got satisfaction it was worth it, every cent of it.

It was unprepossessing enough when it came.

It was a box, small and corrugated, and inside, wrapped in excelsior, was a small lavender enamel-covered machine. A nozzle and hose, also lavender, were attached. Curious, Norma began leafing through the instruction book, and as she read she began to smile because it all became quite plain.

"EFFECTS ARE NOT NECESSARILY PERMANENT," she read aloud, to assuage her conscience. "CAN BE REVERSED BY USING GREEN GAUGE ON THE MACHINE. Oh, Puff," she called, thinking of the white Angora hairs which had sullied so many rugs. "Puffy, come here."

The cat came through the door with a look of insolence.

"Come here," Norma said, aiming the nozzle. "Come on, baby," she said, and when Puff approached, she switched on the machine.

A pervasive hum filled the room, faint but distinct.

Expensive or not it was worth it. She had to admit that none of her household cleansers worked as fast. In less than a second Puff was immobile — walleyed and stiff-backed but immobile, looking particularly fluffy and just as natural as life. Norma arranged the cat artistically in a corner by the TV set and then went looking for Polly Ann's dog. She made Ambrose sit up and beg and just as he snapped for the puppy-biscuit she turned on the machine and ossified him in a split second. When it was over she propped him on the other side of the television set and carefully put away the machine.

Polly Ann cried quite a bit at first.

"Now honey, if we ever get tired of them this way we can reverse the machine wand let them run around again. But right now the house is so *clean*, and see how cute they are? They can see and hear everything you want them to," she said, quelling the child's sticky tears. "And look, you can dress Ambrose up all you want and he won't even squirm."

"I guess so," Polly Ann said, smoothing the front of her velvet dress. She gave Ambrose a little poke.

"And see how little dirt they make."

Polly Ann bent Ambrose's paw in a salute. It stayed. "Okay, Momma. I guess you're right."

Mrs. Brainerd thought the dog and cat were very cute. "How did you *get* them to stay so still?"

"New product," Norma said with a smug smile, and then she wouldn't tell Mrs. Brainerd what product. "I'll get my cake now," she said. "No greasy feel."

"No greasy feel," Mrs. Brainerd said automatically, echoing her, and almost smiled in anticipation.

Moving regally, proud as any queen, Norma brought her coffee tray into the living room. "Now about the coffee hour," she said, presuming because Mrs. Brainerd took up her cup and spoon with an almost admiring look, poking with her fork at the chocolate cake. ("I got the stainless with coupons. You know the kind.")

"The coffee hour," Mrs. Brainerd said, almost mesmerized. Then, looking down, "Oh, what on earth is that?"

And already dreading what she would see, Norma followed Mrs. Brainerd's eyes.

There was a puddle, a distinct puddle, forming under the bathroom door, and as the women watched, it massed and began making a sticky trail down the highly polished linoleum of the hall.

"I'd better . . ." Mrs. Brainerd said, getting up.

"I know," Norma said with resignation. "You'd better go." Then, as she rose and saw her neighbor to the door, she stiffened with a new resolve. "You just come back tomorrow. I can promise you, everything will be just as neat as pie." Then, because she couldn't help herself, "No greasy feel."

"You know," Mrs. Brainerd said ominously, "this kind of thing can only go on for so long. My time is valuable. There are the coffee hours, and the Canasta group . . ."

"I promise you," Norma said. "You'll envy my way with things. You'll tell all your friends. Just come back tomorrow. I'll be ready, I promise you . . ."

Clarice deliberated, unconsciously fingering her Good Luck earrings with one carefully groomed hand. "Oh," she said finally, after a pause which left Norma in a near faint from anxiety. "All right."

"You'll see," Norma said to the closing door. "Wait and see if you don't see."

Then she made her way through the spreading pool of water and knocked on the bathroom door.

"I was making Kool-Aid to sell to all the Daddies," Polly Ann said, gathering all the overflowing cups and jars.

"Come with me, baby," Norma said. "I want you to get all cleaned up and in your very best clothes."

They were all arranged very artistically in the living room, the dog and the cat curled next to the sofa, Polly Ann looking just as pretty as life in her maroon velvet dress with the organdy pinafore. Her eyes were a little glassy and her legs did stick out at a slightly unnatural angle, but Norma had thrown an Afghan over one end of the couch, where she was sitting, and thought the effect, in the long run, was just as good as anything she'd ever seen on a television commercial, and almost as pretty as some of the pictures she had seen in magazines. She noticed with a little pang that there was a certain moist look about the way Polly Ann was watching her, and so she went to the child and patted one waxen hand.

"Don't you worry, honey. When you get big enough to help Momma with her housecleaning, Momma will let you run around for a couple of hours every day. Momma promises."

Then, smoothing the front of her Swirl housedress and refastening her Sweetheart pin, she went to meet Mrs. Brainerd at the door.

"Well," said Mrs. Brainerd in an almost good-natured way. "How nice everything looks."

"No household odor, no stains, no greasy feel to the cake," said Norma anxiously. "This is my little girl."

"What a good child," Mrs. Brainerd said, skirting Polly Ann's legs, which stuck straight out from the couch.

"And our doggy and kitty," Norma said with growing confidence, propping Ambrose against one of Polly Ann's feet because he had begun to slide.

Mrs. Brainerd even smiled. "How cute. How nice."

"Come see the darling kitchen," Norma said, standing so Clarice Brainerd could look into the unclogged drain, the white and pristine sink.

"Just lovely," Clarice said.

"Let me get the cake and coffee," Norma said, leading Clarice Brainerd back to the living room.

"Your windows are just sparkling."

"I know," Norma said, beaming and capable.

"And the rug."

"Glamorene."

"Wonderful." Clarice was hers.

"Here," Norma said, plying her with coffee and cake. "Wonderful coffee," Clarice said. "Call me Clarice. Now about the Garden Club, and the morning coffee hours . . . We go to Marge on Thursday, and Edna Mondays, and Thelma Tuesday afternoons, and . . ." She bit into the proffered piece of cake. "And . . ." she said, turning the morsel over and over in her mouth.

"And . . ." Norma said hopefully.

"And . . ." Mrs. Brainerd said, looking slightly cross-eyed down her nose, as if she were trying to see what was in her mouth. "This cake," she said. "This cake . . ."

"Marvel Mix," Norma said with elan. "No greasy feel . . ."

"I'm sorry," Mrs. Brainerd said, getting up.

"You're—what?"

"Sorry," Mrs. Brainerd said with genuine regret. "It's your cake."

"What about my cake?"

"Why, it's got that greasy feel."

"You—I—it—but the commercial *promised* . . ." Norma was on her feet now, moving automatically. "The cake is so good, and my house is so beautiful . . ." She was in between Mrs. Brainerd and the door now, heading her off in the front hall.

"Sorry," Mrs. Brainerd said. "I won't be seeing you. Now, if you'll just close that closet door so I can get by . . ."

"Close the door?" Norma's eyes were glazed. "I can't. I have to get something off the closet shelf."

"It doesn't matter what you get," Mrs. Brainerd said. "I can't come back. We ladies have so much to do, we don't have time . . ."

"Time," Norma said, getting what she wanted from the shelf.

"Time," Mrs. Brainerd said condescendingly. "Oh. Maybe you'd better not call me Clarice."

"OK, Clarice," Norma said and she let Mrs. Brainerd have it with the lavender machine.

First she propped Mrs. Brainerd up in a corner, where she would be uncomfortable. Then she reversed the nozzle action and brought Polly Ann and Puff and Ambrose back to mobility. Then she brought her box of sewing scraps and all the garbage from the kitchen and began spreading the mess around Mrs. Brainerd's feet and she let Puff rub cat hairs on the furniture and she sent Polly Ann into the back yard for some mud. Ambrose, released, Did It at Mrs. Brainerd's feet.

"So glad you could come, Clarice," Norma said, gratified by the look of horror on Mrs. Brainerd's trapped and frozen face. Then, turning to Polly Ann's laden pinafore, she reached for a handful of mud.

—1964

WINTER

It was late fall when he come to us, there was a scum of ice on all the puddles and I could feel the winter cold and fearsome in my bones, the hunger inside me was already uncurling, it would pace through the first of the year but by spring it would be raging like a tiger, consuming me until the thaw when Maude could hunt again and we would get the truck down the road to town. I was done canning but I got the tomatoes we had hanging in the cellar and I canned some more; Maude went out and brought back every piece of meat she could shoot and all the grain and flour and powdered milk she could bring in one truckload, we had to lay in everything we could before the snow came and sealed us in. The week he come Maude found a jack-rabbit stone dead in the road, it was frozen with its feet sticking straight up, and all the meat hanging in the cold-room had froze. Friday there was rime on the grass and when I looked out I seen footprints in the rime, I said Maude, someone is in the playhouse and we went out and there he was. He was asleep in the mess of clothes we always dressed up in, he had his head on the velvet gown my mother wore to the Exposition and his feet on the satin gown she married Father in, he had pulled her feather boa around his neck and her fox fur was wrapped around his loins.

Before he come, Maude and me would pass the winter talking about how it used to be, we would call up the past between us and look at it and Maude would end by blaming me. I could of married either Lister Hoffman or Harry Mead and left this place for good if it hadn't been for you, Lizzie. I'd tell her, Hell, I never needed you. You didn't marry them because you didn't marry them, you was scared of it and you would use me for an excuse. She would get mad then. It's a lie. Have it your way, I would tell her, just to keep the peace.

We both knew I would of married the first man that asked me, but nobody would, not even with all my money, nobody would ask me because of the taint. If nobody had of known then some man might of married me, but I went down to the field with Miles Harrison once while Father was still alive, and Miles and me, we almost, except that the blackness took me, right there in front of him, and so I never did. Nobody needed to know, but then Miles saw me fall down in the field. I guess it was him that put something between my teeth so I wouldn't bite my tongue, but when I come to myself he was gone. Next time I went to town they all looked at me funny, some of them would try and face up to me and be polite but they was all jumpy, thinking would I do it right there in front of them, would I froth much, would they get hurt, as soon as was decent they would say Excuse me, I got to, anything to get out of there fast. When I run into Miles after that day he wouldn't look at me and there hasn't been a man near me since then, not in more than fifty years, but Miles and me, we almost, and I have never stopped thinking about that.

Now Father is gone and my mother is gone and even Lister Hoffman and Miles Harrison and half the town kids that used to laugh at me, they are all gone, but Maude still reproaches me, we sit after supper and she says If it hadn't been for you I would have grandchildren now and I tell her I would of had them before ever she did because she never liked men, she would only suffer them to get children and that would be too much trouble, it would hurt. That's a lie, Lizzie, she would say, Harry and me used to . . . and I would tell her You never, but Miles and me . . . Then we would both think about being young and having people's hands on us but memory turns Maude bitter and she can never leave it at that, she says, It's all your fault, but I know in my heart that people make their lives what they want them, and all she ever wanted was to be locked in here with nobody to make demands on her, she wanted to stay in this house with me, her dried-up sister, cold and safe, and if the hunger is on her, it has come on her late.

After a while we would start to make up stuff: Once I went with a boy all the way to Portland . . . Once I danced all night and half the morning, he wanted to kiss me on the place where my elbow bends . . . We would try to spin out the winter, but even that was not enough and so we would always be left with the hunger; no matter how much we laid in, the meat was always gone before the thaw and I suppose it was really our lives we was judging but we would decide nothing in the cans looked good to us and so we would sit and dream and hunger and wonder if we would die of it, but finally the thaw would come and Maude would look at me and sigh: If only we had another chance.

Well now perhaps we will.

We found him in the playhouse, maybe it was seeing him being in the playhouse, where we pretended so many times, asleep in the middle of my mother's clothes or maybe it was something of mine; there was this boy, or man, something about him called up our best memories, there was promise wrote all over him. I am too old, I am all dried out, but I have never stopped thinking about that one time, and seeing that boy there, I could pretend he was Miles and I was still young. I guess he sensed us, he woke up fast and went into a crouch, maybe he had a knife, and then I guess he saw it was just too big old ladies in Army boots, he said, I run away from the Marines, I need a place to sleep.

Maude said, I don't care what you need, you got to get out of here, but when he stood up he wobbled. His hair fell across his head like the hair on a boy I used to know and I said, Maude, why don't you say yes to something just this once.

He had on this denim shirt and pants like no uniform I ever seen and he was saying, Two things happened, I found out I might have to shoot somebody in the war and then I made a mistake and they beat me so I cut out of there. He smiled and he looked open. I stared hard at Maude and Maude finally looked at me and said, All right, come up to the house and get something to eat.

He said his name was Arnold but when we asked him Arnold what, he said Never mind. He was in the kitchen by then, he had his head bent over a bowl of oatmeal and some biscuits I had made, and when I looked at Maude she was watching the way the light slid across his hair. When we told him our names he said, You are both beautiful ladies, and I could see Maude's hands go up to her face and she went into her room and when she came back I saw she had put color on her cheeks. While we was alone he said how good the biscuits was and wasn't that beautiful silver, did I keep it polished all by myself and I said well yes, Maude brings in supplies but I am in charge of the house and making all the food. She come back then and saw us with our heads together and said to Arnold, I guess you'll be leaving soon.

I don't know, he said, they'll be out looking for me with guns and dogs.

That's no never mind of ours.

I never done anything bad in the Marines, we just had different ideas. We both figured it was something worse but he looked so sad and tired and besides, it was nice to have him to talk to, he said, I just need a place to hole up for a while.

Maude said, You could always go back to your family.

He said, They never wanted me. They was always meanhearted, not like you.

36

I took her aside and said, It wouldn't kill you to let him stay on. Maude, it's time we had a little life around here.

There won't be enough food for three.

He won't stay long. Besides, he can help you with the chores. She was looking at his bright hair again, she said, like it was all my doing, If you want to let him stay I guess we can let him stay.

He was saying, I could work for my keep.

All right, I said, you can stay on until you get your strength.

My heart jumped. A man, I thought. A man. How can I explain it? It was like being young, having him around. I looked at Maude and saw some of the same things in her eyes, hunger and hope, and I thought, You are ours now, Arnold, you are all ours. We will feed you and take care of you and when you want to wander we will let you wander, but we will never let you go.

Just until things die down a little, he was saying.

Maude had a funny grin. Just until things died down.

Well it must of started snowing right after dark that afternoon, because when we all waked up the house was surrounded. I said, Good thing you got the meat in, Maude, and she looked out, it was still blowing snow and it showed no signs of stopping; she looked out and said, I guess it is.

He was still asleep, he slept the day through except he stumbled down at dusk and dreamed over a bowl of my rabbit stew, I turned to the sink and when I looked back the stew was gone and the biscuits was gone and all the extra in the pot was gone, I had a little flash of fright, it was all disappearing too fast. Then Maude come over to me and hissed, The food, he's eating all the food and I looked at his brown hands and his tender neck and I said, It don't matter, Maude, he's young and strong and if we run short he can go out into the snow and hunt. When we looked around next time he was gone, he had dreamed his way through half a pie and gone right back to bed.

Next morning he was up before the light, we sat together around the kitchen table and I thought how nice it was to have a man in the house, I could look at him and imagine anything I wanted. Then he got up and said, Look, I want to thank you for everything, I got to get along now, and I said, You can't, and he said, I got things to do, I been here long enough, but I told him You can't, and took him over to the window. The sun was up by then and there it was, snow almost to the window ledges, like we have every winter, and all the trees was shrouded, we could watch the sun take the snow and make it sparkle and I said, Beautiful snow, beautiful, and he only shrugged and said, I guess I'll have to wait till it clears off some. I touched his shoulder. I guess you will. I knew not to tell him it would never clear off, not until late spring; maybe he guessed, anyway he looked so sad I gave him Father's silver snuffbox to cheer him up.

He would divide his time between Maude and me, he played Rook with her and made her laugh so hard she gave him her pearl earrings and the brooch Father brought her back from Quebec. I gave him Grandfather's diamond stickpin because he admired it, and for Christmas we gave him the cameos and Father's gold-headed cane. Maude got the flu over New Year's and Arnold and me spent New Year's Eve together, I mulled some wine and he hung up some of Mama's jewelry from the center light, and touched it and made it twirl. We lit candles and played the radio, New Year's Eve in Times Square and somebody's Make-believe Ballroom, I went to pour another cup of wine and his hand was on mine on the bottle, I knew my lips was red for once and next day I gave him Papa's fur-lined coat.

I guess Maude suspected there was something between us, she looked pinched and mean when I went in with her broth at lunch, she said, Where were you at breakfast and I said, Maude, it's New Year's day, I thought I would like to sleep in for once. You were with him. I thought, If she wants to think that about me, let her, and I let my eyes go sleepy and I said, We had to see the New Year in, didn't we? She was out of bed in two days, I have never seen anybody get up so fast after the flu. I think she couldn't stand us being where she couldn't see what we was up to every living minute.

Then I got sick and I knew what torture it must have been for her just laying there, I would call Maude and I would call her, and sometimes she would come and sometimes she wouldn't come and when she finally did look in on me I would say, Maude, where have you been, and she would only giggle and not answer. There was meat cooking all the time, roasts and chops and chicken fricassee, when I said Maude, you're going to use it up, she would only smile and say, I just had to show him who's who in the kitchen, he tells me I'm a better cook than you ever was. After a while I got up, I had to even if I was dizzy and like to throw up, I had to get downstairs where I could keep an eye on them. As soon as I was up to it I made a roast of venison that would put hair on an egg and after that we would vie with each other in the kitchen, Maude and me. Once I had my hand on the skillet handle and she come over and tried to take it away, she was saying, Let me serve it up for him, I said, You're a fool, Maude, I cooked this, and she hissed at me, through the steam, It won't do you no good, Lizzie, it's me he loves, and I just pushed her away and said, You goddam fool, he loves me, and I give him my amethysts just to prove it. A couple of days later I couldn't find neither of them nowhere, I thought I heard noises up in the back room and I went up and if they was in there they wouldn't answer, the door was locked and they wouldn't say nothing, not even when I knocked and knocked and knocked. So the next day I took him up in my room and we locked the door and I told him a story about every piece in my jewel box, even the cheap ones, when Maude tapped and whined outside the door we would just shush, and when we did come out and she said, All right, Lizzie, what was you doing in there, I only giggled and wouldn't tell.

She shouldn't of done it, we was all sitting around the table after dinner and he looked at me hard and said, You know something, Arnold, I wouldn't get too close to Lizzie, she has fits. Arnold only tried to look like it didn't matter, but after Maude went to bed I went down to make sure it was all right. He was still in the kitchen, whittling, and when I tried to touch his hand he pulled away.

I said, Don't be scared, I only throw one in a blue moon.

He said, That don't matter.

Then what's the matter?

I don't know, Miss Lizzie, I just don't think you trust me.

Course I trust you, Arnold, don't I give you everything?

He just looked sad. Everything but trust.

I owe you so much, Arnold, you make me feel so young.

He just smiled for me then. You look younger, Miss Lizzie, you been getting younger every day I been here.

You did it.

If you let me, I could make you really young.

Yes, Arnold, yes.

But I have to know you trust me.

Yes, Arnold.

So I showed him where the money was. By then it was past midnight and we was both tired, he said, Tomorrow, and I let him go off to get his rest.

I don't know what roused us both and brought us out into the hall but I bumped into Maude at dawn, we was both standing in our nightgowns like two ghosts. We crept downstairs together and there was light in the kitchen, the place where we kept the money was open, empty, and there was a crack of light in the door to the coldroom. I remember looking through and thinking, The meat is almost gone. Then we opened the door a crack wider and there he was, he had made a sledge, he must of sneaked down there and worked on it every night. It was piled with stuff, and now he had the door to the outside open, he had dug himself a ramp out of the snow and he was lashing some home-made snowshoes on his feet, in another minute he would cut out of there.

When he heard us he turned.

I had the shotgun and Maude had the axe.

We said, We don't care about the stuff, Arnold. How could we tell him it was our youth he was taking away?'

He looked at us, walleyed. You can have it all, just let me out.

He was going to get away in another minute, so Maude let him have it with the axe.

Afterwards we closed the way to the outside and stood there and looked at each other, I couldn't say what was in my heart so I only looked at Maude, we was both sad, sad, I said, The food is almost gone.

Maude said, Everything is gone. We'll never make it to spring.

I said, We have to make it to spring.

Maude looked at him laying there. You know what he told me? He said, I can make you young.

Me too, I said. There was something in his eyes that made me believe it.

Maude's eyes was glitter, she said, The food is almost gone.

I knew what she meant, he was going to make us young. I don't know how it will work in us, but he is going to make us young, it will be as if the fits had never took me, never in all them years. Maude was looking at me, waiting, and after a minute I looked square at her and I said, I know.

So we et him.

—1967

THE FOOD FARM

So here I am, warden-in-charge, fattening them up for our leader, Tommy Fango; here I am laying on the banana pudding and the milkshakes and the cream-and-brandy cocktails, going about like a technician, gauging their effect on haunch and thigh when all the time it is I who love him, I who could have pleased him eternally if only life had broken differently. But I am scrawny now, I am swept like a leaf around corners, battered by the slightest wind. My elbows rattle against my ribs and I have to spend half the day in bed so a gram or two of what I eat will stay with me for if I do not, the fats and creams will vanish, burned up in my own insatiable furnace, and what little flesh I have will melt away.

Cruel as it may sound, I know where to place the blame.

It was vanity, all vanity, and I hate them most for that. It was not my vanity, for I have always been a simple soul; I reconciled myself early to reinforced chairs and loose garments, to the spattering of remarks. Instead of heeding them I plugged in, and I would have been happy to let it go at that, going through life with my radio in my bodice, for while I never drew cries of admiration, no one ever blanched and turned away.

But they were vain and in their vanity my frail father, my pale, scrawny mother saw me not as an entity but a reflection on themselves. I flush with shame to remember the excuses they made for me. "She takes after May's side of the family," my father would say, denying any responsibility. "It's only baby fat," my mother would say, jabbing her elbow into my soft flank. "Nelly is big for her age." Then she would jerk furiously, pulling my voluminous smock down to cover my knees. That was when they still consented to be seen with me. In that period they would stuff me with pies and roasts before we went anywhere, filling me up so I would not gorge myself in public. Even so I had to take thirds, fourths, fifths and so I was a humiliation to them.

In time I was too much for them and they stopped taking me out; they made no more attempts to explain. Instead they tried to think of ways to make me look better; the doctors tried the fool's poor battery of pills: they tried to make me join a club. For a while my mother and I did exercises; we would sit on the floor, she in a black leotard, I in my smock. Then she would do the brisk one-two, one-two and I would make a few passes at my toes. But I had to listen, I had to plug in, and after I was plugged in naturally I had to find something to eat; Tommy might sing and I always ate when Tommy sang, and so I would leave her there on the floor, still going one-two, one-two. For a while after that they tried locking up the food. Then they began to cut into my meals.

That was the cruelest time. They would refuse me bread, they would plead and cry, plying me with lettuce and telling me it was all for my own good. My own good. Couldn't they hear my vitals crying out? I fought. I screamed, and when that failed I suffered in silent obedience until finally hunger drove me into the streets. I would lie in bed, made brave by the Monets and Barry Arkin and the Philadons coming in over the radio, and Tommy (there was never enough; I heard him a hundred times a day and it was never enough; how bitter that seems now!). I would open the first pie or the first half-gallon off ice cream and then, as I began, I would plug in.

Tommy, beautiful Tommy Fango, the others paled to nothing next to him. Everybody heard him in those days; they played him two or three times an hour but you never knew when it would be so you were plugged in and listening hard every living moment; you ate, you slept, you drew breath for the moment when they would put on one of Tommy's records, you waited for his voice to fill the room. Cold cuts and cupcakes and game hens came and went during that period in my life but one thing was constant: I always had a cream pie thawing and when they played the first bars of "When a Widow" and Tommy's voice first flexed and uncurled, I was ready, I would eat the cream pie during Tommy's midnight show. The whole world waited in those days; we waited through endless sunlight, through nights of drumbeats and monotony, we all waited for Tommy Fango's records, and we waited for that whole unbroken hour of Tommy, his midnight show. He came on live at midnight in those days; he sang, broadcasting from the Hotel Riverside, and that was beautiful, but more important, he talked, and while he was talking he made everything all right. Nobody was lonely when Tommy talked; he brought us all together on that midnight show, he talked and made us powerful, he talked and finally he sang. You have to imagine what it was like, me in the night, Tommy, the pie. In a while I would go to a place where I had to live on Tommy and only Tommy, to a time when hearing Tommy would bring back the pie, all the poor lost pies . . .

Tommy's records, his show, the pie . . . that was perhaps the happiest period of my life. I would sit and listen and I would eat and eat and eat. So great was my bliss that it became torture to put away the food at daybreak; it grew harder and harder for me to hide the cartons and the cans and the bottles, all the residue of my happiness. Perhaps a bit of bacon fell into the register; perhaps an egg rolled under the bed and began to smell. All right, perhaps I did become careless, continuing my revels into the morning, or I may have been thoughtless enough to leave a jelly roll unfinished on the rug. I became aware that they were watching, lurking just outside my door, plotting as I ate. In time they broke in on me, weeping and pleading, lamenting over every ice cream carton and crumb of pie; then they threatened. Finally they restored the food they had taken from me in the daytime, thinking to curtail my eating at night. Folly. By that time I needed it all. I shut myself in with it and would not listen. I ignored their cries of hurt pride, their outpouring of wounded vanity, their puny little threats. Even if I had listened, I could not have forestalled what happened next.

I was so happy that last day. There was a Smithfield ham, mine, and I remember a jar of cherry preserves, mine, and I remember bacon, pale and white on Italian bread. I remember sounds downstairs and before I could take warning, an assault, a company of uniformed attendants, the sting of a hypodermic gun. Then the ten of them closed in and grappled me into a sling, or net, and heaving and straining, they bore me down the stairs. I'll never forgive you, I cried as they bundled me into the ambulance. I'll never forgive you, I bellowed as my mother in a last betrayal took away my radio, and I cried out one last time, as my father removed a hambone from my breast: I'll never forgive you. And I never have.

It is painful to describe what happened next. I remember three days of horror and agony, of being too weak, finally, to cry out or claw the walls. Then at last I was quiet and they moved me into a sunny, pastel, chintz-bedizened room. I remember that there were flowers on the dresser and someone was watching me.

"What are you in for?" she said.

I could barely speak for weakness. "Despair."

"Hell with that," she said, chewing. "You're in for food."

"What are you eating?" I tried to raise my head.

"Chewing. Inside of the mouth. It helps."

"I'm going to die."

"Everybody thinks that at first. I did." She tilted her head in an attitude of grace. "You know, this is a very exclusive school."

Her name was Ramona and as I wept silently, she filled me in. This was a last resort for the few who could afford to send their children here. They prettied it up with a schedule of therapy, exercise, massage; we would wear dainty pink smocks and talk of art and theater; from time to time we would attend classes in elocution and hygiene. Our parents would say with pride that we were away at Faircrest, an elegant finishing school; we knew better—it was a prison and we were being starved.

"It's a world I never made," said Ramona, and I knew that her parents were to blame, even as mine were. Her mother liked to take the children into hotels and casinos, wearing her thin daughters like a garland of jewels. Her father followed the sun on his private yacht, with the pennants flying and his children on the fantail, lithe and tanned. He would pat his flat, tanned belly and look at Ramona in disgust. When it was no longer possible to hide her, he gave in to blind pride. One night they came in a launch and took her away. She had been here six months now, and had lost almost a hundred pounds. She must have been monumental in her prime; she was still huge.

"We live from day to day," she said. "But you don't know the worst."

"My radio," I said in a spasm of fear. "They took away my radio."

"There is a reason," she said. "They call it therapy."

I was mumbling in my throat, in a minute I would scream.

"Wait." With ceremony, she pushed aside a picture and touched a tiny switch and then, like sweet balm for my panic, Tommy's voice flowed into the room.

When I was quiet she said, "You only hear him once a day."

"No."

"But you can hear him any time you want to. You hear him when you need him most."

But we were missing the first few bars and so we shut up and listened, and after "When a Widow" was over we sat quietly for a moment, her resigned, me weeping, and then Ramona threw another switch and the Sound filtered into the room, and it was almost like being plugged in.

"Try not to think about it."

"I'll die."

"If you think about it you *will* die. You have to learn to use it instead. In a minute they will come with lunch," Ramona said and as The Screamers sang sweet background, she want on in a monotone: "One chop. One lousy chop with a piece of lettuce and maybe some gluten bread. I pretend it's a leg of lamb, that works if you eat very, very slowly and think about Tommy the whole time; then if you look at your picture of Tommy you can turn the lettuce into anything you want, Caesar salad or a whole smorgasbord, and if you say his name over and over you can pretend a whole bombe or torte if you want to and . . ."

"I'm going to pretend a ham and kidney pie and a watermelon filled with chopped fruits and Tommy and I are in the Rainbow Room and we're going to finish up with Fudge Royale . . ." I almost drowned in my own saliva; in the background I could almost hear Tommy and I could hear Ramona saying, "Capon, Tommy would like capon, canard à l'orange, Napoleons, tomorrow we will save Tommy for lunch and listen while we eat . . ." and I thought about that, I thought about listening and imagining whole cream pies and I went on, ". . . lemon pie, rice pudding, a whole Edam cheese . . . I think I'm going to live."

The matron came in the next morning at breakfast and stood as she would every day, tapping red fingernails on one svelte hip, looking on in revulsion as we fell on the glass of orange juice and the hard-boiled egg. I was too weak to control myself; I heard a shrill sniveling sound and realized only from her expression that it was my own voice: "Please, just some bread, a stick of butter, anything. I could lick the dishes if you'd let me, only please don't leave me like this, please . . ." I can still see her sneer as she turned her back.

I felt Ramona's loyal hand on my shoulder. "There's always toothpaste but don't use too much at once or they'll come and take it away from you."

I was too weak to rise and so she brought it and we shared the tube and talked about all the banquets we had ever known, and when we got tired of that we talked about Tommy and when that failed, Ramona went to the switch and we heard "When a Widow," and that helped for a while, and then we decided that tomorrow we would put off "When a Widow" until bedtime because then we would have something to look forward to all day. Then lunch came and we both wept.

It was not just hunger: after a while the stomach begins to devour itself and the few grams you toss it at mealtimes assuage it so that in time the appetite itself begins to fail. After hunger comes depression. I lay there, still too weak to get about, and in my misery I realized that they could bring me roast pork and watermelon and Boston cream pie without ceasing; they could gratify all my dreams and I would only weep helplessly, because I no longer had the strength to eat. Even then, when I thought I had reached rock bottom, I had not comprehended the worst. I noticed it first in Ramona. Watching her at the mirror, I said, in fear:

"You're thinner."

She turned with tears in her eyes. "Nelly, I'm not the only one."

I looked around at my own arms and saw that she was right: there was one less fold of flesh above the elbow; there was one less wrinkle at the wrist. I turned my face to the wall and all Ramona's talk of food and Tommy did not comfort me. In desperation she turned on Tommy's voice, but as he sang I lay back and contemplated the melting of my own flesh.

"If we stole a radio we could hear him again," Ramona said, trying to soothe me. "We could hear him when he sings tonight."

Tommy came to Faircrest on a visit two days later, for reasons I could not then understand. All the other girls lumbered into the assembly hall to see him, thousands of pounds of agitated flesh. It was that morning that I discovered I could walk again, and I was on my feet, struggling into the pink tent in a fury to get to Tommy, when the matron intercepted me.

"Not you, Nelly."

"I have to get to Tommy. I have to hear him sing."

"Next time, maybe." With a look of naked cruelty she added, "You're a disgrace. You're still too gross."

I lunged but it was too late; she had already shot the bolt. And so I sat in the midst of my diminishing body, suffering while every other girl in the place listened to him sing. I knew then that I had to act; I would regain myself somehow, I would find food and regain my flesh and then I would go to Tommy. I would use force if I had to, but I would hear him sing. I raged through the room all that morning, hearing the shrieks of five hundred girls, the thunder of their feet, but even when I pressed myself against the wall I could not hear Tommy's voice.

Yet Ramona, when she came back to the room, said the most interesting thing. It was some time before she could speak at all, but in her generosity she played "When a Widow" while she regained herself, and then she spoke:

"He came for something, Nelly. He came for something he didn't find."

"Tell about what he was wearing. Tell what his throat did when he sang."

"He looked at all the *before* pictures, Nelly. The matron was trying to make him look at the *afters* but he kept looking at the befores and shaking his head and then he found one and put it in his pocket and if he hadn't found it, he wasn't going to sing."

I could feel my spine stiffen. "Ramona, you've got to help me. I must go to him."

That night we staged a daring break. We clubbed the attendant when he brought dinner, and once we had him under the bed we ate all the chops and gluten bread on his cart and then we went down the corridor, lifting bolts, and when we were a hundred strong we locked the matron in her office and raided the dining hall, howling and eating everything we could find. I ate that night, how I ate, but even as I ate I was aware of a fatal lightness in my bones, a failure in capacity, and so they found me in the frozen food locker, weeping over a chain of link sausage, inconsolable because I understood that they had spoiled it for me, they with their chops and their gluten bread; I could never eat as I once had, I would never be myself again.

In my fury I went after the matron with a ham hock, and when I had them all at bay I took a loin of pork for sustenance and I broke out of that place. I had to get to Tommy before I got any thinner; I had to try. Outside the gate I stopped a car and hit the driver with the loin of pork and then I drove to the Hotel Riverside, where Tommy always stayed. I made my way up the fire stairs on little cat feet and when the valet went to his suite with one of his velveteen suits I followed, quick as a tigress, and the next moment I was inside. When all was quiet I tiptoed to his door and stepped inside.

He was magnificent. He stood at the window, gaunt and beautiful; his blond hair fell to his waist and his shoulders shriveled under a heartbreaking double-breasted pea-green velvet suit. He did not see me at first; I drank in his image and then, delicately, cleared my throat. In the second that he turned and saw me, everything seemed possible.

"It's you." His voice throbbed.

"I had to come."

Our eyes fused and in that moment I believed that we two could meet, burning as a single, lambent flame, but in the next second his face had crumpled in disappointment; he brought a picture from his pocket, a fingered, cracked photograph, and he looked from it to me and back at the photograph, saying, "My darling, you've fallen off."

"Maybe it's not too late," I cried, but we both knew I would fail.

And fail I did, even though I ate for days, for five desperate, heroic weeks; I threw pies into the breach, fresh hams and whole sides of beef, but those sad days at the food farm, the starvation and the drugs have so upset my chemistry that it cannot be restored; no matter what I eat I fall off and I continue to fall off; my body is a halfway house for foods I can no longer assimilate. Tommy watches, and because he knows he almost had me, huge and round and beautiful, Tommy mourns. He eats less and less now. He eats like a bird and lately he has refused to sing; strangely, his records have begun to disappear.

And so a whole nation waits.

"I almost had her," he says when they beg him to resume his midnight shows; he will not sing, he won't talk, but his hands describe the mountain of woman he has longed for all his life.

And so I have lost Tommy, and he has lost me, but I am doing my best to make it up to him. I own Faircrest now, and in the place where Ramona and I once suffered I use my skills on the girls Tommy wants me to cultivate. I can put twenty pounds on a girl in a couple of weeks and I don't mean bloat. I mean solid fat. Ramona and I feed them up and once a week we weigh and I poke the upper arm with a special stick and I will not be satisfied until the stick goes in and does not rebound because all resiliency is gone. Each week I bring out my best and Tommy shakes his head in misery because the best is not yet good enough, none of them are what I once was. But one day the time and the girl will be right—would that it were me—the time and the girl will be right and Tommy will sing again. In the meantime, the whole world waits; in the meantime, in a private wing well away from the others, I keep my special cases: the matron, who grows fatter as I watch her. And Mom. And Dad.

—1967

IN BEHALF OF THE PRODUCT

Of course I owe everything I am today to Mr. Manuel Omerta, my personal representative, who arranged for practically everything, including the dental surgery and the annulment, but I want all of you wonderful people to know that I couldn't have done any of it without the help and support of the most wonderful person of all, my Mom. It was Mom who kept coming with the superenriched formula and the vitamins, she was the one who twirled my hair around her finger every time she washed it, it was Mom who put Vaseline on my eyelashes and paid for the trampoline lessons because she had faith in me. Anybody coming in off the street might have thought I was just an ordinary little girl, but not my mom: why, the first thing I remember is her standing me up on a table in front of everybody. I had on my baby tapshoes and a big smile and Mom was saying, Vonnie is going to be Miss Wonderful Land of Ours someday.

Even then she knew.

Well, here I am, and I can't tell you how happy I am to be up here, queen of the nation, an inspiration and a model for all those millions and billions of American girls who can grow up to be just like me. And this is only the beginning. Why, after I spend a year touring the country, meeting the people and introducing them to the product, after I walk down the runway at next year's pageant and put the American eagle floral piece into the arms of my successor, and she cries, anything can happen. I might go on to a career as an internationally famous television personality, or if I'd rather, I could become a movie queen or a spot welder, or I could marry Stanley, if he's still speaking to me, and raise my own little Miss Wonderful Land of Ours. Why, the world is mine, except of course for the iron curtain countries and their sympathizers, and after this wonderful year, who knows?

I just wish Daddy could be here to share this moment, but I guess that's just too much to hope, and I want you to know, Daddy, wherever you are out there, I forgive you, and if you'll only turn yourself in and make a public confession, I know the authorities will be lenient with you.

And that goes for you too, Sal. I know it was hard on you, always being the ugly older sister, but I really don't think you should have done what you did, and to show you how big I can be, if the acid scars came out as bad as I think they did, Mom and I are perfectly willing to let bygones be bygones and sink half the prize money into plastic surgery for you. I mean, after all, it's the least we can do. Why, there aren't even any charges outstanding against you; after all, nobody was really hurt—I mean, since Mr. Omerta happened to come in when he did and bumped your arm, and the acid went all over you instead of me.

I know I am the center of all eyes standing up here, I am the envy of millions, and I love the way the silver gown feels, slithering down over me like so much baby oil. I even love the weight of the twenty-foot-long red, white and blue velvet cloak, and every once in a while I want to reach up and touch the rhinestone stars and lightning bolts in my tiara but of course I can't because I am still holding the American eagle floral piece, the emblem of everything I have ever wanted. Of course you girls envy me. I used to get a stomachache just from looking at the pageant on TV. I would look at the winner smiling out over the Great Seal and I would think: Die, and let it be me. I just want you girls to know it hasn't all been bread and roses, there have been sacrifices, and Mom and Mr. Omerta had to work very hard, so if you're out there watching and thinking: What did she do to deserve that? let me tell you, the answer is, Plenty.

The thing is, without Mr. Omerta, poor Mom and I wouldn't have known where to begin. Before Mr. Omerta we were just rookies in the ballgame of life; we didn't have a prayer. There we were at the locals in the Miss Tiny Miss contest, me in my pink tutu and the little sequined tiara, I even had a wand; it was my first outing and I came in with a fourth runner-up. If it had been up to me I would have turned in my wand right then and there. Maybe Mom would have given up too, if it hadn't been for Mr. Omerta, but there must have been something about me, star quality, because he picked me out of all those other little girls, *me*. He didn't even give the winner a second look, he just came over to us in his elegant kidskin suit and the metallic shoes. We didn't know it then but it was Mr. Manuel Omerta, and he was going to change my life.

I was a loser, I must have looked a mess; the winner and the first runner-up were over on the platform crying for the camera and pinching each other in between lovey-dovey hugs, it was all over for the day, Mom and I were hanging up our cleats and packing away our uniforms when Mr. Omerta licked Mom's ear and said, "You two did a lot of things wrong today, but I want to tell you I like your style." I said, Oh thank you, and went on crying but Mom, she shushed me and hissed at me to listen up. She knew what she was doing too; she wasn't just going to say, Oh, thank you, and take the whole thing sitting down. She said, "What do you mean, a few things wrong?" and Mr. Omerta said, "Listen, I can give you a few pointers. Come over here." I couldn't hear what he said to her but she kept nodding and looking over at me and by the time I went over to tell them they were closing the armory and we had better get out, they were winding up the agreement; Mr. Omerta said, "And I'll only take fifty per cent."

"Don't you fifty per cent me," Mom said. "You know she's got the goods or you never would have picked her."

"All right," he said, "forty-five per cent."

Mom said, "She has naturally curly hair."

"You're trying to ruin me."

First Mr. Omerta pretended to walk out on Mom and then Mom pretended to take me away and they finally settled it; he would become my personal representative, success guaranteed, and he would take forty-two point eight per cent off the top. "The first thing," he said. "Tap dancing is a lousy talent. No big winner has ever made it on tap dancing alone. You have to throw in a gimmick, like pantomime. Something really different."

"Sword swallowing," Mom said in a flash.

"Keep coming, I really like your style." They bashed it back and forth for another few minutes. "Another thing," Mr. Omerta said, "We've got to fix those teeth; they look kind of, I don't know, *foreign*."

Mom said, "Got it Mr. Omerta, I think we're going to make a winning team."

It turned out Mr. Omerta was more or less between things and besides, to do a good job he was going to have to be on the spot, so he ended up coming home with us. Dad was a little surprised at first but he got used to it, or at least he acted like he was used to it; he only yelled first thing in the morning, while Sal and I were still hiding in our beds and Mr. Omerta was still out on the sun porch with the pillow over his head, stacking Zs. We fixed the sun porch up for Mr. Omerta; the only inconvenience was when you wanted to watch TV you had to go in and sit on the end of the Hide-a-Bed and sometimes it made him mad and other times it didn't; you were in trouble either way. Sal used to hit him on the knuckles with her leg brace; she said if you just kept smacking him he would get the idea and quit. He didn't bother me much. I was five at the time, and later on I was, you know, the Property; in the end I was going to be up against the Virginity Test and even when you passed that they did a lot of close checking to be sure you hadn't been fooling around. If you are going to represent this

Wonderful Land of Ours, you have to be a model for all American woman-hood; I mean, you wouldn't put pasties on Columbia the Gem of the Ocean or photograph the Statue of Liberty without her concrete robe, which is why I am so grateful to Mr. Omerta for busting in on Stanley and me in Elkton, Maryland, even if we *were* legally married by a justice of the peace. We could have taken care of the married part, but there was the other thing; it isn't widely known but if you flunk the Test in the semifinals you are tied to the Great Seal in front of everybody and all the other con-testants get to cast the first stone.

I cried but Mr. Omerta said not to be foolish, I was only engaging in the classic search for daddy anyway, just like in all the books. I suppose he was right, except that by the time Stanley and I ran away together Daddy had been gone for ten years. We were sitting around one night when I was eight. I had just won the state Miss Subteen title and Mr. Omerta and Mom were clashing glasses; before he put the prize check less his percent-age into my campaign fund, Mr. Omerta had lost his head and bought us a couple of bottles of pink champagne. Then Daddy got fed up or some-thing, he threw down his glass and stood up, yelling, "You're turning my daughter into a Kewpie doll." Sally started giggling and Mom slapped her and let my father have it all in one fluid motion. She said, "Henry, it's the patriotic thing to do." He said, "I don't see what that has to do with any-thing, and besides . . ."

I got terribly quiet. Mom and Mr. Omerta were both leaning forward, saying, "Besides?"

I tried to shut him up but it was too late.

"Besides, what's so wonderful about a country that lets this kind of thing go on?"

"Oh, *Daddy*," I cried, but it was already too late. Mr. Omerta was al-ready on the hot line to the House Un-American Activities Committee Pa-trol Headquarters; he didn't even hear Daddy yelling that the whole thing was a gimmick to help sell the war. By that time we could hear sirens. Daddy crashed through the back window and landed in the flower bed and that was the last anybody ever saw of him.

Well, we do have to go and visit the troops a lot and we do lead those victory rallies as part of our public appearance tour in behalf of the prod-uct, but it's not anything like Daddy said. I mean, any girl would do as much, and if you happen to be named Miss Wonderful Land of Ours, it's an honor and a privilege. I keep dreaming that when I start my nationwide personal appearance tour I will find Daddy standing in the audience in Detroit or Nebraska, he will be carrying a huge UP AMERICA sign and I can take him to my bosom and forgive him and he'll come back home to live.

Now that I think about it, Stanley does look a little bit like Daddy, and maybe that's why I was attracted to him. I mean, it's no fun growing up in a household where there are no men around, unless, of course, you want to count Mr. Omerta, who did keep saying he wanted to be a father to me, but that wasn't exactly what he meant. I was allowed to go to public high school so I could be a cheerleader because that can make or break you if you're going for Miss Teen-Age Wonderful Land of Ours, which of course is only a way station, but it's a lot of good personal experience. As it turned out I only got to the state finals. I could have gone to the nationals as an alternate but Mr. Omerta said it would be bad exposure and besides, we made enough out of the state contest to see us through until it was time for the main event. Anyway, Stanley was captain of the football team the year I made head cheerleader, and at first Mr. Omerta encouraged us because he could take pictures of us sitting in the local soda fountain, one soda and two straws, or me handing a big armful of goldenrod to Stanley after the big game. The thing I liked about Stanley, he wasn't interested in One Thing Only, he really loved me for my soul. When I came in after a date Mr. Omerta would sneak upstairs and sit on the end of my bed in his bathrobe while I told him all about it: you would have thought we were college roommates after the junior prom. Stanley loved me so much I know he would have waited but I decided there were more important things than being Miss Wonderful Land of Ours so the night of graduation we ran off to Elkton, Maryland, and if Mr. Omerta had gotten there five minutes later it would have been too late.

Whatever you might think about what he did to Stanley, you've got to give him credit for doing his job. He was my personal representative, he got me through the Miss Preteen and the Miss Adolescent with flying colors, and saw me through Miss Teen-Age Wonderful Land of Ours; he got me named Miss Our Town and it was all only a matter of time, I was a cinch for Miss State, and once I got to the nationals, well, with my talent gig, I was a natural, but here I was in Elkton, Maryland, I was just about to throw it all away for a pot of marriage when Mr. Omerta came crashing in and saved the day. What happened was, I was just melting into Stanley's arms when the door banged open and there were about a hundred people in the room, Mr. Omerta in the vanguard. I could have killed him then and there and he knew it. He took me by the shoulders and he looked me in the eye and said, "Brace up, baby, you owe it to your country. I will not let you smirch yourself before the pageant. Death before dishonor," Mr. Omerta said, and then he yelled, "There he is, grab him," and they dragged poor Stanley away. I'll never know how he managed to tail us, but he had the propaganda squad with him and before I could do a thing they had poor Stanley arrested on charges of menacing a national monument, they threw in a couple of perversion charges so Mr. Omerta could push through the annulment, and now poor Stanley is on ice until the end of next year. By that time my tour as Miss Wonderful Land of Ours will be over and maybe Mr. Omerta will let bygones be bygones and clear Stanley's name so he and I can get married again; after all, that's the only way I will ever be eligible to become *Mrs.* Wonderful Land of Ours, and you can't let yourself slip into retirement just because you've already been to the top.

But I haven't told you anything about my talent. I mean, it's possible to take lessons in Frankness and Sincerity, but talent is the one thing you can't fake. Mr. Omerta told us right off that tap dancing alone just wouldn't make it, but every time I tried sword swallowing (Mom's idea) I gagged and had to stop, but the trouble with fire eating was that the first time I burned my face, so naturally after that they couldn't even get me to try tapping and twirling the flaming baton. We thought about pantomime but of course that would rule out that and just then Mr. Omerta had an inspiration; he got me an accordion. So I went into the Miss Tiny Miss contest the next year tapping and playing the accordion, but there was a girl who sang patriotic songs and tapped the V for Victory in Morse code, and that gave Mr. Omerta an even better idea. To make a long story short, when I got up here tonight to do my talent for the last time, it was a routine we have been working on for years, and I owe it all to Mr. Omerta, with an extra little bow for Mom, whose idea it was to dress me in the Betsy Ross costume with the cutouts and the skirt ripped off at the crotch, our tattered forefathers and all that, and if you all enjoyed my interpretation of "O Beautiful, for Spacious Skies" done in song and dance and pantomime with interludes on the accordion, I want to say a humble thank you, thank you one and all.

I guess not many of you wonderful people know how close I came to not making it. First there was that terrible moment in the semi finals when we went back to find that my entire pageant wardrobe had been stolen, but I want you to know that Miss Massachusetts has been apprehended and they made her give me her wardrobe because between the ripping and the ink she had more or less ruined mine, and I have begged them to go easy on her because we are all working under such a terrible strain. And then there was the thing where they wouldn't let my mom into the rehearsals but they settled that very nicely and she is watching right now from her very own private room in the hospital and they will let her come home as soon as she is able to relate. Thanks for everything, Mom, and as soon as we get off TV I'm coming over and give you a great big kiss even if you don't know it's me. Then there's the thing about Mr. Omerta, and I feel just terrible, but it had to be done. I mean, he just snapped last night, he got past all the chaperones and came up to my hotel room. I said, "Oh, Mr. Omerta, you shouldn't *be* here, I could be disqualified," and the next thing I knew he had thrown himself down on my feet. He said, "Vonnie, I love you, I adore you." It was disgusting. He said, "Throw it all over and run away with me." Well, there I was not twenty-four hours from the big title; it was terrible. I said, "Oh, come on, Mr. Omerta, don't start that now, not after what you did to Stanley," and when he wouldn't stop kissing my ankles I kicked him a couple of times and said, "Come on, all you've ever thought about is money, money," and when he said there were more important things than money I started screaming, "Help me, somebody come and help me, this man is making an indecent advance," and the matrons came like lightning and carried him off to jail. Well, what did he expect? He's spent the last thirteen years training me for this day.

So when the big moment came tonight I was the one with the perfect figure, the perfect walk, the perfect talent, I wowed them in the charm department and . . . I don't know, there has just been this guy up here, the All-American Master of Ceremonies; you thought he was kissing my cheek and handing me another bouquet but instead he was whispering in my ear, "OK, sweetie, enough's enough." There seems to be something wrong; it turns out I am not reaching you wonderful people out there, my subjects. You can see my lips moving but that's not me you hear on the PA system, it's a prerecorded speech. He says . . . he says I'm perfect in almost every respect but there's this one thing wrong, they found out too late so they're going to have to go through with it. I guess they found out when I got up here and tried to make this speech. I am a weeny bit too frank to be a typical Miss Wonderful Land of Ours, he says I have too many regrets, but adjust as soon as I get down from here and they run the last commercial, they're going to take care of that. He says I'll be ready to begin my nationwide personal appearance tour in behalf of the product just as soon as they finish the lobotomy.

—1973

SONGS OF WAR

For some weeks now a fire had burned day and night on a hillside just beyond the town limits; standing at her kitchen sink, Sally Hall could see the smoke rising over the trees. It curled upward in promise but she could not be sure what it promised, and despite the fact that she was contented with her work and her family, Sally found herself stirred by the bright autumn air, the column of smoke.

Nobody seemed to want to talk much about the fire, or what it meant. Her husband, Zack, passed it off with a shrug, saying it was probably just another commune. June Goodall, her neighbor, said it was coming from Ellen Ferguson's place; she owned the land and it was her business what she did with it. Sally said what if she had been taken prisoner. Vic Goodall said not to be ridiculous, if Ellen Ferguson wanted those people off her place, all she had to do was call the police and get them off, and in the meantime it was nobody's business.

Still there was something commanding about the presence of the fire; the smoke rose steadily and could be seen for miles, and Sally, working at her drawing board, and a number of other women, going about their daily business, found themselves yearning after the smoke column with complex feelings. Some may have been recalling a primal past in which men conked large animals and dragged them into camp, and the only housework involved was a little gutting before they roasted the bloody chunks over the fire. The grease used to sink into the dirt and afterward the diners, smeared with blood and fat, would roll around in a happy tangle. Other women were stirred by all the adventure tales they had stored up from childhood; people would run away without even bothering to pack or leave a note, they always found food one way or another and they met new friends in the woods. Together they would tell stories over a campfire, and when they had eaten they would walk away from the bones to some high excitement that had nothing to do with the business of living from day to day. A few women, thinking of Castro and his happy guerrilla band, in the carefree, glamorous days before he came to power, were closer to the truth. Thinking wistfully of campfire camaraderie, of everybody marching together in a common cause, they were already dreaming of revolution.

Despite the haircut and the cheap suit supplied by the Acme Vacuum Cleaner company, Andy Ellis was an underachiever college dropout who could care less about vacuum cleaners. Until this week he had been a beautiful, carefree kid and now, with a dying mother to support, with the wraiths of unpaid bills and unsold Marvelvacs trailing behind him like Marley's chains, he was still beautiful, which is why the women opened their doors to him.

He was supposed to say, "Good morning, I'm from the Acme Vacuum Cleaner Company and I'm here to clean your living room, no obligation, absolutely free of charge." Then, with the room clean and the Marvel-sweep with twenty attachments and ten optional features spread all over the rug, he was supposed to make his pitch.

The first woman he called on said he did good work but her husband would have to decide, so Andy sighed and began collecting the Flutes-noot, the Miracle Whoosher and all the other attachments and putting them back into the patented Bomb Bay Door.

"Well thanks anyway . . ."

"Oh, thank *you*," she said. He was astounded to discover that she was unbuttoning him here and there.

"Does this mean you want the vacuum after all?"

She covered him with hungry kisses. "Shut up and deal."

At the next house, he began again. "Good morning, I'm from the Acme Vacuum Cleaner company . . ."

"Never mind that. Come in."

At the third house, he and the lady of the house grappled in the midst of her unfinished novel, rolling here and there between the unfinished tapestry and the unfinished wire sculpture.

"If he would let me alone for a minute I would get some of these things done," she said. "All he ever thinks about is sex."

"If you don't like it, why are we doing this?"

"To get even," she said.

On his second day as a vacuum cleaner salesman, Andy changed his approach. Instead of going into his pitch, he would say, "Want to screw?" By the third day he had refined it to, "My place or yours?"

Friday his mother died so he was able to turn in his Marvelvac, which he thought was just as well, because he was exhausted and depressed, and, for all his efforts, he had made only one tentative sale, which was contingent upon his picking up the payments in person every week for the next twelve years. Standing over his mother's coffin, he could not for the life of him understand what had happened to women—not good old Mom, who had more or less liked her family and at any rate had died uncomplaining—but the others, all the women in every condition in all the houses he had gone to this week. Why weren't any of them happy?

Up in the hills, sitting around the fire, the women in the vanguard were talking about just that; the vagaries of life, and woman's condition. They had to think it was only that. If they were going to go on, they would have to be able to decide the problem was X, whatever X was. It had to be something they could name, so that, together, they could do something about it.

They were of a mind to free themselves. One of the things was to free themselves of the necessity of being thought of as sexual objects, which turned out to mean only that certain obvious concessions, like lipstick and pretty clothes, had by ukase been done away with. Still, there were those who wore their khakis and bandoliers with a difference. Whether or not they shaved their legs and armpits, whether or not they smelled, the pretty ones were still pretty and the others were not; the ones with good bodies walked in an unconscious pride and the others tried to ignore the differences and settled into their flesh, saying: Now, we are all equal.

There were great disputes as to what they were going to do and which things they would do first. It was fairly well agreed that although the law said that they were equal, nothing much was changed. There was still the monthly bleeding. Dr. Ora Fessenden, the noted gynecologist, had showed them a trick which was supposed to take care of all that, but nothing short of surgery or menopause would halt the process altogether; what man had to undergo such indignities? There was still pregnancy, but the women all agreed they were on top of that problem. That left the rest; men still looked down on them, in part because in the main, women were shorter; they were more or less free to pursue their careers, assuming they could keep a babysitter, but there were still midafternoon depressions, dishes, the wash; despite all the changes, life was much the same. More drastic action was needed.

They decided to form an army.

At the time, nobody was agreed on what they were going to do or how they would go about it, but they were all agreed that it was time for a change. things could not go on as they were; life was often boring, and too hard.

She wrote a note:
Dear Ralph,
I am running away to realize my full potential. I know you have always said I could do anything I want but what you meant was, I could do anything as long as it didn't mess you up, which is not exactly the same thing now, is it? Don't bother to look for me.

No longer yours,
Lory

Then she went to join the women in the hills.
I would like to go, Suellen thought, *but what if they wouldn't let me have my baby?*

Jolene's uncle in the country always had a liver-colored setter named Fido. The name remained the same and the dogs were more or less interchangeable. Jolene called all her lovers Mike, and because they were more or less interchangeable, eventually she tired of them and went to join the women in the hills.

"You're not going," Herb Chandler said.
Annie said, "I am."
He grabbed her as she reached the door. "The hell you are, I need you."
"You don't need me, you need a maid." She slapped the side of his head. "Now let me go."
"You're mine," he said, aiming a karate chop at her neck. She wriggled and he missed.
"Just like your ox and your ass, huh." She had gotten hold of a lamp and she let him have it on top of the head.
"Ow," he said, and crumpled to the floor.
"Nobody owns me," she said, throwing the vase of flowers she kept on the side table, just for good measure. "I'll be back when it's over." Stepping over him, she went out the door.

After everybody left that morning, June mooned around the living room, picking up the scattered newspapers, collecting her and Vic's empty coffee cups and marching out to face the kitchen table, which looked the same way every morning at this time, glossy with spilled milk and clotted cereal, which meant that she had to go through the same motions every morning at this time, feeling more and more like that jerk, whatever his name was, who for eternity kept on pushing the same recalcitrant stone up the hill; he was never going to get it to the top because it kept falling back on him and she was never going to get to the top, wherever that was, because there would always be the kitchen table, and the wash, and the crumbs on the rug, and besides she didn't know where the top was because she had gotten married right after Sweetbriar and the next minute, bang, there was the kitchen table and, give or take a few babies, give or take a few stabs at night classes in something or other, that seemed to be her life. There it was in the morning, there it was again at noon, there it was at night; when people said, at parties, "What do you do?" she could only move her hands helplessly because there was no answer she could give that would please either herself or them. *I clean the kitchen table,* she thought, because there was no other way to describe it. Occasionally she thought about running away but where would she go, and how would she live? Besides, she would miss Vic and the kids and her favorite chair in the television room. Sometimes she thought she might grab the milkman or the next delivery boy, but she knew she would be too embarrassed, either that or she would start laughing, or the delivery boy would, and even if they didn't she would never be able to face Vic. She thought she had begun to disappear, like the television or the washing machine; after a while nobody would see her at all. They might complain if she wasn't working properly, but in the main she was just another household appliance, and so she mooned, wondering if this was all there was ever going to be: herself in the house, the kitchen table.

Then the notice came.

JOIN NOW

It was in the morning mail, hastily mimeographed and addressed to her by name. If she had been in a different mood she might have tossed it out with the rest of the junk mail, or called a few of her friends to see if they'd gotten it too. As it was, she read it through, chewing over certain catchy phrases in this call to arms, surprised to find her blood quickening. Then she packed and wrote her note:

Dear Vic,

There are clean sheets on all the beds and three casseroles in the freezer and one in the oven. The veal one should do for two meals. I have done all the wash and a thorough vacuuming. If Sandy's cough doesn't get any better you should take her in to see Dr. Weixelbaum, and don't forget Jimmy is supposed to have his braces tightened on the 12th. Don't look for me.

Love,
June

Then she went to join the women in the hills.

Glenda Thompson taught psychology at the university; it was the semester break and she thought she might go to the women's encampment in an open spirit of inquiry. If she liked what they were doing she might chuck Richard, who was only an instructor while she was an assistant professor, and join them. To keep the appearance of objectivity, she would take notes.

Of course she was going to have to figure out what to do with the children while she was gone. No matter how many hours she and Richard taught, the children were her responsibility, and if they were both working in the house, she had to leave her typewriter and shush the children because of the way Richard got when he was disturbed. None of the sitters she called could come; Mrs. Birdsall, their regular sitter, had taken off without notice again, to see her son the freshman in Miami, and she exhausted the list of student sitters without any luck. She thought briefly of leaving them at Richard's office, but she couldn't trust him to remember them at the end of the day. She reflected bitterly that men who wanted to work just got up and went to the office, it had never seemed fair.

"Oh hell," she said finally, and because it was easier, she packed Tommy and Bobby and took them along.

Marva and Patsy and Betts were sitting around in Marva's room; it was two days before the junior prom and not one of them had a date, or even a nibble, there weren't even any blind dates to be had.

"I know what let's do," Marva said, "let's go up to Ferguson's and join the women's army."

Betts said, "I didn't know they had an *army*."

"Nobody knows what they have up there," Patsy said.

They left a note so Marva's mother would be sure and call them in case somebody asked for a date at the last minute and they got invited to the prom after all.

Sally felt a twinge of guilt when she opened the flier.

JOIN NOW

After she read it she went to the window and looked at the smoke column in open disappointment: *Oh, so that's all it is.* Yearning after it in the early autumn twilight, she had thought it might represent something more: excitement, escape, but she supposed she should have guessed. There was no great getaway, just a bunch of people who needed more people to help. She knew she probably ought to go up and help out for a while, she could design posters and ads they could never afford if they went to a regular graphics studio. Still, all those women . . . She couldn't bring herself to make the first move.

"I'm not a joiner," she said aloud, but that wasn't really it; she had always worked at home, her studio took up one wing of the house and she made her own hours; when she tired of working she could pick at the breakfast dishes or take a nap on the lumpy couch at one end of the studio; when the kids came home she was always there and besides, she didn't like going places without Zack.

At the camp, Dr. Ora Fessenden was leading an indoctrination program for new recruits. She herself was in the stirrups, lecturing coolly while everybody filed by.

One little girl, lifted up by her mother, began to whisper: "Ashphasp-hazzzzzz-pzz."

The mother muttered, "Mumumumumummmmmm . . ."

Ellen Ferguson, who was holding the light, turned it on the child for a moment. "Well, what does *she* want?"

"She wants to know what a man's looks like."

Dr. Ora Fessenden took hold, barking from the stirrups, "With luck, she'll never have to see."

"Right on," the butch sisters chorused, but the others began to look at one another in growing discomfiture, which as the weeks passed would ripen into alarm.

By the time she reached the camp, June was already worried about the casseroles she had left for Vic and the kids. Would the one she had left in the oven go bad at room temperature? Maybe she ought to call Vic and tell him to let it bubble for an extra half hour just in case. Would Vic really keep an eye on Sandy, and if she got worse would he get her to the doctor in time? What about Jimmy's braces? She almost turned back.

But she was already at the gate to Ellen Ferguson's farm. and she was surprised to see a hastily constructed guardhouse, with Ellen herself in khakis, standing with a carbine at the ready and she said, "Don't shoot, Ellen, it's me."

"For God's sake, June, I'm not going to shoot you." Ellen pushed her glasses up on her forehead so she could look into June's face. "I never thought you'd have the guts."

"I guess I needed a change."

"Isn't it thrilling?"

"I feel funny without the children." June was trying to remember when she had last seen Ellen: over a bridge table? at Weight Watchers? "How did you get into this?"

"I needed something to live for," Ellen said.

By that time two other women with rifles had impounded her car and then she was in a jeep bouncing up the dirt road to headquarters. The women behind the table all had on khakis, but they looked not at all alike in them. One was tall and tawny and called herself Sheena; there was a tough, funny-looking one named Rap and the third was Margy, still redolent of the kitchen sink. Sheena made the welcoming speech, and then Rap took her particulars while Margy wrote everything down.

She lied a little about her weight, and was already on the defensive when Rap looked at her over her glasses, saying, "Occupation?"

"Uh, household manager."

"Oh shit, another housewife. Skills?"

"Well, I used to paint a little, and . . ."

Rap snorted.

"I'm pretty good at conversational French."

"Kitchen detail," Rap said to Margy and Margy checked off a box and flipped over to the next sheet.

"But I'm tired of all that," June said.

Rap said, "Next."

Oh it was good sitting around the campfire, swapping stories about the men at work and the men at home; every woman had a horror story, because even the men who claimed to be behind them weren't really behind them, they were playing lip service to avoid a higher price, and even the best among them would make those terrible verbal slips. It was good to talk to other women who were smarter than their husbands and tired of having to pretend they weren't. It was good to be able to sprawl in front of the fire without having to think about Richard and what time he would be home. The kids were safely stashed down at the day care compound, along with everybody else's kids, and for the first time in at least eight years Glenda could relax and think about herself. She listened drowsily to that night's speeches, three examples of wildly diverging cant, and she would have taken notes except that she was full, digesting a dinner she hadn't had to cook, and for almost the first time in eight years she wasn't going to have to go out in the kitchen and face the dishes.

Marva, Patsy and Betts took turns admiring each other in their new uniforms and they sat at the edge of the group, hugging their knees and listening in growing excitement. Why, they didn't have to worry about what they looked like, what wasn't going to matter in the new scheme of things. It didn't *matter* whether or not they had dates. By the time the new order was established, they weren't even going to *want* dates. Although they would rather die than admit it, they all felt a little pang at this. Goodbye hope chest, goodbye wedding trip to Nassau and picture in the papers in the long white veil. Patsy, who wanted to be a corporation lawyer, thought: Why can't I have it *all*.

Now that his mother was dead and he didn't need to sell vacuum cleaners any more, Andy Ellis was thrown back on his own resources. He spent three hours in the shower and three days sleeping, and on the fourth day he emerged to find out his girl had left him for the koto player across the hall. "Well shit," he said, and wandered into the street.

He had only been asleep for three days but everything was subtly different. The people in the corner market were mostly men, stocking up on TV dinners and chunky soups or else buying cooking wines and herbs, kidneys, beef liver and tripe. The usual girl was gone from the checkout counter, the butcher was running the register instead, and when Andy asked about it Freddy the manager said, "She joined up."

"Are you kidding?"

"Some girl scout camp up at Ferguson's. The tails revolt."

Just then a jeep sped by in the street outside, there was a crash and they both hit the floor, rising to their elbows after the object that had shattered the front window did not explode. It was a rock with a note attached. Andy picked his way through the glass to retrieve it. It read:

WE WILL BURY YOU

"See?" Freddy said, ugly and vindictive. "See? See?"

The local hospital admitted several cases of temporary blindness in men who had been attacked by night with women's deodorant spray.

All over town the men whose wives remained lay next to them in growing unease. Although they all feigned sleep, they were aware that the stillness was too profound: the women were thinking.

The women trashed a porn movie house. Among them was the wife of the manager, who said, as she threw an open can of film over the balcony, watching it unroll, "I'm doing this for us."

So it had begun. For the time being, Rap and her cadre, who were in charge of the military operation, intended to satisfy themselves with guerrilla tactics; so far, nobody had been able to link the sniping and materiel bombing with the women on the hill, but they all knew it was only a matter of time before the first police cruiser came up to Ellen Ferguson's gate with a search warrant, and they were going to have to wage open war.

By this time one of the back pastures had been converted to a rifle range, and even poor June had to spend at least one hour of every day in practice. She began to take an embarrassing pleasure in it, thinking, as she potted away:

Aha, Vic, there's a nick in your scalp. Maybe you'll remember what I look like next time you leave the house for the day.

OK, kids, I am not the maid.

All right, Sally, you and your damn career. You're still only the maid.

Then, surprisingly, *This is for you, Sheena. How dare you go around looking like that, when I have to look like this.*

This is for every rapist on the block.

By the time she fired her last shot her vision was blurred by tears. *June, you are stupid, stupid, you always have been and you know perfectly well nothing is going to make any difference.*

Two places away, Glenda saw Richard's outline in the target. She made a bullseye. *All right, damn you, pick up that toilet brush.*

Going back to camp in the truck they all sang "Up Women" and "The

Internacionale," and June began to feel a little better. It reminded her of the good old days at camp in middle childhood, when girls and boys played together as if there wasn't any difference. She longed for that old androgynous body, the time before sexual responsibility. Sitting next to her on the bench, Glenda sang along but her mind was at the university; she didn't know what she was going to do if she got the Guggenheim because Richard had applied without success for so long that he had given up trying. What should she do, lie about it? It would be in all the papers. She wondered how convincing she would be, saying, Shit, honey, it doesn't mean anything. She would have to give up the revolution and get back to her work; her book was only half-written, she would have to go back to juggling kids and house and work, it was going to be hard, hard. She decided finally that she would let the Guggenheim Foundation make the decision for her. She would wait until late February and then write and tell Richard where to forward her mail.

Leading the song, Rap looked at her group. Even the softest ones had calluses now, but it was going to be some time before she made real fighters out of them. She wondered why women had all buried the instinct to kill. It was those damn babies, she decided, grunt, strain, pain, *Baby*. Hand a mother a gun and tell her to kill and she will say, *After I went to all that trouble?* Well if you are going to make sacrifices you are going to have to make sacrifices, she thought, and led them in a chorus of the battle anthem, watching to see just who did and who didn't throw herself into the last chorus, which ended: kill, kill, *kill*.

Sally was watching the smoke again. Zack said, "I wish you would come away from that window."

She kept looking for longer than he would have liked her to, and when she turned she said, "Zack, why did you marry me?"

"Couldn't live without you."

"No, really."

"Because I wanted to love you and decorate you and take care of you for the rest of your life."

"Why me?"

"I thought we could be friends for a long time."

"I guess I didn't mean why did you marry *me*, I meant, why did you *marry* me."

He looked into his palms. "I wanted you to take care of me too."

"Is that all?"

He could see she was serious and because she was not going to let go he thought for a minute and said at last, "Nobody wants to die alone."

Down the street, June Goodall's husband, Vic, had called every hospital in the county without results. The police had no reports of middle-aged housewives losing their memory in Sears or getting raped, robbed or poleaxed anywhere within the city limits. The police sergeant said, "Mr. Goodall, we've got more serious things on our minds. These bombings, for one thing, and the leaflets and the ripoffs. Do you know that women have been walking out of supermarkets with full shopping carts without paying a cent?" There seemed to be a thousand cases like June's, and if the department ever got a minute for them it would have to be first come first served.

So Vic languished in his darkening house. He had managed to get the kids off to school by himself the past couple of days. He gave them money for hot lunches but they were running out of clean clothes and he could not bring himself to sort through those disgusting smelly things in the clothes hamper to run a load of wash. They had run through June's casseroles and they were going to have to start eating out; they would probably go to the Big Beef Plaza tonight, and have pizza tomorrow and chicken the next night and Chinese the next, and if June wasn't back by that time he didn't know what he was going to do because he was at his wits' end. The dishes were piling up in the kitchen and he couldn't understand why everything looked so grimy; he couldn't quite figure out why, but the toilet had begun to smell. One of these days he was going to have to try and get his mother over to clean things up a little. It was annoying, not having any clean underwear. He wished June would come back.

For the fifth straight day, Richard Thompson, Glenda's husband, opened *The French Chef* to a new recipe and prepared himself an exquisite dinner. Once it was finished he relaxed in the blissful silence. Now that Glenda was gone he was able to keep things the way he liked them; he didn't break his neck on Matchbox racers every time he went to put a little Vivaldi on the record player. It was refreshing not to have to meet Glenda's eyes, where, to his growing dissatisfaction, he perpetually measured himself. Without her demands, without the kids around to distract him, he would be able to finish his monograph on Lyly's *Euphues*. He might even begin to write his book. Setting aside Glenda's half-finished manuscript with a certain satisfaction, he cleared a space for himself at the desk and tried to begin.

Castrated, he thought half an hour later. *Her and her damned career, she has castrated me.*

He went to the phone and began calling names on his secret list. For some reason most of them weren't home, but on the fifth call he came up with Jennifer, the biology major who wanted to write poetry, and within minutes the two of them were reaffirming his masculinity on the living room rug, and if a few pages of Glenda's half-finished manuscript got mislaid in the tussle, who was there to protest? If she was going to be off there, farting around in the woods with all those women, she never would get it finished.

In the hills, the number of women had swelled, and it was apparent to Sheena, Ellen and Rap that it was time to stop hit-and-run terrorism and operate on a larger scale. They would mount a final recruiting campaign. Once that was completed, they would be ready to take their first objective. Sheena had decided the Sunnydell Shopping Center would be their base for a sweep of the entire country. They were fairly sure retaliation would be slow, and to impede it further, they had prepared an advertising campaign built on the slogan: YOU WOULDN'T SHOOT YOUR MOTHER, WOULD YOU? As soon as they could they would co-opt some television equipment and make their first nationwide telecast from Sunnydell. Volunteers would flock in from fifty states and in time the country would be theirs.

There was some difference of opinion as to what they were going to do with it. Rap was advocating a scorched-earth policy; the women would rise like phoenixes from the ashes and build a new nation from the rubble, more or less alone. Sheena raised the idea of an auxiliary made up of male sympathizers. The women would rule, but with men at hand. Margy secretly felt that both Rap and Sheena were too militant; she didn't want things to be completely different, only a little better. Ellen Ferguson wanted to annex all the land surrounding her place. She envisioned it as the capitol city of the new world. The butch sisters wanted special legislation that would outlaw contact, social or sexual, with men, with, perhaps, special provisions for social meetings with their gay brethren. Certain of the straight sisters were made uncomfortable by their association with the butch sisters and wished there were some way the battle could progress without them. At least half of these women wanted their men back, once victory was assured, and the other half were looking into ways of perpetuating the race by means of parthenogenesis, or, at worst, sperm banks and AI techniques. One highly vocal splinter group wanted mandatory sterilization for everybody, and a portion of the lunatic fringe was demanding transsexual operations. Because nobody could agree, the women decided for the time being to skip over the issues and concentrate on the war effort itself.

By this time word had spread and the volunteers were coming in, so it was easy to ignore issues because logistics were more pressing. It was still warm enough for the extras to bunk in the fields, but winter was coming on and the women were going to have to manage food, shelters and uniforms for an unpredictable number. There had been a temporary windfall when Rap's bunch hijacked a couple of semis filled with frozen dinners and surplus clothes, but Rap and Sheena and the others could sense the hounds of hunger and need not far away and so they worked feverishly to prepare for the invasion. Unless they could take the town by the end of the month, they were lost.

"We won't have to hurt our *fathers*, will we?" Although she was now an expert marksman and had been placed in charge of a platoon, Patsy was still not at ease with the cause.

Rap avoided her eyes. "Don't be ridiculous."

"I just couldn't do that to anybody I *loved*," Patsy said. She reassembled her rifle, driving the bolt into place with a click. "Don't you worry about it," Rap said. "All you have to worry about is looking good when you lead that recruiting detail."

"Okay." Patsy tossed her hair. She knew how she and her platoon looked, charging into the wind; she could feel the whole wild group around her, on the run with their heads high and their bright hair streaming. *I wish the boys at school could see,* she thought, and turned away hastily before Rap could guess what she was thinking.

I wonder if any woman academic can be happy. Glenda was on latrine detail and this always made her reflective. *Maybe if they marry garage mechanics.* In the old days there had been academic types: single, tweedy, sturdy in orthopedic shoes, but somewhere along the way these types had been supplanted by married women of every conceivable type, who pressed forward in wildly varied disciplines, having in common only the singular harried look which marked them all. The rubric was more or less set: if you were good, you always had to worry about whether you were shortchanging your family; if you weren't as good as he was, you would always have to wonder whether it was because of all the other duties: babies, meals, the house; if despite everything you turned out to be better than he was, then you had to decide whether to try and minimize it, or prepare yourself for the wise looks on the one side, on the other, his look of uncomprehending reproach. If you *were* better than he was, then why should you be wasting your time with *him*? She felt light years removed from the time when girls used to be advised to let him win the tennis match; everybody played to win now, but she had the uncomfortable feeling that there might never be any real victories. Whether or not you won there were too many impediments; if he had a job and you didn't, then tough; if you both had jobs but he didn't get tenure, then you had to quit and move with him to a new place. She poured Lysol into the last toilet and turned her back on it, thinking: *Maybe that's why those Hollywood marriages are always breaking up.*

Sally finished putting the children to bed and came back into the living room, where Zack was waiting for her on the couch. By this time she had heard the women's broadcasts, she was well aware of what was going on at Ellen Ferguson's place and knew as well that this was where June was, and June was so inept, so soft and incapable that she really ought to be up there helping June, helping *them*; it was a job that ought to be done, on what scale she could not be sure, but the fire was warm and Zack was waiting; he and the children, her career, were all more important than that abstraction in the hills; she had negotiated her own peace—let them take care of theirs. Settling in next to Zack, she thought: *I don't love my little pink dishmop. I don't, but everybody has to shovel* some *shit.* Then: *God help the sailors and poor fishermen who have to be abroad on a night like this.*

June had requisitioned a jeep and was on her way into town to knock over the corner market, because food was already in short supply. She had on the housedress she had worn when she enlisted, and she would carry somebody's old pink coat over her arm to hide the pistol and the grenade she would use to hold her hostages at bay while the grocery boys filled up the jeep. She had meant to go directly to her own corner market, thinking, among other things, that the manager might recognize her and tell Vic, after which, of course, he would track her back to the camp and force her to come home to him and the children. Somehow or other she went right by the market and ended up at the corner of her street.

She knew she was making a mistake but she parked and began to prowl the neighborhood. The curtains in Sally's window were drawn but the light behind them gave out a rosy glow, which called up in her longings that she could not have identified; they had very little to do with her own home, or her life with Vic; they dated, rather, from her childhood, when she had imagined marriage, had prepared herself for it with an amorphous but unshakeable idea of what it would be like.

Vic had forgotten to put out the garbage; overflowing cans crowded the back porch and one of them was overturned. Walking on self-conscious cat feet, June made her way up on the porch and peered into the kitchen: just as she had suspected, a mess. A portion of her was tempted to go in and do a swift, secret cleaning—*the phantom housewife strikes*—but the risk of being discovered was too great. Well, let him clean up his own damn messes from now on. She tiptoed back down the steps and went around the house, crunching through bushes to look into the living room. She had hoped to get a glimpse of the children, but they were already in bed. She thought about waking Juney with pebbles on her window, whispering: Don't worry, mother's all right, but she wasn't strong enough; if she saw the children she would never be able to walk away and return to camp. She assuaged herself by thinking she would come back for Juney and Victor Junior just as soon as victory was assured. The living room had an abandoned look, with dust visible and papers strewn, a chair overturned and Vic himself asleep on the couch, just another neglected object in this neglected house. Surprised at how little she felt, she shrugged and turned away. On her way back to the jeep she did stop to right the garbage can.

The holdup went off all right; she could hear distant sirens building behind her, but so far as she knew, she wasn't followed.

The worst thing turned out to be finding Rap, Sheena and Ellen Ferguson gathered around the stove in the main cabin; they didn't hear her come in.

". . . so damn fat and soft," Rap was saying.

Sheena said, "You have to take your soldiers where you can find them."

Ellen said, "An army travels on its stomach."

"As soon as it's over we dump the housewives," Rap said. "Every single one."

June cleared her throat. "I've brought the food."

"Politics may make strange bedfellows," Glenda said, "but this is ridiculous."

"Have it your way," she said huffily—whoever she was—and left the way she had come in.

Patsy was in charge of the recruiting platoon, which visited the high school, and she thought the principal was really impressed when he saw that it was her. Her girls bound and gagged the faculty and held the boys at bay with M-1s while she made her pitch. She was successful but drained when she finished, pale and exhausted, and while her girls were processing the recruits (all but one percent of the girl students, as it turned out) and waiting for the bus to take them all to camp, Patsy put Marva in charge and simply drifted away, surprised to find herself in front of the sweetie shop two blocks from school. The place was empty except for Andy Ellis, who had just begun work as a counter boy.

He brought her a double dip milkshake and lingered.

She tried to wave him away with her rifle. "We don't have to pay."

"That isn't it." He yearned, drawn to her.

She couldn't help seeing how beautiful he was. "Bug off."

Andy said, "Beautiful."

She lifted her head, aglow. "Really?"

"No kidding. Give me a minute. I'm going to fall in love with you."

"You can't," she said, remembering her part in the eleventh grade production of *Romeo and Juliet*. "I'm some kind of Montague."

"OK, then, I'll be the Capulet."

"I . . ." Patsy leaned forward over the counter so they could kiss. She drew back at the sound of a distant shot. "I have to go."

"When can I see you?"

Patsy said, "I'll sneak out tonight."

Sheena was in charge of the recruiting detail that visited Sally's neighborhood. Although she had been an obscure first-year medical student when the upheaval started, she was emerging as the heroine of the revolution. The newspapers and television newscasters all knew who she was and so Sally knew, and was undeniably flattered that she had come in person.

She and Sally met on a high level; if there is an aristocracy of achievement, then they spoke aristocrat to aristocrat. Sheena spoke of talent and obligation; she spoke of need and duty; she spoke of service. She said the women needed Sally's help, and when Sally said, Let them help themselves, she said, They can't. They were still arguing when the kids came home from school, they were still arguing when Zack came home. Sheena spoke of the common cause and a better world. She spoke once more of the relationship between gifts and service. Sally turned to Zack, murmuring, and he said:

"If you think you have to do it, then I guess you'd better do it."

She said: "The sooner I go the sooner this thing will be over."

Zack said, "I hope you're right."

Sheena stood aside so they could make their goodbyes. Sally hugged the children, and when they begged to go with her she said, "it's no place for kids."

Climbing into the truck, she looked back at Zack and thought: *I could not love thee half so much loved I not honor more.* What she said was, "I must be out of my mind."

Zack stood in the street with his arms around the kids, saying, "She'll be back soon. Some day they'll come marching down our street."

In the truck, Sheena said, "Don't worry. When we occupy, we'll see that he gets a break."

They were going so fast now that there was no jumping off the truck; the other women at the camp seemed to be so grateful to see her that she knew there would be no jumping off the truck until it was over.

June whispered, "To be perfectly honest, I was beginning to have my doubts about the whole thing, but with *you* along . . ."

They made Sally a member of the council.

The next day the women took the Sunnydell Shopping Center, which included two supermarkets, a discount house, a fast-food place and a cinema; they selected it because it was close to camp and they could change guard details with a minimum of difficulty. The markets would solve the food problem for the time being, at least.

In battle, they used M-1s, one submachine gun and a variety of sidearms and grenades. They took the place without firing a shot.

The truth was that until this moment, the men had not taken the revolution seriously.

The men had thought: After all, it's only women.

They had thought: Let them have their fun. We can stop this thing whenever we like.

They had thought: What difference does it make? They'll come crawling back to us.

In this first foray the men, who were, after all, unarmed, fled in surprise. Because the women had not been able to agree upon policy, they let their vanquished enemy go; for the time being, they would take no prisoners.

They were sitting around the victory fire that night, already aware that it was chilly and when the flames burned down a bit they were going to have to go back inside. It was then, for the first time, that Sheena raised the question of allies.

She said, "Sooner or later we have to face facts. We can't make it alone."

Sally brightened, thinking of Zack. "I think you're right."

Rap leaned forward. "Are you serious ?"

Sheena tossed her hair. "What's the matter with sympathetic men?"

"The only sympathetic man is a dead man," Rap said.

Sally rose. "Wait a minute."

Ellen Ferguson pulled her down. "Relax. All she means is, at this stage we can't afford any risks. Infiltration. Spies."

Sheena said, "We could use a few men."

Sally heard herself, *sotto voce*. "You're not kidding."

Dr. Ora Fessenden rose, in stages. She said, with force, "Look here, Sheena, if you are going to take a stance, you are going to have to take a stance."

If she had been there, Patsy would have risen to speak in favor of a men's auxiliary. As it was, she had sneaked out to meet Andy. They were down in the shadow of the conquered shopping center, falling in love.

In the command shack, much later, Sheena paced moodily. "They aren't going to be satisfied with the shopping center for long."

Sally said, "I think things are going to get out of hand."

"They can't." Sheena kept on pacing. "We have too much to do."

"Your friend Rap and the doctor are out for blood. Lord knows how many of the others are going to go along." Sally sat at the desk, doodling on the roll sheet. "Maybe you ought to dump them."

"We need muscle, Sally."

Margy, who seemed to be dusting, said, "I go along with Sally."

"No." Lory was in the corner, transcribing Sheena's remarks of the evening. "Sheena's absolutely right."

It was morning, and Ellen Ferguson paced the perimeter of the camp. "We're going to need fortifications here, and more over here."

Glenda, who followed with the clipboard, said, "What are you expecting?"

"I don't know, but I want to be ready for it."

"Shouldn't we be concentrating on *offense?*"

"Not me," Ellen said, with her feet set wide in the dirt. "This is my place. This is where I make my stand."

"Allies. That woman is a marshmallow. *Allies.*" Rap was still seething. "I think we ought to go ahead and make our play."

"We still need them," Dr. Ora Fessenden said. The two of them were squatting in the woods above the camp. "When we get strong enough, then . . ." She drew her finger across her throat. "Zzzzt."

"Dammit to hell, Ora." Rap was on her feet, punching a tree trunk. "If you're going to fight, you're going to have to kill."

"You know it and I know it," Dr. Ora Fessenden said. "Now try and tell that to the rest of the girls."

As she settled into the routine, Sally missed Zack more and more and, partly because she missed him so much, she began making a few inquiries. The consensus was that women had to free themselves from every kind of dependence, both emotional and physical; sexual demands would be treated on the level of other bodily functions, any old toilet would do.

"Hello, Ralph?"

"Yes?"

"It's me, Lory. Listen, did you read bout what we did?"

"About what *who* did?"

"Stop trying to pretend you don't know. Listen, Ralph, that was us that took over out at Sunnydale. *Me.*"

"You and what army?"

"The women's army. Oh, I see, you're being sarcastic. Well listen, Ralph, I said I was going to realize myself as a person and I have. I'm a sublieutenant now. A sublieutenant, imagine."

"What about your novel you were going to write about your rotten marriage?"

"Don't pick nits. I'm Sheena's secretary now. You were holding me

75

back, Ralph, all those years you were dragging me down. Well now I'm a free agent. Free."

"Terrific."

"Look, I have to go; we have uniform inspection now and worst luck, I drew KP."

"Listen," Rap was saying to a group of intent women, "You're going along minding your own business and wham, he swoops down like the wolf upon the fold. It's the ultimate weapon."

Dr. Ora Fessenden said bitterly, "And you just try and rape him back."

Margy said, "I thought men were, you know, supposed to protect women from all that."

Annie Chandler, who had emerged as one of the militants, threw her knife into a tree. "Try and convince them it ever happened. The cops say you must have led him on."

Dr. Ora Fessenden drew a picture of the woman as a ruined city, with gestures.

"I don't know what I would do if one of them tried to . . ."

Betts said to Patsy. "What would you do?"

Oh, Andy. Patsy said, "I don't know."

"There's only one thing *to* do," Rap said, with force. "Shoot on sight."

It was hard to say what their expectations had been after this first victory. There were probably almost as many expectations as there were women. A certain segment of the group was disappointed because Vic/Richard/Tom-Dick-Harry had not come crawling up the hill crying, My God how I have missed you, come home and everything will be different. Rap and the others would have wished for more carnage, and as the days passed the thirst for blood heaped dust in their mouths. Sheena was secretly disappointed that there had not been wider coverage of the battle in the press and on nationwide TV. The mood in the camp after that first victory was one of anticlimax, indefinable but growing discontent.

Petty fights broke out in the rank and file.

There arose, around this time, some differences between the rank-and-file women, some of whom had children, and the Mothers' Escadrille, an elite corps of women who saw themselves as professional mothers. As a group, they looked down on people like Glenda, who sent their children off to the day care compound. The Mothers' Escadrille would admit, when pressed, that their goal in banding together was the eventual elimination of the role of the man in the family, for man, with his incessant demands, interfered with the primary function of the mother. Still, they had to admit that, since they had no other profession, they were going to have to be assured some kind of financial support in the ultimate scheme of things. They also wanted more respect from the other women, who seemed to look down on them because they lacked technical or professional skills, and so they conducted their allotted duties in a growing atmosphere of hostility.

It was after a heated discussion with one of the mothers that Glenda, suffering guilt pangs and feelings of inadequacy, went down to the day care compound to see her own children. She picked them out at once, playing in the middle of a tangle of preschoolers, but she saw with a pang that Bobby was reluctant to leave the group to come and talk to her, and even after she said, "It's Mommy," it took Tommy a measurable number of seconds before he recognized her.

The price, she thought in some bitterness. *I hope in the end it turns out to be worth the price.*

Betts had tried running across the field both with and without her bra, and except for the time when she wrapped herself in the Ace bandage, she definitely bounced. At the moment nobody in the camp was agreed as to whether it was a good or a bad thing to bounce; it was either another one of those things the world at large was going to have to, by God, learn to ignore, or else it was a sign of weakness. Either way it was uncomfortable, but so was the Ace bandage uncomfortable.

Sally was drawn toward home but at the same time, looking around at the disparate women and their growing discontent, she knew she ought to stay on until the revolution had put itself in order. The women were unable to agree what the next step would be, or to consolidate their gains, and so she met late into the night with Sheena, and walked around among the others. She had the feeling that she could help, that whatever her own circumstance, the others were so patently miserable that she must help.

"Listen," said Zack, when Sally called him to explain, "it's no picnic being a guy, either."

The fear of rape had become epidemic. Perhaps because there had been no overt assault on the women's camp, no army battalions, not even any police cruisers, the women expected more subtle and more brutal retaliation. The older women were outraged because some of the younger women said what difference did it make? If you were going to make it, what did the circumstances matter? Still, the women talked about it around the campfire and at last it was agreed that regardless of individual reactions, for ideological reasons sit was important that it be made impossible; the propaganda value to the enemy would be too great, and so, at Rap's suggestion, each woman was instructed to carry her handweapon at all times and to shoot first and ask questions later.

Patsy and Andy Ellis were finding more and more ways to be together, but no matter how much they were together it didn't seem to be enough. Since Andy's hair was long, they thought briefly of disguising him as a woman and getting him into camp, but a number of things: whiskers, figure, musculature, would give him way and Patsy decided it would be too dangerous.

"Look, I'm in love with you," Andy said. "Why don't you run away?"

"Oh, I couldn't do that," Patsy said, trying to hide herself in his arms. "And besides . . ."

He hid his face in her hair. "Besides nothing."

"No, really. Besides. Everybody has guns now, everybody has different feelings, but they all hate deserters. We have a new policy."

"They'd never find us."

She looked into Andy's face. "Don't you want to hear about the new policy?"

"OK, what?"

"About deserters." She spelled it out, more than a little surprised at how far she had come. "It's hunt down and shave and kill."

"They wouldn't really do that."

"We had the first one last night, this poor old lady about forty. She got homesick for her family and tried to run away."

Andy was still amused. "They shaved all her hair off?"

"That wasn't all," Patsy said. "When they got finished they really did it. Firing squad, the works."

Although June would not have been sensitive to it, there were diverging feelings in the camp about who did what, and what there was to do. All she knew was she was sick and tired of working in the day care compound and when she went to Sheena and complained, Sheena, with exquisite sensitivity, put her in charge of the detail that guarded the shopping center. It was a temporary assignment but it gave June a chance to put on a cartridge belt and all the other paraphernalia of victory, so she cut an impressive figure for Vic, when he came along.

"It's me, honey, don't you know me?"

"Go away," she said with some satisfaction. "No civilians allowed."

"Oh for God's sake."

To their mutual astonishment, she raised her rifle. "Bug off, fella."

"You don't really think you can get away with this."

"Bug off or I'll shoot."

"We're just letting you do this, to get it out of your system." Vic moved as if to relieve her of the rifle. "If it makes you feel a little better . . ."

"This is your last warning."

"Listen," Vic said, a study in male outrage, "one step too far and, *tschoom*, federal troops."

She fired a warning shot so he left.

Glenda was a little sensitive about the fact that various husbands had found ways to smuggle in messages, some had even come looking for their wives, but not Richard. One poor bastard had been shot when he came in too close to the fire; they heard an outcry and a thrashing in the bushes but when they looked for him the next morning there was no body, so he must have dragged himself away. There had been notes in food consignments and one husband had hired a skywriter, but so far she had neither word nor sign from Richard, and she wasn't altogether convinced she cared. He seemed to have drifted off into time past along with her job, her students and her book. Once her greatest hope had been to read her first chapter at the national psychological conference; now she wondered whether there would even be any more conferences. If she and the others were successful, that would break down, along with a number of other things. Still, in the end she would have had her definitive work on the women's revolu-

79

tion, but so far the day-to-day talk had been so engrossing that she hadn't had a minute to begin. Right now, there was too much to do.

They made their first nationwide telecast from a specifically erected podium in front of the captured shopping center. For various complicated reasons the leaders made Sally speak first, and, as they had anticipated, she espoused the moderate view: this was a matter of service, women were going to have to give up a few things to help better the lot of their sisters. Once the job was done everything would be improved, but not really different.

Sheena came next, throwing back her bright hair and issuing the call to arms. The mail she drew would include several spirited letters from male volunteers who were already in love with her and would follow here anywhere; because the women had pledged never to take allies, these letters would be destroyed before they ever reached her.

Dr. Ora Fessenden was all threats, fire and brimstone. Rap took up where she left off.

"We're going to fight until there's not a man left standing . . ."

Annie Chandler yelled, "Right on."

Margy was trying to speak. ". . . just a few concessions."

Rap's eyes glittered. "Only sisters, and you guys . . ."

Ellen Ferguson said, "Up, women, out of slavery."

Rap's voice rose. ". . . you guys are going to burn."

Sally was saying, ". . . reason with you."

Rap hissed, "Bury you."

It was hard to say which parts of these messages reached the viewing public, as the women all interrupted and overrode each other and the cameramen concentrated on Sheena, who was to become the sign and symbol of the revolution. None of the women on the platform seemed to be listening to any of the others, which may have been just as well; the only reason they had been able to come this far together was because nobody ever did.

The letters began to come.

"Dear Sheena, I would like to join, but I already have nine children and now I am pregnant again . . ."

"Dear Sheena, I am a wife and mother but I will throw it all over in an instant if you will only glance my way . . ."

"Dear Sheena, our group has occupied the town hall in Gillespie, Indiana, but we are running out of ammo and the water supply is low. Several of the women have been stricken with plague, and we are running out of food . . ."

"First I made him lick my boots and then I killed him but now I have this terrible problem with the body, the kids don't want me to get rid of him . . ."

"Who do you think you are, running this war when you don't even know what you are doing, what you have to do is kill every last damn one of them and the ones you don't kill you had better cut off their Things . . ."

"Sheena, baby, if you will only give up this half-assed revolution you and I can make beautiful music together. I have signed this letter Maud to escape the censors but if you look underneath the stamp you can see who I really am."

The volunteers were arriving in dozens. The first thing was that there was not housing for all of them; there was not equipment, and so the woman in charge had to cut off enlistments at a certain point and send the others back to make war in their own home towns.

The second thing was that, with the increase in numbers, there was an increasing bitterness about the chores. Nobody wanted to do them; in secret truth nobody ever had, but so far the volunteers had all borne it, up to a point, because they sincerely believed that in the new order there would be no chores. Now they understood that the more people there were banded together, the more chores there would be. Laundry and garbage were piling up. At some point around the time of the occupation of the shopping center, the women had begun to understand that no matter what they accomplished, there would always be ugly things to do: the chores, and now, because there seemed to be so *much* work, there were terrible disagreements as to who was supposed to do what, and as a consequence they had all more or less stopped doing any of it.

Meals around the camp were catch as catch can.

The time was approaching when nobody in the camp would have clean underwear.

The latrines were unspeakable.

The children were getting out of hand; some of them were forming packs and making raids of their own, so that the quartermaster never had any clear idea of what she would find in the storehouse. Most of the women in the detail that had been put in charge of the day care compound were fed up.

By this time Sheena was a national figure; her picture was on the cover of both newsmagazines in the same week and there were nationally distributed lines of sweatshirts and toothbrush glasses bearing her picture and her name. She received love mail and hate mail in such quantity that Lory, who had joined the women to realize her potential as an individual, had to give up her other duties to concentrate on Sheena's mail. She would have to admit that it was better than KP, and besides, if Sheena went on to better things, maybe she would get to go along.

The air of dissatisfaction grew. Nobody agreed any more, not even all those who had agreed to agree for the sake of the cause. Fights broke out like flash fires; some women were given to sulks and inexplicable silences, others to blows and helpless tears quickly forgotten. On advice from Sally, Sheena called a council to try and bring everybody together, but it got off on the wrong foot.

Dr. Ora Fessenden said, "Are we going to sit around on our butts, or what?"

Sheena said, "National opinion is running in our favor. We have to consolidate our gains."

Rap said, "Gains hell. What kind of war is this? Where are the scalps?"

Sheena drew herself up. "We are not Amazons."

Rap said, "That's a crock of shit," and she and Dr. Ora Fessenden stamped out.

"Rape," Rap screamed, running from the far left to the far right and then making a complete circuit of the clearing. "Rape," she shouted, taking careful note of who came running and who didn't. "Raaaaaaaaape."

Dr. Ora Fessenden rushed to her side, the figure of outraged woman-hood. They both watched until a suitable number of women had assembled and then she said, in stentorian tones, "We cannot let this go unavenged."

"My God," Sheena said, looking at the blackened object in Rap's hand. "What are you doing with that thing?"

Blood-smeared and grinning, Rap said, "When you're trying to make a point, you have to go ahead and make your point." She thrust her trophy into Sheena's face.

Sheena averted her eyes quickly; she thought it was an ear. "That's supposed to be a *rhetorical* point."

"Listen, baby, this world doesn't give marks for good conduct."

Sheena stiffened. "You keep your girls in line or you're finished."

Rap was smoldering; she pushed her face up to Sheena's, saying, "You can't do without us and you know it."

"If we have to, we'll learn."

"Aieeee." One of Rap's cadre had taken the trophy from her and tied it on a string; now she ran through the camp swinging it around her head, and dozens of throats opened to echo her shout. "Aieeeeee."

Patsy and Andy were together in the bushes near the camp; proximity to danger made their pleasure more intense. Andy said, "Leave with me."

She said, "I can't. I told you what they do to deserters."

"They'll never catch us."

"You don't know these women," Patsy said. "Look, Andy, you'd better go."

"Just a minute more." Andy buried his face in her hair. "Just a little minute more."

"Rape," Rap shouted again, running through the clearing with her voice raised like a trumpet. "Raaaaaaaape."

Although she knew it was a mistake, Sally had sneaked away to see Zack and the children. The camp seemed strangely deserted, and nobody was there to sign out the jeep she took. She had an uncanny intimation of trouble at a great distance, but she shook it off and drove to her house. She would have expected barricades and guards: state of war, but the streets were virtually empty and she reached her neighborhood without trouble.

Zack and the children embraced her and wanted to know when she was coming home.

"Soon, I think. They're all frightened of us now."

Zack said, "I'm not so sure."

"There doesn't seem to be any resistance."

"Oh," he said, "they've decided to let you have the town."

"What did I tell you?"

"Sop," he said. "You can have anything you want. Up to a point."

Sally was thinking of Rap and Dr. Ora Fessenden. "What if we take more?"

"Wipeout," Zack said. "You'll see."

"Oh Lord," she said, vaulting into the jeep. "Maybe it'll be over sooner than I thought."

She was already too late. She saw the flames shooting skyward as she came out of the drive.

"It's Flowermont."

Because she had to make sure, she wrenched the jeep in that direction and rode to the garden apartments; smoke filled the streets for blocks around.

Looking at the devastation, Sally was reminded of Indian massacres in the movies of her childhood: the smoking ruins, the carnage, the moans of the single survivor who would bubble out his story in her arms. She could not be sure about the bodies: whether there were any, whether there were as many as she thought, but she was sure those were charred corpses in the rubble. Rap and Dr. Ora Fessenden had devised a flag and hoisted it from a tree: the symbol of the women's movement, altered to suit their mood — the crudely executed fist reduced to clenched bones and surrounded by flames. The single survivor died before he could bubble out his story in her arms.

In the camp, Rap and Dr. Ora Fessenden had a victory celebration around the fire. They had taken unspeakable trophies in their raid and could not understand why many of the women refused to wear them.

Patsy and Andy, in the bushes, watched with growing alarm. Even from their safe distance, Andy was fairly sure he saw what he thought he saw and he whispered, "Look, we've got to get out of here."

"Not now," Patsy said, pulling him closer. "Tonight. The patrols."

By now the little girls had been brought up from the day care compound and they had joined the dance, their fat cheeks smeared with blood. Rap's women were in heated discussion with the Mothers' Escadrille about the disposition of the boy children: would they be destroyed or reared as slaves? While they were talking, one of the mothers who had never felt at home in any faction sneaked down to the compound and freed the lot of them. Now she was running around in helpless tears, flapping her arms and sobbing broken messages, but no matter what she said to the children, she couldn't seem to get any of them to flee.

Sheena and her lieutenant, Margy, and Lory, her secretary, came out of the command shack at the same moment Sally arrived in camp; she rushed to join them, and together they extracted Rap and Dr. Ora Fessenden from the dance for a meeting of the council.

When they entered the shack, Ellen Ferguson hung up the phone in clattering haste and turned to confront them with a confusing mixture of expressions; Sally thought the foremost one was probably guilt.

Sally waited until they were all silent and then said, "The place is surrounded. They let me through to bring the message. They have tanks."

Ellen Ferguson said, "They just delivered their ultimatum. Stop the raids and pull back to camp or they'll have bombers level this place."

"Pull back hell," Rap said.

Dr. Ora Fessenden shook a bloody fist. "We'll show them."

"We'll fight to the death."

Ellen said, quietly, "I already agreed."

Down at the main gate, Marva, who was on guard duty, leaned across the barbed wire to talk to the captain of the tank detail. She thought he was kind of cute.

"Don't anybody panic," Rap was saying. "We can handle this thing. We can fight them off."

"We can fight them in the hedgerows," Dr. Ora Fessenden said in rising tones. "We can fight them in the ditches, we can hit them with everything we've got . . ."

"Not from here you can't."

"We can burn and bomb and kill and . . . What did you say?"

"I said, not from here." Because they were all staring, Ellen Ferguson

85

covered quickly, saying, "I mean, if I'm going to be of any value to the movement, I have to have this place in good condition."

Sheena said quietly, "That's not what you mean."

Ellen was near tears. "All right, dammit. This place is all I have."

"My God," Annie Chandler shrieked. "Rape." She parted the bushes to reveal Patsy and Andy, who hugged each other in silence. "Rape," Annie screamed, and everybody who could hear above the din came running. "Kill the bastard, rape, rape, rape."

Patsy rose to her feet and drew Andy up with her, shouting to make herself heard. "I said, it isn't rape."

Rap and Dr. Ora Fessenden were advancing on Ellen Ferguson. "You're not going to compromise us. We'll kill you first."

"Oh," Ellen said, backing away. "That's another thing. They wanted the two of you. I had to promise we'd send you out."

The two women lunged, and then retreated, mute with fury. Ellen had produced a gun from her desk drawer and now she had them covered.

"Son of a bitch," Rap said. "Son of a bitch."

"Kill them."

"Burn them."

"Hurt them."

"Make an example of them."

"I love you, Patsy."

"Oh, Andy, I love you."

Sally said softly, "So it's all over."

"Only parts of it," Ellen said. "It will never really be over, as long as there are women left to fight. We'll be better off without these two and their cannibals; we can retrench and make a new start."

"I guess this as good a time as any." Sheena got to her feet. "I might as well tell you, I'm splitting."

They turned to face her, Ellen being careful to keep the gun on Dr. Ora Fessenden and Rap.

"You're what?"

"I can do a hell of a lot more good on my new show. Prime time, nightly, nationwide TV."

Rap snarled, "The hell you say."

"Look, Rap, I'll interview you."

"Stuff it."

"Think what I can do for the movement. I can reach sixty million people, you'll see."

Ellen Ferguson said, with some satisfaction, "That's not really what you mean."

"Maybe it isn't. It's been you, you, you all this time." Sheena picked up her clipboard, her notebooks and papers; Lory and Margy both moved as if to follow her but she rebuffed them with a single sweep of her arm. "Well it's high time I started thinking about me."

Outside, the women had raised a stake and now Patsy and Andy were lashed to it, standing back to back.

In the shack, Rap and Dr. Ora Fessenden had turned as one and advanced on Ellen Ferguson, pushing the gun aside.

The good doctor said, "I knew you wouldn't have the guts to shoot. You never had any guts."

Ellen cried out, "Sheena, help me."

But Sheena was already in the doorway, and she hesitated for only a moment, saying, "Listen, it's *sauve qui peut* in this day and time, sweetie, and the sooner you realize it, the better."

Rap finished pushing Ellen down and took the gun. She stood over her victim for a minute, grinning. "In the battle of the sexes, there are only allies." Then she put a bullet through Ellen's favorite moosehead so Ellen would have something to remember her by.

The women had collected twigs and they were just about to set fire to Patsy and Andy when Sheena came out, closely followed by Dr. Ora Fessenden and a warlike Rap.

Everybody started shouting at once and in the imbroglio that followed, Patsy and Andy escaped. They would surface years later in a small town in Minnesota, with an ecologically alarming number of children; they would both be able to pursue their chosen careers in the law because they worked hand in hand to take care of all the children and the house, and they would love each other until they died.

Ellen Ferguson sat with her elbows on her knees and her head drooping, saying, "I can't believe it's all over, after I worked so hard, I gave so much . . ."

Sally said, "It isn't over. Remember what you said, as long as there are women, there will be a fight."

"But we've lost our leaders."

"You could . . ."

"No, I couldn't."

"Don't worry, there are plenty of others."

As Sally spoke, the door opened and Glenda stepped in to take Sheena's place.

When the melee in the clearing was over, Dr. Ora Fessenden and Rap had escaped with their followers. They knew the lay of the land and so they were able to elude the troop concentration, which surrounded the camp, and began to lay plans to regroup and fight another day.

A number of women, disgusted by the orgy of violence, chose to pack their things and go. The Mothers' Escadrille deserted en masse, taking their children and a few children who didn't even belong to them.

Ellen said, "You're going to have to go down there and parley. I'm not used to talking to men."

And so Sally found herself going down to the gate to conduct negotiations.

She said, "The two you wanted got away. The rest of them—I mean us—are acting in good faith." She lifted her chin. "If you want to go ahead and bomb anyway, you'll have to go ahead and bomb."

The captain lifted her and set her on the hood of the jeep. He was grinning. "Shit, little lady, we just wanted to throw a scare into you."

"You don't understand." She wanted to get down off the hood but he had propped his arms on either side of her. She knew she ought to be furious, but instead she kept thinking how much she missed Zack. Speaking with as much dignity as she could under the circumstances, she outlined the women's complaints; she already knew it was hopeless to list them as demands.

"Don't you worry about a thing, honey." He lifted her down and gave her a slap on the rump to speed her on her way. "Everything is going to be real different from now on."

"I bet."

Coming back up the hill to camp, she saw how sad everything looked, and she could not for the life of her decide whether it was because the women who had been gathered here had been inadequate in the cause or whether it was, rather, that the cause itself had been insufficiently identified; she suspected that they had come up against the human condition, failed to recognize it and so tried to attack a single part, which seemed to involve attacking the only allies they would ever have. As for the specific campaign, as far as she could tell, it was possible to change some of the surface or superficial details but once that was done things were still going to be more or less the way they were, and all the best will in the world would not make any real difference.

In the clearing, Lory stood at Glenda's elbow. "Of course you're going to need a lieutenant."

Glenda said, "I guess so."

Ellen Ferguson was brooding over a row of birches that had been trashed during the struggle. If she could stake them back up in time, they might reroot.

June said, "OK, I'm going to be mess sergeant."

Margy said, "The hell you will," and pushed her in the face.

Glenda said, thoughtfully, "Maybe we could mount a Lysistrata campaign."

Lory snorted. "If their wives won't do it, there are plenty of girls who will."

Zack sent a message:

WE HAVE TO HELP EACH OTHER.

Sally sent back:

I KNOW.

Before she went home, Sally had to say goodbye to Ellen Ferguson. Ellen's huge, homely face sagged. "Not you too."

Sally looked at the desultory groups policing the wreckage, at the separate councils convening in every corner. "I don't know why I came. I guess I thought we could really *do* something."

Ellen made a half-turn, taking in the command shack, the compound, the women who remained. "Isn't this enough?"

"I have to get on with my life ."

Ellen said, "This is mine."

"Oh, Vic, I've been so stupid." June was sobbing in Vic's arms. She was also lying in her teeth but she didn't care, she was sick of the revolution and she was going to have to go through this formula before Vic would allow her to resume her place at his kitchen sink. The work was still boring and stupid but at least there was less of it than there had been at camp; her bed was softer, and since it was coming on winter, she was always grateful for the storm sashes, which Vic put up every November, and the warmth of the oil burner, which he took apart and cleaned with his own hands every fall.

Sally found her house in good order, thanks to Zack, but there were several weeks' work piled up in her studio, and she had lost a couple of commissions. She opened her drawer to discover, with a smile, that Zack had washed at least one load of underwear with something red.

"I think we do better together," Zack said.

Sally said, "We always have."

In the wake of fraternization with the military guard detail, Marva discovered she was pregnant. She knew what Dr. Ora Fessenden said she was supposed to do, but she didn't think she wanted to.

As weeks passed, the women continued to drift away. "It's nice here and all," Betts said apologetically, "but there's a certain *je ne sais quoi* missing; I don't know what it is, but I'm going back in there and see if I can find it."

Glenda said, "Yeah, well. So long as there is a yang, I guess there is going to have to be a yin."

"Don't you mean, so long as there is a yin, there is going to have to be a yang?"

Glenda looked in the general direction of town, knowing there was nothing there for her to go back to. "I don't know what I mean any more."

Activity and numbers at the camp had decreased to the point where federal troops could be withdrawn. They were needed, as it turned out, to deal with wildcat raids in another part of the state. Those who had been on the scene came back with reports of incredible viciousness.

Standing at their windows in the town, the women could look up to the hills and see the camp fire still burning, but as the months wore on, fewer and fewer of them looked and the column of smoke diminished in size because the remaining women were running out of volunteers whose turn it was to feed the fire.

Now that it was over, things went on more or less as they had before.

—1974

THE WEREMOTHER

Often in that period in her life, when she least expected it, she would feel the change creeping over her. It would start in the middle of an intense conversation with her younger son or with her daughter, behind whose newly finished face she saw her past and intimations of her future flickering silently, waiting to break cover. Black hairs would begin creeping down the backs of her hands and claws would spring from her fingertips. She could feel her lip lifting over her incisors as she snarled: "Can't you remember *anything*?" or: "Stop picking your face."

She had to concentrate on standing erect then, determined to defeat her own worst instincts just once more, but she knew it was only a matter of time before she fell into the feral crouch. In spite of her best efforts she would end up loping on all fours, slinking through alleys and stretching her long belly as she slid over fences; she would find herself hammering on her older son's window, or deviling him on the phone: Yes we are adults together, we are even friends, but do you look decent for the office? Even when he faced her without guile, as he would any ordinary person, she could feel the howl bubbling in her throat: Did you remember to use your face medicine?

Beware, she is never far from us; she will stalk us to the death, wreaking her will and spoiling our best moments, threatening our future, devouring our past. Beware the weremother when the moon is high and you and the one you love are sinking to earth; look sharp or she will spring upon you; she will tear you apart to save you if she has to, bloodying tooth and claw in the inadvertency of love.

Lash me to the porch she cried, knowing what was coming, chain me to the beds, but she could not stop thinking what might happen to the older son if he married the wrong girl, whom he is in love with. Who would iron his shirts? Would she know how to take care of him? It's his decision now; he's a grown man and we are adults together, but I am his mother, and older. I have a longer past than he does and can divine the future.

This is for your own good.

She and the man she married were at a party years before they even had children. Someone introduced the identity game. Tell who you are in three sentences. After you finished, the woman who started the game diagnosed you. She said you valued what you put first. Somebody began, My name is Martha, I'm a mother. She remembers looking at that alien woman, thinking, A mother? Is that all you want to be? What does that make of the man sitting next to you? She thinks: I know who I am. I know my marriage. I know my ambitions. I am those three things and by the way I am a mother. I would never list it first in this or any other game.

On the other hand, she can't shake the identity.

Here is an old story she hates. It is called The Mother's Heart. The cherished only son fell into debt and murdered his adoring mother for her money. He had been ordered to tear out her heart and take it to his debtors as proof. On the way he fell. Rolling out of the basket, the heart cried: "Are you hurt, my son?"

Damn fool.

Nobody wanted that. Not him, not her.

As a child she had always hated little girls who told everybody they wanted to grow up to be mothers.

She goes to visit her own mother, who may get sick at any moment and need care for the rest of her life. She comes into the tiny apartment in a combined guilt and love that render her speechless. On these visits she slips helplessly into childhood, her mind seething with unspoken complexities while her lips shape the expected speeches.

What was it like for you?

"How are you feeling?"

Did you and he enjoy it and how did you keep that a secret?

"That's too bad. Your African violets look wonderful."

93

Why won't you ever give me a straight answer?

"Do you really want Kitty up there with the plants? I wish you'd get someone in to help you clean."

I wish I didn't have to worry. I went from child who depended to woman struggling for freedom to this, without ever once passing through a safe zone in which neither of us really needed the other.

"That dress is beautiful, Mother, but you don't look warm enough."

I know you think I dress to embarrass you.

The aging woman whose gracious manner comes out of a forgotten time says, "As long as it looks nice, I can put up with being chilly."

Just before the mother looks away her daughter sees a flash of the captive girl. The old lady's flesh has burned away, leaving the skin quite close to her skull. Stepping off the curb, she is uncertain. Caged behind her mother's face is her own future.

As they go out the door the old mother tries to brush a strand of hair off her grown daughter's forehead; the old lady would like to replace her daughter's wardrobe with clothes more like her own.

Stop that. Please don't do that.

She thinks, Mother, I'm sorry your old age is lonely, but something else snags at the back of her mind. Why was my childhood lonely? She will lavish her own children with company: siblings, people to sleep over. She will answer all their questions in full. She will never insist on anything that isn't important.

All her friends have mothers. In one way or another all those mothers have driven their grown daughters crazy.

"She pretended to know me," says Diana, who had flown all the way to Yorkshire to be with her. "Then on the fourth day we were in the sitting room when she showed me a picture. I asked who it was and she said this was her daughter Diana, who was married and living in America. She had erased me."

Another says: "When I was little she praised everything I did, even if it wasn't any good. She praises everything so much that you know she means, Is that all?"

"She says, You can't do that, whatever it is, when what she means is that she couldn't do it. When I told her in spite of the family and the job I'd made the Law Review she said, 'You're doing too much,' when what she meant was: It's your funeral."

94

"The world has gone past her, and at some level she is jealous."

Every one of the women says, "She thinks my house is never clean enough."

"She thinks families always love each other and dinners are delicious and everything is always fine, and if it isn't, then it's my failure."

We are never going to be like that.

As their children grow older they try to remain open, friendly, honest, tolerant, but behind their eyes the question rises and will not be put down. Will we be like that after all?

Beware for she is lurking, as the full moon approaches she will beg her captors to lock the cell tightly and chain her to the bars, but when the moon completes itself she will break through steel to get to you and when she does she will spring on your best moments and savage them, the bloody saliva spraying for your own good for she never does anything she does except out of love.

And she does love you.

Says her own mother, whom she has just asked what she's going to do when she gets out of the hospital:

"We'll see."

It is the same answer her mother gave when she was a child and asking, Are we going to the movies? Can I have some candy? Is my life going to come out all right? It infuriates her because it means nothing.

(She will always give her own children straight answers. She will tell them more than they want to know about things they may not have asked.)

She is trembling with rage. The aging woman looks at her with that same heedless smile, magnificently negligent. How will she manage alone with a mending hip?

We'll see. That smile!

She cannot know whether this is folly or bravery. In her secret self she can feel the yoke descending.

I will never be like that.

Can she keep her hand from twitching when she sees her daughter's hair out of control? Can she be still when the oldest flies to Europe and his brother wants to leave school/move away/hitchhike to Florida and sleep on beaches? Will she be able to pretend these decisions are theirs to make or will she begin to replicate those maternal patterns of duplicity? Kissing the cheek to detect fever, giving the gift designed to improve the recipient, making remarks that pretend to be idle but stampede her young in the direction she has chosen. She never wants to do that.

She wants to be herself, is all.

Is that such a big thing to want?

Her problem is that she wishes to believe she has more than one function.

Lash me to the . . .

Are you sure you know what you're doing?

Are you all right?

I was just asking.

Beware the weremother, for even when you have hung the room with wolfsbane and sealed the door and bolted it with a crucifix, even as you light the candles she is abroad and there is no power to prevent her; cross yourself and stay alert for she will spring upon you and her bite has the power to transform even the strong est. Barricade yourself and never take anything for granted even when you think you're safe, for even in that last moment, when you think you have killed her with the silver bullet or stopped her once for all with the stake at the crossroads her power lives; when everything else is finished there will be the guilt.

—1979

CHICKEN SOUP

When he was little Harry loved being sick. He would stay in bed with his books and toys spread out on the blankets and wait for his mother to bring him things. She would come in with orange juice and aspirin at midmorning; at lunchtime she always brought him chicken soup with Floating Island for dessert, and when he had eaten she would straighten the pillow and smooth his covers and settle him for his nap. As long as he was sick he could stay in this nest of his own devising, safe from schoolmates' teasing and teachers who might lose their tempers, and falling down and getting hurt. He could wake up and read or drowse in front of the television, perfectly content. Some time late in the afternoon, when his throat was scratchy and boredom was threatening his contentment, he would start watching the bedroom door. The shadows would be long by that time and Harry restless and perhaps faintly threatened by longer shadows that lurked outside his safe little room: the first intimations of anxiety, accident and risk. Finally he would hear her step on the stair, the clink of ice in their best glass pitcher, and she would come in with cookies and lemonade. He would gulp the first glass all at once and then, while she poured him another, he would feel his own forehead in hopes it would be hot enough to entitle him to another day. He would say: I think my head is hot. What do you think? She would touch his forehead in loving complicity. Then the two of them would sit there together, Harry and Mommy, happy as happy in the snug world they had made.

Harry's father had left his widow well fixed, which meant Mommy didn't have to have a job, so she had all the time in the world to make the house pretty and cook beautiful meals for Harry and do everything he needed even when he wasn't sick. She would wake him early so they could sit down to a good hot breakfast together, pancakes with sausage and orange juice, after which they would read to each other out of the paper until it was time for Harry to go. They always talked over the day when he came home from school and then, being a good mother, she would say, Don't you want to play with a little friend? She always made cookies when his friends came over, rolling out the dough and cutting it in neat circles with the rim of a wine glass dusted with sugar. She sat in the front row at every violin and flute recital, and when Harry had trouble with a teacher, any kind of trouble at all, she would go up to the grammar school and have it out with him. Harry's bed was made for him and his lunches carefully wrapped and, although nobody would find out until they reached middle school and took communal showers, Harry's mother ironed his underwear. In return, Harry emptied the garbage and made the phone calls and did most of the things the man of the house would have done, if he had been there.

Like all happy couples they had their fights, which lasted only an hour or two and cleared the air nicely. Usually they ended with one of them apologizing and the other saying, with admirable largesse, I forgive you. In fact the only bad patch they had came in the spring of the year Harry was twelve, when Charles appeared with a bottle of wine and an old college yearbook in which he and Harry's father were featured. Naturally Mommy invited him to dinner and Harry was shocked to come out of the kitchen with the bottle opener just in time to hear his mother saying, "You don't know what a relief it is to have an adult to talk to for a change."

Didn't Harry get asthma that night, and wasn't he home sick for the rest of the week? He did not spend his usual happy sick time because his mother seemed distracted almost to the point of being neglectful, and he was absolutely astonished at lemonade time that Friday. There were two sets of footsteps on the stairs.

Mommy came in first. "Oh Harry, I have a surprise for you."

"I'm too sick."

She managed to keep the smile in her voice. "It's Charles. He's brought you a present."

"I don't want it." He flopped on his stomach and put the pillows over his head.

"Oh Harry."

"Let me handle this." There was Charles's voice in his bedroom, his bedroom, that had always been sacrosanct. Harry wanted to rage and drive him out, he might even brain him with a bookend, but that would involve showing himself, and as long as he stayed under the pillows there was the chance Charles would give up and go away.

There was something wriggling on his bed.

"Help. What's that?"

"It's a puppy."

"Go away."

"Charles had brought you a lovely puppy."

"A puppy?"

There it was. He was so busy playing with it that he only half-heard when Mommy said the puppy's name was Ralph and Ralph was going to keep him company while she and Charles went out for a little while. Wait, Harry said, or tried to, but the puppy was warm under his hands and he couldn't keep his mind on what he was saying. It had already wet the blanket, and Harry was riveted by the experience. The wet was soaking right through the blanket and the sheet and into Harry's pajama leg, and by the time he had responded to the horror and the wonder of it, Mommy had already kissed him and she and Charles were gone.

For the first hour or two he and the puppy were happy together, but just as he began to take it into his confidence, convincing himself that it was company enough, the puppy flopped on its side and slept like a stone, leaving Harry alone in the room, jabbering to the gathering shadows. He clutched the covers under his chin and kept on talking, but the empty house was terrifying in its silence, so that Harry too felt silent, certain that both he and the house were listening.

She took forever to come home. When she did come in she was voluble and glowing, absently noting that she had forgotten to leave him anything for supper, passing it off with a half-hearted apology and a long recital of everything Charles had said and thought. She approached the bed with the air of a jeweler unveiling his finest creation and proffered a piece of Black Forest cake she had wrapped carefully right there in the restaurant and brought halfway across town cradled in her lap.

Harry did the only logical thing under the circumstances. He started wheezing. The puppy woke and blundered across the blanket to butt him with its head. He picked it up, murmuring to it between wheezes.

"Harry, Harry, what's the matter?"

He said to the puppy, "I told you I was sick."

"Harry, please!" She proffered cough medicine and he spurned it; she held out the inhaler and he knocked it away.

He said, not to her, but to the puppy, "Mommy left me alone when I was sick."

"Harry, please."

"Right, puppy?"

"Oh Harry, please take your medicine."

"It's you and me, puppy. You and me."

Harry and the puppy were thick as thieves for the next couple of days. They refused to read the paper with his mother when she came in with breakfast and they wouldn't touch anything on any of her trays. Instead they bided their time and sneaked down to raid the kitchen when she was asleep. They talked only to each other, refusing all her advances, brooking no excuses and no apologies.

On the third day she cracked. She came to Harry's room empty-handed and weeping. "All right, what do you want me to do?"

He answered in a flash. "Never leave me alone when I'm sick."

"Is that all?"

"I don't like that guy."

"Charles?"

"I don't like him."

Her face was a study: whatever she felt for Charles in a tug-of-war with the ancient, visceral pull. After a pause she said, "I don't like him either."

Harry smiled. "Mommy, I'm hungry."

"I'll bring you a nice bowl of chicken soup."

That was the end of Charles.

After that Harry and his mother were closer than ever. If it cost her anything to say goodbye to romance she was gallant about it and kept her feelings well hidden. There was Harry to think about. She was the one who argued with his teachers over that last quarter of a point and prepped him for tests and sent the coach packing when he suggested that, with his build, Harry was a natural for basketball; and if Harry seemed at all reluctant to give up the team trips, boys and girls together on a dark and crowded bus, his mother pointed out that it would be the worst possible thing for his asthma. It was his mother who badgered the dean of admissions until Harry was enrolled in the college of his choice, located three convenient blocks from their house. They were both astonished when, at the end of the first term, the dean suggested that he take a year off because he needed to mature. Harry and his mother talked about it privately and concluded that, for whatever reasons, the administration objected to the presence of a middle-aged woman, however attractive, at the college hangout and in various seminars and waiting with Harry on the bench outside the dean's office until it was his turn to go in.

"Who needs college?" she said.

Harry thought, but did not say: Hey, wait.

"After all," she was saying. "We both know you're going to be an artist."

Harry was not so sure. His mother had enrolled him in the class because she had always wanted art lessons and so she assumed he would want them too, and Harry dutifully went to the Institute on Tuesday to do still lifes of fruit of the season with the same old clay wine bottle, in pencil, charcoal, pastels and acrylics. His colors all ran together and the shapes were hideous, but his mother admired them all the same.

"Oh Harry," she would say, promiscuous in her approval, "that's just beautiful."

"That's what you always say." It irritated him because it meant nothing, so that he was both flattered and fascinated when the cute girl from the next class came in just as he was finishing a depressing oil of the same old wine bottle, with dead leaves and acorns this time, and said, in hushed tones:

"Gee, that really stinks."

"Do you really think so?"

"Sorry, I just . . ."

"You're the first person who's ever told the truth. What's your name?"

"Marianne."

Harry fell in love with her.

It was around this time that his mother began to get on his nerves. If he lingered after class to talk to Marianne or buy her a cup of coffee, his mother would spring out the front door before he put his key in the lock. She would be a one-woman pageant of anxiety. Where have you been? What kept you? I thought you'd been hit by a taxi or run over by a truck, oh Harry, don't frighten me like that again. He would say, aw, Ma, but she would already be saying: The least you could do is call when you're going to be late. She managed to be in the hall every time he used the phone, and when he began to go out with Marianne she could not keep herself from asking where he was going, how long he would be; it didn't matter whether he came home at ten or twelve or two or four a.m., she would be rattling in the kitchen, her voice would take on the high hum of hysteria: I couldn't sleep.

He should have known better than to bring Marianne home to meet her. She didn't do much, she didn't say much, but she brought in his puppy, which was no longer a puppy but instead was aging, balding, with broken, rotting teeth. When Harry squatted to pet the dog his mother looked at Marianne over his head. "That's the only thing Harry has ever loved. Can't sleep without him."

Marianne looked at her in shock. "What?"

"Right next to him on the pillow, too. Head to head. I tried to get him to put that thing in the cellar, but all I have to do is mention it and Harry starts to wheeze."

"Harry wheezes?"

"Oh all the time," his mother said cheerfully, opening the front door for her.

When she was gone, Harry turned on his mother in a rage, but she managed to stop him in his tracks. "I only do these things because I love you. Think of what I have given up for you." She was wheezing herself, as she confronted him with their whole past history in her face.

"Oh Mother, I—"

"I don't like Marianne."

All their years together accumulated and piled into him like the cars of a fast express. "I don't like her either," he said.

At the same time he knew he could not stand the force of his mother's love, wanted to leave her because he was suffocating; did not know how. He didn't know whether he would ever find another girl who loved him but if he did, he was going to handle it differently.

His first vain thought was to marry his mother off, but she would not even accept a date. "You might need me," she said, in spite of all his protests that he was grown now, would do fine without her. "I wouldn't do that to you."

It was implied that he wouldn't do that to her, either, but he would in a flash, if he could only figure out how. It was around this time that he started going into the library in the evenings, and it was natural that he should find himself attracted to one of the librarians. She liked him too, and they had a nice thing going there in the stacks, late-night sandwiches and hurried kisses. But one night Harry heard a distinct rustling in the next aisle, and when he came around the end of Q-S and into T-Z he found his mother crouching, just as the girl he had been fondling saw her and began to scream . . .

When he stamped into the house that night she greeted him with a big smile and an apple pie.

"Mother, how could you?"

"Look, Harry, I baked this for you. Your favorite"

"How could you do a thing like that?"

"Why Harry, you know I would do anything for you."

"But you . . . damn . . . ruined . . ." He was frothing, raging and inarticulate. He looked into that face suffused by blind mother love and in his fury took desperate measures to dramatize his anger and frustration. "You . . ." He snatched the pie from her, ignoring her craven smile. "Have . . ." He raised it above his head, overriding her hurried "It's-your-favorite," and screamed: "Got to stop." He took the fruit of her loving labor and dashed it to the floor. There.

He was exhausted, quivering and triumphant. He had made her understand. She had to understand.

When the red film cleared and he could see again she was on here
hands and knees in front of him, scraping bits of pie off the rug as if nothing could make her happier. "Oh Harry," she said, imperturbable in her
love, "you know I would do anything for you."

A less determined son would have given up at that point, sinking into
the morass of mother love, but two things happened to Harry around that
time, each peculiarly liberating. First his puppy died. Then they began life
classes at the Institute and Harry, who up to that point had seen only selected fragments of his mother, saw his first woman nude.

Her name was Coral and he fell in love with her. They began to stay after class, Harry pretending to keep sketching, Coral pretending to pose,
until the night their hands met as he pretended to adjust her drape, and
Coral murmured into his ear and Harry took her home. He may have been
aware of rustling in the bushes outside the studio, or of somebody following as they went up the drive to Coral's bungalow; he may have sensed a
determined, feral presence under Coral's bedroom window, but he tried to
push back the awareness, to begin what Coral appeared to be so ready to
begin. He would have, too, kissing her as he took off his shirt, but as he
clasped her to him Coral went rigid and began to scream. He turned
quickly to see what had frightened her and although he caught only a
glimpse of the face in the window it was enough.

"Harry, what is it?"

He lied. "Only a prowler. I think it's gone." He knew it wasn't.

"Then kiss me."

"I can't." He just couldn't.

"Please."

"I can't—yet. There's something I have to take care of."

"Don't go."

"I have to."

"When will you come back?"

"As soon as I can. It may not be until tomorrow."

"Tomorrow, then." Gradually, she let go. "Tomorrow or never. Harry, I
don't wait."

"I promise." He was buttoning his shirt. "But right now there's something I have to do."

She was waiting for him at the end of the driveway, proffering something. He didn't know how she got there because he had taken the car; he
had the idea she might have run the whole way because she was breathing

hard and her clothes were matted with brambles; her stockings were torn and muddy at the knees. Her face was a confusing mixture of love and apprehension, and as he came toward her she shrank.

"I thought you might need your sweater."

He looked at her without speaking.

"I only do these things because I love you."

He opened the car door.

"Harry, you know I'd do anything for you."

He still did not speak.

"If you're mad at me, go ahead and get good and mad at me. You know I'll forgive you, no matter what you do."

"Get in."

She made one more stab. "It's raining, Harry. I thought you might be cold."

Later, when they made the turn away from their house and up the road into the foothills, she said, "Harry, where are we going? Where are you taking me?"

His response was dredged from millennia of parent-child dialogs. He leaned forward, taking the car into rocky, forbidding country, up an increasingly sharp grade. He said, "We'll see."

Maybe he only planned to frighten her, but at that last terrible moment she said, blindly, "I'll always be there when you need me."

He got rid of her by pushing her into Dumbman's Gorge. She got right out of the car when he told her to—she would have done any thing to keep on his right side—and when he pushed her she looked back over her shoulder with an inexorable motherly smile. There were dozens of jagged tree stumps and sharp projecting rocks and she seemed to ricochet off every single one of them going down but, in spite of that and perhaps because of the purity of the air and the enormous distance she had to tumble, he thought he heard her calling to him over her shoulder, I forgive you— the words trailing behind her in a dying fall.

He didn't know whether it was guilt or the simple result of going all the way to the peak above Dumbman's Gorge and standing out there arguing in such rotten weather, but he was sick by the next evening, either flu or pneumonia, and there was no going to Coral's house that evening to take his reward. He telephoned her instead and she came to him, looking hurried and distracted and shying off when he began to cough and sneeze.

"I really want to, Harry, but right now you're too contagious."

"But Coral." He could hardly breathe.

"As soon as you get better." She closed the bedroom door behind her.

When he tried to get up to plead with her he found he was too weak to stand. "But Coral," he said feebly from his bed.

"I'll lock the front door behind me," she said, her voice rising behind her as she descended the stairs. "Do you want some chicken soup?"

His voice was thin but he managed to say, "Anything but that." He heard the thump as she closed the front door.

Despairing, he fell into a fevered sleep.

It may have been partly the depression of illness, the frustration of having his triumph with Coral postponed, it may have been partly delirium and partly the newly perceived flickering just beyond the circle of his vision: the gathering shadows of mortality. It may only have been a sound that woke him. All Harry knew was that he woke suddenly around midnight, gasping for breath and sitting bolt upright, swaying in the dark. He was paralyzed, trembling in the fearful certainty that something ominous was approaching, coming slowly from a long way off. When he found that his trunk could not support itself and his legs would no longer move he sank back into the pillows, bloating with dread.

There had been a sound: something on the walk, sliding heavily and falling against the front door.

I came as soon as I could.

"What?" Why couldn't he sit up?

He did not know how much time passed but, whatever it was, it was in the house now. It seemed to be dragging itself through the downstairs hall. Was that it in the kitchen? In his terror and delirium he may have blacked out. He came to, returning from nowhere, thought he might have been hallucinating, tried to slow his heart. Then he heard it again. It was on the stairs leading to his room, mounting tortuously.

You're sick.

"My God." He tried to move.

The sound was in the hall outside his room now, parts of whatever it was were thumping or sliding wetly against his bedroom door in a travesty of a knock. In another second it would start to fumble with the knob. He cried out in terrible foreknowledge: "Who's there?"

Harry, it's Mother.

—1980

PILOTS OF THE PURPLE TWILIGHT

The wives spent every day by the pool at the Miramar, not far from the base, waiting for word about their men. The rents were cheap and nobody bothered them, which meant that no one came to patch the rotting stucco or kill centipedes for them or pull out the weeds growing up through the cracks in the cement. They were surrounded by lush undergrowth and bright flowers nobody knew the names for, and although they talked about going into town to shop or taking off for home, wherever that was, they needed to be together by the pool because this was where the men had left them and they seemed to need to keep claustrophobia as one of the conditions of their waiting.

On good days they revolved slowly in the sunlight, redolent of suntan oil and thorough in the exposure of all their surfaces because they wanted the tans to be *right* for the homecoming, but they also knew they had plenty of time. If it rained they would huddle under the fading canopy and play bridge and canasta and gin, keeping scores into the hundreds of thousands even though they were sick of cards. They did their nails and eyebrows and read Perry Mason paperbacks until they were bored to extinction, bitching and waiting for the mail. Everybody took jealous note of the letters received, which never matched the number of letters sent because mail was never forwarded after a man was reported missing. The women wrote anyway, and every day at ten they swarmed down the rutted drive to fall on the mailman like black widow spiders, ravenous. Most of the letters were for the wretches whose husbands had already come *home*, for God's sake, whisking them away to endlessly messy kitchens and perpetual heaps of laundry in dream houses mortgaged on the GI Bill. Embarrassed by joy, they had left the Miramar without a backward glance, and for the same reason they always wrote at least once, stuffing their letters with vapid-looking snapshots of first babies, posting them from suburbs on the other side of the world.

At suppertime they all went into the rambling stucco building, wrenching open the rusting casements because it seemed important to keep sight of the road. Just before the shadows merged to make darkness they would drift outside again, listening, because planes still flew out from the nearby base every morning and, waiting, they were fixed on the idea of counting them back in. Most of their men had left in ships or on foot but still they waited. To the women at the Miramar every dawn patrol hinted at a twilight return, and the distant Fokkers or P-38s or F-87s seemed appropriate emblems for their own hopes, the suspense a fitting shape to place on the tautening stomachs, the straining ears, the dread of the telegram.

They all knew what they would do when the men came back even though they had written their love scenes privately. There would be the reunion in the crowded station, the embrace that would shut out everybody else. She would be standing at the sink when he came up from behind and put his arms around her waist, or she would be darning or reading, not thinking about him just for once, when a door would open and she would hear him: Honey, I'm home. There would be the embrace at the end of the driveway, the embrace in plain view, the embrace in the field. None of them thought about what he would be like when they embraced, what he must look like now, the way he really smelled, because their memories had been stamped with images distilled, perfected by the quality of their own waiting, the balance they tried to keep between thinking about it and not thinking about it. *If I can just manage not to think about it*, Elise still told herself, *then maybe he will come.*

Watching the sky, even after all these years, she would be sure she heard the distant vibration of motors drumming, or maybe it was the jet sound, tearing the sky like a scythe; she had been there since Chateau Thierry, or was it Amiens, and she knew the exact moment at which it became too dark to hope. "Tomorrow," she would say, and because the others preferred to think she was the oldest and so was the best at waiting, they would follow her inside. They all secretly feared that there was an even older woman bedridden in the tower, and that her husband had sailed with Enoch Arden, but nobody wanted to know for sure. They preferred to look to Elise, who kept herself beautifully and was still smiling; she had survived.

They were soft at night, jellied with anticipation and memory, one in spirit with Elise, but each morning found them clattering out to the chaises with Pam and Marge, hard and bright. Pam and Marge were the leaders of a group of self-styled girls in their fifties, who had graying hair and thickening waists. They liked to kid and whistled songs like "Praise the Lord and Pass the Ammunition" through their teeth. They shared a home-front camaraderie that enraged Donna, who was younger, and who had sent her husband off to a war nobody much remembered. She and Sharon and a couple of others in their forties would press their temples with their fists, grumbling about grandstanding, and people who still thought fighting was to be admired. Anxious, bored, frazzled by waiting, these two groups indulged in a number of diverting games: who had the most mail and who was going to sit at the round table at supper, who was hogging all the sunlight. They chose to ignore the newcomers, mere slips of things who had sent their men off to—where was it—Nam, or someplace worse.

Pam and Marge were tugging back and forth with Donna and Sharon this particular morning, wrangling over who was going to sit next to Elise, when Peggy walked in. Her shoes were sandy from the walk up the long driveway and her brave going-away outfit was already rusty with sweat. Bill had put her in a cab for the Miramar because, as he pointed out, he wasn't going to be gone for long and she would be better off with other service wives, they would have so much in common.

"Bitch," Marge was saying, "look what you did to my magazines."

Donna dumped her makeup kit and portable radio on the chaise. "It serves you right."

Marge was red-faced and hot, she may not even have heard herself lashing out. "I hope it crashes."

Even Pam was shocked. "Marge!"

"It would serve her right."

Peggy dropped her overnight bag. "Stop it." Donna had gone white.

"Don't ever say that." "Stop." Peggy set her fist against her teeth.

"Girls." Elise stood between them, frail and ladylike in voile. "What would Harry and Ralph think if they could see you now?"

Donna and Marge stood back, pink with shame.

"What is the new girl going to think?"

"I'm sorry," Marge said, and she and Donna hugged.

Elise saw that Peggy was backing away, ready to make a break for it. The perfect hostess, she put a hand on her arm. "Come and sit by me, ah . . ." She inclined her head graciously.

"Peggy."

"Come, Peggy." She patted the chaise. "I want you to meet Donna, her Ralph is in the Kula gulf, and Pam and Marge both have husbands at, yes, that's it, Corregidor."

"But they couldn't."

Elise said, serenely, "Won't you have some iced tea?"

Peggy was gauging the distance between her and the overnight bag, looking for a gap in the overgrown greenery. "I can't stay."

"You'll have to excuse the girls," Elise said. "Everybody is a little taut, you understand."

"I don't belong here, I'm . . ."

Elise spoke gently, overlapping, ". . . only here for a little while. I know."

"Bill promised."

"Of course he did."

Later, when she felt better, Peggy let Elise lead her inside the cavernous building. She unpacked her things and after she had changed into her bikini she went out to take her place by the pool. She thought she would join the other girls in bikinis, who looked closer to her age, but they sat in closed ranks at the far end of the pool, giving her guarded looks of such hostility that she hurried back to her place by Elise.

"Don't mind them," Elise said. "It takes time to adjust."

Going down to dinner, Peggy understood how important it was to be well groomed. The room was bright with printed playsuits and pretty shifts in floral patterns chosen in fits of bravery. Although there were only women in the room, each of them had taken care with her hair and makeup, pressing her outfit because it was important; if they flagged, the men might discover them and be disgusted, or else the word would get out that they had given up, and there was no telling what grief that would bring. Either way they would never be forgiven. Whether or not the men came they would face each dinner hour tanned and combed and carefully made up and no matter what it cost, they would be smiling.

That night Pam and Marge were never better; they had on their shark-skin shorts and the bright jersey shirts knotted under their breasts to expose brown bellies, and when Betty joined them at the end of the dining room they went into their Andrews Sisters imitation with a verve that left everybody shouting. Jane played the intro again and again, and even though they were spent and gasping, they came tapdancing back. There was a mood of antic pleasure which had partly to do with the new girl in the audience, and partly with the possibility that the men just might come back and discover them at a high point: *See how well we do without you. Look how pretty we are, how lively. How could you bear to leave us for long?* They imagined the men laughing and hooting the way they did for USO shows; at the finale, the women would bring them up on stage.

Bernice was next with "I'll be seeing you," and they were all completely still by the time Donna took the microphone and sang, "Fly the Ocean in a Silver Plane." Then it was time to go outside.

"Tell me about him," Elise said, leading Peggy through the trees.

Peggy said, "He has blue eyes."

"Of course he does. Gailliard has blue eyes."

"Who?"

"Gailliard. He crushed my two hands in one of his, and when I cried out he said, Did I hurt you, and I had to let him think he had pinched my fingers because I didn't want to let him know I was afraid." She whimpered. "I'm still afraid."

This old lady? Peggy wanted to support her. *Oh Lord.*

"Harry always kisses me very sweetly," Pam was saying to Marge, "he only opens his mouth a little."

Marge said, "Dave promised to bring me a dish carved out of Koa wood. Have you ever seen Koa wood?"

Donna and her group muttered together; they had been schooled to believe it was important not to let any of it show.

None of the young things seemed to know what they thought about the parting. Still they came out into the evening with all the others, straining as if they too were convinced of the return. Marva knew they didn't even speak the same language as the old ladies, who would talk abut duty and patriotism and, what was it, the job that had to be done. She and Ben and a whole bunch of others had been together in the commune, like puppies, until they came for him because he had thrown away the piece of paper with the draft call, the MP kicked him and said, Son, you ought to be damn glad to go. Now here was this new girl not any older than Marva but her husband was what they called a career man, she probably believed in all that junk the old ladies believed in, so she could learn to play canasta and go to hell.

At first Peggy was afraid of the shadows; then the figures in the field sorted themselves out so that she could see which were trees and which were women running across the grass like little girls, stretching their arms upwards, and she found herself swallowing rage because this place was worse than any ghetto. The women were all either stringy and bitter or big-assed and foolish and Bill had dumped her here as if she were no better than the rest of them. When Elise tried to take her hand she pulled away.

"It's going to be all right."

"This is terrible."

"You'll get used to it."

"Listen." Marge's voice lifted. "Do you hear anything?" Waiting, they all stood apart because each departure shimmered in the air at this moment of possible return.

Elise remembered that Gailliard had taken her to the balcony at the Officers Club. He had set her up on the rail in her grey chiffon with the grey suede slippers and then he stood back to regard her, so handsome that she wanted to cry out, and she remembered that at the time they were so steeped in innocence that each departure of necessity spelled victory and swift return. She wondered if old ladies were supposed to feel the hunger that stirred her when she remembered his body. She wondered if he was still loyal, after all these years. In retrospect their love was so perfect that she knew he would always be beautiful, as she remembered him, and true.

Pam and Marge had said goodbye in peacetime; when Harry and Dave flew out from Pearl in April of that year it had seemed like just another departure. Marge could remember dancing with Dave's picture, relieved, in a way, because the picture never belched or scratched its belly, although she and Pam stoutly believed that if they had known there was going to be a war they could have surrounded the parting with the right number of tears and misgivings, enough prayers to prepare for the return. Their fears would have been camouflaged by bright grins because, when you were a service wife, you had to treat every parting like every other parting. Still . . .

Bernice's husband Rob enlisted in the first flush of patriotism after Pearl Harbor. "Go," she said, clenching her fists to keep from grabbing him. He looked back once: "At least I'm doing the right thing." *He's off there accomplishing things with a bunch of other guys, they're busy all day and at night they relax and horse around while I am stuck here, getting older, with nothing to do except sing that song on Saturday nights . . .* Donna remembered her and Ralph on the bed, wondering what sense it made for him to go into the mess in Korea. There was no choice and so, laying resignation between them like a knife-blade, they made love one last time. Marva remembered being stoned in that commune near Camp Pendleton, Ben would come in looking like Donald Duck in that uniform and all the kids would laugh, but the last time he made her pick up her bedroll and he brought her here, he told her he would be back and maybe he would.

Peggy nursed a secret hurt: what Bill said to her in a rage right before he dumped her at the Miramar: "If you can't wait more than five minutes, why should I bother to come back," and her riposte: "Don't bother," so when Marge yelled, "I think I hear something," she had to run to the edge of the clearing with the rest of them; at the first sound they would light the flares. She heard herself calling aloud, thinking if anything happened to Bill it would be her fault, for willing it, and that if she spread her arms and cried, "They're coming," it might bring them.

She discovered that the days were exquisitely organized around their waiting; no one sunned or played cards or read for too long in any one day because it would distort the schedule; they had to keep the division between the segments because it made the hours keep marching. Although fights were a constant, no quarrel could be too violent to preclude a reconciliation because they had to continue together, even as they had to silence any suggestion that even one of them might be disappointed; when the men came back they were all coming, down to the last one. Unless this was so, there was no way for the women to live together.

Pam and Marge organized a softball team, mostly thick-waisted "girls" from their own age group. They got Peggy to play, and after some consideration Donna joined them.

"Wait till you meet Dave," Marge said, sprawling in the grass in the outfield. "I would see him at the end of the walk in his uniform and that was when I loved him most. He'll never change."

"Everybody changes," Donna said gently.

"Not my Dave."

"Now Bill . . ." Peggy began, but when she tried to think of Bill there was a blur and what she remembered was not what he looked like but what she wanted him to look like because she had always been bothered by the hair growing in his nostrils, his wide Mongol cheekbones, covered by too much flesh, so she recomposed his face to her liking: If I can't have what I had, then at least let me make it what I want. "Bill looks like something out of the movies."

Somebody decided it would be a good idea to have bonfires ready; if the planes should come by daylight they would see the smoke columns. Every few weeks the women could rebuild the heaps of firewood, taking out anything that looked wet or rotten. Bernice organized a duplicate bridge tournament. Marva and some of the younger girls meditated for half an hour before breakfast and again before supper and, grudgingly, asked Peggy to join them.

She and Peggy were the first at the chaises one bright morning and they exchanged stories, grumbling about being stuck with all these old biddies, no better off than anybody else.

"I don't know," Marva was saying, "at least the meals come regular. I got sick of granola."

Peggy said, "I never had a tan like this before."

"But they act like we're going to be here forever." Marva looked at Marge, wabbling out on wedgies. "It's obscene."

Peggy said bravely, "We're not like them."

"We'll never be like them."

"We just have to hang in here for the time being." Peggy settled herself, feeling the sun on her belly. "For the time being we're in the same boat."

Elise seemed especially drawn to Peggy; she would pat the chaise next to her and wait for Peggy to join her. Then she would put the name, Gailliard, into the air between them and sit contemplating it, assuming that Peggy shared some of the same feelings. She told herself Peggy was young enough to be her daughter but that was a lie; she could be Peggy's grandmother, and knew it. Still it seemed important to her to keep the pretense of youth, even as it was important to keep herself exquisitely groomed and to greet each morning with the same generous smile, the same air of hope because to the others she was a fixed point, which they could sight from, and until she flagged they would not waver. She did her best to suspend Peggy in that same network of waiting, to keep her safe with the rest.

"You ought to talk to Donna," she said, "I think you have a lot in common."

"I'm afraid of her because she seems so sad."

"You could learn from her," Elise said. "She keeps herself well."

Peggy knew what Elise meant. Pam and Marge and their group played records over and over and mooned and dithered like a bunch of girls but Donna kept her dignity, fixed in a purity of waiting which Elise would admire because it resembled her own. There was no way for Peggy to explain that she and Bill had parted in anger, that she was pledged to wait but she had already jeopardized everything she was waiting for, that in her failure of will she might already have wished Bill to his death.

Please bring him back, she thought. *I would give anything to have him back.*

By the time she thought this she had already been there longer than she realized; time blurred, and as she sent out her wish she heard the distant drumming of engines and the sky darkened with planes returning, the message running ahead of them, singing in the air at the Miramar, hanging before them as clearly as anything in writing:

I'M BACK

so that Peggy had to hide her head and rock with anxiety and it was Donna who was the first to acknowledge it, addressing the sky gently, her voice soft with several lifetimes of regret.

She said, so nobody else heard her: "I'm afraid it's too late."

Elise found her hands fluttering about her face and her loins weak and her head buzzing in panic. Even with her eyes closed she was aware of Gailliard shimmering before her, beautiful and unscathed, and she pulled a towel up to cover her, murmuring, "He'll see me, he'll *see* me," because she knew that he would come to her with his beauty preserved at the moment when his life went out like a spark and she was well past seventy now,

113

beautifully groomed but old, wrinkled, with all her systems crumbling, diminished even further by his relentless beauty, and if he recognized her at all he would say, You're so *old*. She pulled the towel closer, like a shroud, whispering, "Please don't let him see me."

HONEY, IT'S ME

(Donna murmured, "There's nothing left here.")

"You bastard, wasting me like this, while you stayed young." Bernice went to her room and pulled the curtains and slammed the door.

Marge was ablaze with love, and she sang, or prayed: Dave, let me keep you out there, perfect and unchanged. If you come you will have a beer belly, just like me, you will have gotten gray. As she sang, or prayed, she imagined she heard him responding: How could I, I've been dead, and she said, aloud, "Dave, let me keep you the way I thought you were."

DON'T YOU HEAR ME

(In the tower, the oldest lady turned milky eyes to the ceiling; she could no longer speak but she made herself understood: *It was all used up by waiting*.)

Peggy cowered; they were supposed to light the flares or something— set off fires. Remembering the story of the monkey's paw she thought her last wish had come true and that Bill was struggling out of some distant heap of wreckage at this very minute, and he would be mangled, dreadful, dragging toward her . . .

"The meals aren't bad," Marva was saying, doing her best to override the thunder of the engines; the sky above was black now but she pushed on, "And Ben, he never really gave a damn." Shrugging as if to brush aside the shadows of the wings, she said, "Hey, Peg, do you hear anything?"

. . . either that or he would try and yank her away from this place that she loved just to go on making her unhappy. He would be Enoch Arden, at the window, and she would turn to face him: Oh, it's you.

"No," Peggy said firmly, as the planes passed over, "I don't hear anything."

—1981

FRONTIERS

Every time he left home Gunnar Morgan had the same misgivings: as he kissed Anne and the twins goodbye he was visited by all the farewell scenes in all those old Westerns: the settler kissing the wife and young ones and going off to town only to come back and find the homestead flattened, with an Indian spear planted in the wreckage and some child's rag doll abandoned next to a naked, charred ribcage, still smoking in the ruins. The settler would weep over the remains in the full knowledge that in such circumstances, the dead were always better off than the ones that were captured. In the movies the settler always seemed surprised, while Gunnar and the rest of the audience knew ahead of time, from the moment at which they parted. Now that he had a family of his own Gunnar thought perhaps the settler had known too, but in the frontier society there were times when a man had to go ahead and do that which needed doing.

Still he held Anne too tight at the last moment; she must have guessed at some of it because she ran her hands behind her back and took his hands firmly, helping him to release her. "Gunnar, don't worry."

"Alone out here. One woman alone, with nobody but a couple of children."

"The sooner you go, the sooner you'll be back."

Why did that sound so familiar? Troubled by echoes, he said, "It's so wild out here, I just hate to leave you."

"I don't care. I like it."

He looked at the glint in her eyes and thought perhaps she did. "Take care of yourself."

She lifted her head. "I always do." She seemed compelled to add: "The girls like it too."

"Oh Anne, please be careful."

"Don't worry, there's nothing out there."

"Still . . ." What was he afraid of, really?

"Gunnar, go!" She was about to loose her temper. It was hard, he supposed, all of them shut in here with no place to go and no place to be alone. These days he and Anne grappled over the smallest issues, sawing back and forth over each petty decision. At the end she always smiled and deferred to him, saying, "After all, you're the boss here." In another circumstance she would be the boss and they both knew it; he blamed himself for these clashes; it was his fault that they were stuck out here; he put her lapses down to cabin fever.

The twins were hanging on his waist. "Bring us a present from Flagstaff, Daddy."

Reluctant to let go of Anne's fingers, he looked down at them: Jenna, who moved like a willow whip, and practical little Betsy. "What do you want me to bring you?"

Betsy said, "A book I haven't read."

Jenna's face blossomed. "Anything, just as long as it's pretty."

"I never should have brought you to this Godforsaken place," he said over their heads. "You should have friends, you should be going to exciting places."

Anne lifted her head with an odd smile. "This will have to do for the time being." She was helping him to leave. "I need you to go now, we're running out of everything. And if you can find that fabric I've been waiting for, it will make all the difference."

"Oh Anne." His voice failed him.

"Hurry. When you get back, we'll have a party."

"I love you, Anne."

"I know it."

She'll be all right, he told himself, riding out. This is a different story altogether. He waited outside the dome until she had secured the airlock. Now nothing could get in or out and as far as he knew, nothing moved in the vast, dead lands outside it. Anne had sidearms and emergency beepers in addition to the laser cannon, but his heart contracted every time he had to go away and he would walk with his jaw taut and his shoulders high until he came riding back over the last ridge and saw her standing next to the airlock, waving to him through the dome's tough, transparent surface.

He had to go to Flagstaff to pick up supplies and a new chip for his communicator because the thing kept missing digits, which meant he also had to deliver the month's observations to the government office in person. Before the cataclysm everything was easier; computer systems were reliable and they could be checked and augmented by voice transmission. After the failure of Fail-Safe and the cataclysm, a great many things simply stopped working. Even now, with civilization more or less reassembled, they were still not working. Gunnar felt badly about this but, he thought, he owed his job to the disaster. How would he keep Anne and the twins without it? They lived in comfort in the dome, maintaining one of the outposts Gunnar had established. It was Gunnar's job to collect data because somebody in Washington reasoned that if the air ever cleared, it would happen first in the remote areas. How long would it take? Would it ever happen? Gunnar did not know; he only knew that he had to go on as if this would happen because when there is no choice, hoping is always better than not hoping.

Flagstaff depressed him. It was crowded and ugly under the enormous dome, with too many people clogging the passages, all looking gaunt and frantic.

It always took him a week to finish his business, not because he had that much to do but because of the lines at the government offices. He shaved the time a little by sleeping in the waiting room instead of paying someone to hold his place at night, but he tossed restlessly, and when he did sleep he dreamed of painted savages swarming over the ramparts in enormous numbers. At the supply depot, he could not find half the things Annie had asked for. There were flawed fabrics, meat tinned in spite of the maggots, weevilly flour. He did the best he could, knowing whatever he brought, Anne would pretend to be delighted. Then she would take it and transform it as she had the outpost, making pretty little curtains and tablecloths, constructing beautiful dinners out of the meanest ingredients.

Oh Anne. He had robbed her of her job and her society; they both pretended she could sell her designs from the outpost and if she could not—well, he was going to figure out some way for her to get them to the fashion center. Until he did, it was important for him to encourage her to keep working and for both of them to pretend this was somehow possible. He bought her a piece of artificial turquoise and picked up some candy for the twins and, as an afterthought, a piece of colored glass for Jenna. Then he headed out across the darkening badlands, already imagining what Anne would have prepared for the homecoming dinner, what he would say when the twins swamped him with the drawings they had made to surprise him. In the ruined world he fixed on the life at home, which he had wrought with his bare hands and which would be going on as always, waiting for him to walk back into it. Once he had shut himself in and sealed the airlock, he could believe the world was at rights because, inside the dome, he and Anne tried to make the life they wanted.

Leaving Flagstaff, he thought the color of the sky had altered in the week he had been there. He was certain the air was denser. Sunset bloodied the desert and as the broken shells of buildings outside the dome gave way to broken rock shapes and ruined mesas, shadows fell like knifeblades across the path Gunnar traveled. Once he thought he saw something moving and he kicked the air-cushion on the scooter a little higher and checked the shield. He told himself this was routine; after all, these were contaminated lands and he needed to protect himself, but he was running the scooter too fast and he understood that there was more. He had the idea that some thing had changed, there were strange forces stirring. What was the matter? Just nerves, he told himself: too many days away from the family, but that did not explain it. He could not say exactly what he feared, only that he feared it. He would not feel easy until he had ridden up over the last rise and could see Anne under the lights inside the airlock, waving. It was near dawn by the time he made the approach and as the sky began to pale he started in alarm and jerked around to look at the long ridge off to his right. In the flash before he turned and saw nothing he had imagined he saw this: a frieze of people naked as the figures on a Greek urn streaming over the crest and away from him.

Coming downhill, he was relieved to see the dome exactly as he had left it. There were Anne's plants in hanging baskets, just inside the airlock; the emission tube was steaming, which meant that she was preparing his homecoming dinner in spite of the hour. He strained to see her and when he did not he thought she must be in the house, releasing the catch for the decontamination hangar. He gunned the scooter inside, started the process and waited until the gauges told him it was safe.

Everything was as he had left it. Anne's little garden was flourishing under the artificial light; she had picked tomatoes for the homecoming meal and left them in the grass. He was surprised to see the knife stuck into the earth next to them; usually she was not so careless. He picked up the basket and went to the house, calling.

"Anne, I'm home."

When she did not answer he thought she must be in the bathroom; the rotten supplies made them sick more often than they would have admitted.

"Anne," he said a little louder. "Are you all right?"

He imagined he heard her answer.

"I brought in the tomatoes."

The sound turned out to be the kettle whistling in the neat little kitchen. The sauce was just beginning to burn off the cutlets she had been making. He turned off the stove and went down the hall.

"Anne, are you in there?"

The bathroom turned out to be empty.

"All right, if you're hiding, I give up."

Nobody answered and nobody came.

"Game's over, OK?"

He went into the twins' room. Jenna's bed had not been slept in. She was like a little spook sometimes, flitting around the dome in the middle of the night; they would find her asleep in the garden the next morning. Betsy had been in her bed not five minutes ago; there was the dent her head left in the pillow. He put his face in it, smelling the young girl smell of soap and musk and candy. It was still warm.

"Come on, dammit, everybody."

He was tired, it did not seem like a good game; they weren't in the house and he searched the garden in growing exasperation. They would have to lie flat in the synthetic earth to elude him and yet he could not see anybody. He searched the house from the gable to the crawlspace underneath. In a panic, he made certain Anne's clothes were where she had left them. If she ran away where would she go anyway, and how would she get out? There was not another scooter between here and Flagstaff. Mourning, he went into the kitchen. In addition to the cutlets, Anne had been making a dessert and a bowl of cream substitute; the cream mixture was still frothing. She must have run out in a hurry. Run out. She couldn't. Their suits were still hanging by the airlock and they were good only for short distances. He would have found their bodies within a few feet of the dome.

"Oh, Anne! Is it something I did?"

His voice tore through the silence in the dome but all he heard was the reverberation, circling and coming back to mock him.

He had not really expected an answer.

Frantic, he inserted the new chip and punched an emergency message into the console. FAMILY MISSING. UNEXPLAINED. All he got back was the usual: MESSAGE BEING PROCESSED. It would be days before they got back to him. He got in the scooter and began sweeping the surrounding wastelands in widening circles, not because he thought he would find them alive, even if he did find them, but because a portion of his life had been stolen and he would not feel right until he could restore it. Circling hopelessly, he called them by name, not because he imagined they would hear him through the shield or across the terrifying distances, but because he could imagine they were still his at least for as long as he kept calling them. By the time he gave up altogether, which was not for several weeks, he had covered hundreds of miles, ranging wide in spite of his fears, the sinister shadows and crevices in the empty, blasted lands.

119

Finally the terminal acknowledged his first transmission:
ABSENCE UNEXPLAINED.

He sent back: PLEASE EXPLAIN IT.

DON'T WORRY.

EXPLAIN. He tapped out this last in growing impatience. The exchange had taken several weeks and when he returned from his last foray the terminal was displaying what would turn out to be the last message on the subject.

THIS KIND OF THING HAPPENS ALL THE TIME.

"Like hell it does!"

It was almost more than he could bear, he thought, and he tapped in his last response: BUT THEY LOVED ME.

Preparing for yet another sweep he stopped, suddenly, in the middle of filling his pack with provisions. He was riveted by Anne's cutlets, petrifying in their sauce. The mold growing on the abandoned cream substitute filled him with sadness, and then anger. *Damned if I'll eat her food*, he thought, *not until I've had an explanation.*

Whose fault was this, anyway, his, for leaving them alone, or hers, for being careless? What were the last things they'd said to each other? He scoured his memory, trying to remember her exact tone the last time he saw her. What was it? Love, or exasperation? If the latter, whose fault was it, his, for bringing her out here to this awful place, or hers, for losing faith? Should he have loved her better or was it her fault, for not loving him, or was it out of their hands altogether?

It came to him in a flash. *This is not my fault. It is beyond my power.*

He would settle in here, and try to reconcile himself. In the next second, of course, his mouth went dry and his heart thudded to a stop: *My God, what if somebody out there stole her?*

KIDNAPPERS? He tapped it into the console.

IMPOSSIBLE. It took a week for this response to come: a week in which he reluctantly disposed of the last meal Anne had cooked for him, and began setting the house to rights. The letters formed: ENVIRONS UNINHABIT-ABLE.

UNINHABITABLE REALLY?

The machine corrected itself. UNINHABITED.

"Then this is all her fault. Hers," he said aloud, although at the moment he could not have said whether or how this followed.

Now that he had the house shipshape he gave up looking for them, on the premise that the next move was not his, but hers. Once he had begun keeping the place and performing his duties in a regular way, he found himself immeasurably comforted by routine and gave himself the solace of ritual. He did not know what he was going to do without his wife and children but at the same time he found he had plenty to do: there were the observations to record and transmit; he had to keep the place tidy; he needed to plan and make and clean up after meals, he had to exercise. He occupied almost all of their king-sized bed now, sleeping spreadeagled, and he told himself again and again that this was wonderful: the peace and quiet.

Then why did he find himself standing under the dome in the middle of the night, waking from a sound sleep to find himself drenched with sweat and screaming at the red-rimmed moon:

"You bitch, how could you do this to me?"

When it was time to make another run to Flagstaff, he secured the dome as best he could and got in the scooter with a premonitory chill: as if at strange footsteps approaching. He shook it off and kicked the scooter into high, running quickly into the city. When he got back this time with his scooter laden with supplies, he thought at first that nothing had been disturbed. Everything in the dome seemed right but not quite right; it took him several hours to locate the difference. All the presents he had brought in after the last trip and abandoned in a corner of the twins' room, were missing.

He woke before dawn with a roaring in his ears and his insides trembling. He ran out and battered like a moth against the inside of the dome, plastering himself against the transparent surface. In the next fevered seconds he either did or did not see a wild procession peeling off from a circle in the desert; he could not be certain because they were already at the top of the ridge, pouring over the horizon; even if he did see this he could not know whether it was illusion or whether that was really Anne with her hair flying and naked breasts gleaming in the poisoned air, running along with them. He threw himself onto the scooter and hurtled out, cursing the seconds it took to move through the ejection stages. Delayed as he was, he knew if there was anything out there he would catch up with it in a matter of seconds. By the time he came over the ridge, there was nothing moving and no trace of anything.

"Oh Anne," he shouted to the deadlands.

Then he thought: *It's your fault I'm going crazy.*

What would he do if he did come upon her, cowering in the rubble? He did not know.

He searched for a long time.

That night he slept without dreams, and when he woke he was weeping.

After that he got hold of himself. He added several new elements to his routine: the late-morning coffee, the afternoon drink. He liked being alone, he thought. He had always liked it.

If this was true, then what was the matter with him? He found himself pressed against the dome at odd hours, staring into the night without being sure how he got there. Once he thought he saw somebody staring in: a naked man, the color of the red sand; he thought he saw other naked people standing in the shadows behind him. Another time he imagined he saw Anne and the twins and another time, the naked man with Anne at his shoulder.

In the morning everything always looked more or less the same, and by the time Gunnar had finished his morning rounds, the fevered visions would have faded.

Still one night when a sudden wind swept away most of the haze, he saw them again and this time he was certain the savage, if that was what it was, had something bright on a thong at its throat, and touched it just before it laughed and vanished: the turquoise he had brought Anne from Flagstaff.

Damn you Anne! Damn you anyway.

He knew he could not have seen this because nothing could live out there. Still he hardened his heart against her.

Gunnar, Gunnar, please.

He sat up in bed, certain he had been dreaming. He sat in the dark with his eyes wide and his jaws open as if that would help him hear better.

The dome reverberated with her pounding. *Please, Gunnar.*

"Go to hell, he said aloud, and then covered his head with pillows. She had put him through too much; she was gone forever, he could live with that. Still he could hear the drumming. He reached for the sleeping capsule he always kept next to the bed and crunched it between his teeth.

When he woke it was still night; the sky outside was touched with beginning light and Anne, if it was Anne, was still out there.

He ran outside. It was her, or somebody who looked just like her, splendidly naked, pressing herself against the dome and calling.

"Go away."

Did she answer? *Oh Gunnar, please let me in.*

"I can't, you're dead."

Not dead. Changed.

"Oh Anne, why did you leave me?"

I didn't leave you, I was taken.

The thought shook him with rage. "You don't love me." She threw her hands in the air. *I couldn't help it.*

"Now I suppose you want to come back."

Oh Gunnar, please. I want to come home. We all do. The twins came out of the murk and stood next to her: taller, beginning to be women.

"Where were you? Where were you all this time?"

Oh Gunnar, it doesn't matter.

He was torn: caution and resentment pulled him one way, desire the other. "If you loved me, you never would have gone."

We couldn't help it. Really. Please let us in.

He said, "I can't," but his hands were already pressed against hers, separated only by the dome's glassy surface. He was thinking about the apparitions in the night: the savage with the flash of turquoise at the throat; he was thinking about what she and the savage would have done together and he was both enraged and maddened. "This is impossible. Everything outside is poison."

That's what you think.

"The air is poison."

That's only what you think. She danced back a few steps and shook herself.

"You must be poison."

She threw back her head and lifted her arms. *Do I look poison?*

He cried out, putting all the loss and frustration of the last months into his voice. "What were you doing all this time?"

Don't make me stand out here begging. Then she added that which he needed to hear to make what came next possible. *I love you.*

He thought he knew what he was letting into the dome: doubt and anger, along with whatever contamination their bodies would have collected, but Gunnar found himself moving toward the airlock in spite of himself, passing trembling hands over the dials and switches that would open it to her, and as he did so he could feel his throat close and his body quicken with a sweet, wild desire.

He hesitated.

This might be a trick.

She might be trying to destroy him. He realized it didn't really matter.

She was back, enhanced by her absence and whatever had happened to her in it and he knew he would have her.

"I love you too," he said and threw the last switch. The last seal opened and she came in to him, and even as he held out his arms and Anne walked into them without apology or explanation, he could see the twins tumbling in behind her, could see the crazed look in Betsy's eyes, which were all whites, the fact that Jenna's teeth were bared; in the second before he buried his face in Anne's neck he saw lodged in Jenna's dense hair: the jawbone of some long-dead small animal, two brightly colored feathers.

—1982

THE BRIDE OF BIGFOOT

Imagine the two of us together, the sound of our flesh colliding; the smell of him. The smell of me.

At first I was afraid. Who would not be frightened by stirring shadows, leaves that shiver inexplicably, the suspicion that just outside the circle of bug lamps and firelight something huge has passed? If there was a Thing at all it was reported to be shy; the best photographs are blurred and of questionable origin; hunters said it would not attack even if provoked, but still . . . The silence it left behind was enormous; I could feel my heart shudder in my chest. With gross figures roaming, who would not be afraid?

We did not see or hear it; there was only the intimation. It had been there. It was gone. Thomas, whom I married six months ago, said, Listen. I said, I don't hear anything. Roberta said, I'm cold. Thomas persisted: I thought I heard something. Did you hear anything? I did not speak but Malcolm, who was torturing steaks on our behalf, spoke politely. Everybody's so quiet, it must be twenty of or twenty after. Then Roberta said, Something just walked over my grave. I tried to laugh, but I was cold.

This was the night of our first cookout of the summer, shortly before I found certain pieces of my underwear missing from the line.

Our house is on the outer ring of streets here, so that instead of our neighbors' carports and arrangements for eating outside we look out at a wooded hillside, dense undergrowth and slender trees marching up the slope.

If it weren't for dust and attrition and human failure our house would be picture perfect. I used to want to go to live in one of our arrangements; the future would find me among the plant stands, splayfooted and supporting a begonia; I would be both beautiful and functional, a true work of art. Or I would be discovered on the sofa among the pillows, my permanent face fixed in a perpetual smile. I would face the future with no worries and no obligations, just one more pretty, blameless thing. It's a long road that knows no turning but an even longer one we women go. Each night even as I surveyed my creation I could see fresh dust settling on my polished surfaces, crumbs collecting on my kitchen floor, and I knew soon the light would change and leaves drop from my plants no matter what I did. Each night I knew I had to turn from my creations and start dinner because although Thomas and I both worked, it was I who must prepare the food. Because women are free and we are in the new society I was not forced to do these things; I had to do them by choice.

But it was summer, we opened all the windows and went in the yard without coats. We had that first cookout and maybe it was the curling smoke that wakened it, or maybe it saw me in my bathing suit . . . All I can tell you is that I lost certain underthings: my satin panties, my gossamer sheen bra. When I came home from work at night I went directly into the back yard. I tried to penetrate the woods, staring at the screen of leaves for so long that I was certain I had seen something move. The summer air was already dense with its scent, but what it was I did not know; I could not be sure whether that was a tuft of hair caught in the wild honeysuckle or only fur. Every night I lingered and therefore had to apologize to Thomas because dinner was late.

Something dragged a flowering bush to our back stoop. Outside our bedroom the flowers were flattened mysteriously. I got up at dawn and listened to the woods. Did I imagine the sound of soft breath? Did I catch a flash of gold among the leaves, the pattern of shadows dappling a naked flank?

In midsummer something left a dead bird with some flowers on my kitchen table and I stopped going outside. I stopped leaving the windows open too; I told Thomas we would sleep better with the air conditioning. I should have known none of our arrangements are permanent. Even with the house sealed and the air conditioner whirring I could hear something crashing in the woods. I ran to the back door to see and when I found nothing I stood a moment longer so that even though I could not see it, it would see me. When we went to bed that night it was not Thomas I imagined next to me, but something else.

In August I retreated to the kitchen; with the oven fan going and the radio on, the blender whizzing and all my whisks and ladles and spatulas laid out I could pretend there was nothing funny happening. We had seafood soufflé one night and the next we had veal medallions, one of my best efforts. When we went to bed Thomas turned to me and I tried to be attentive but I was already torn. I was as uneasy as a girl waiting for somebody new to come in to the high school party—one of those strange, tough boys that shows up unexpectedly, with the black T-shirt and the long, slick

hair, who stands there with his pelvis on the slant and the slightly dangerous look that lets you know your mother would never approve.

On Friday I made salmon mayonnaise, which I decorated with cress
and dill, and for dessert I made a raspberry fool, after which I put on my
lavender shift and opened the back door. In spite of the heat I stood there
until Thomas came in the front door. Then I touched the corners of the
mats and napkins on my pretty table and aligned the wineglasses and the
water tumblers because Thomas and I had pretty arrangements and we set
store by them.

Honey, why such a big kiss?

I missed you, I said. How was your day?

Much the same.

So we sat down at the little table with all our precious objects: the crys-
tal candle holders, the wedding china, the Waterford, him, me. I asked if
he liked his dinner.

Mmmm.

All right; I tried to slip it in. Am I doing something wrong?

I'm just a little tired.

Tell me about your day, you never do.

Mmm.

Outside, the thing in the woods was stirring.

Thomas, love is to man a thing apart, it's woman's whole existence.

Mmmmm.

In the woods there was the thunder of air curdling: something stopping
in mid-rush.

I love you, Thomas.

I love you.

Honey, are you sure?

Mmmmm.

I put out a dish of milk for it.

No, Lieutenant, there were no signs of a struggle, one reason I didn't
think to call you right away. I thought she had just stepped out and was
coming back. When I got home from work Monday she was gone. Nothing out of order, nothing to raise your suspicions, no broken windows or
torn screens. The house was shining clean. She had even left a chicken pie
for me. But there was this strange, wild stink in the bedroom, plus which
later I found *this* stuck in the ornamental palm tree on our screen door,
your lab could tell you if it's hair, or fur.

127

I wish I could give you more details, like whether the thing knocked my wife out or tied her up or what, but I wasn't too careful looking for clues because I didn't even know there was a Thing. For all I knew she had run over to a neighbor's, or down to the store to pick up some wine, which is what I thought in spite of the heap of clothes by the bed, thought even after it got dark.

By midnight when I hadn't heard I called her folks. You can imagine. Then I checked the closet with my heart going, clunk, clunk. Nothing gone. Her bankbook and wallet were in her purse. All right, I should have called you but to tell the truth I thought it was something I could handle by myself. Ought to handle. A man has a right to protect what's his, *droit de seigneur*, OK? Besides, I didn't think it was kidnappers. That grey fur. The smell. It had to be some kind of wild animal, an element with which I am equipped to cope. I used to hunt with my father, and I know what animals do when they're spooked. Your cordon of men or police helicopter could panic it into doing something we would all be sorry for. I figured if it was a bear or wolf or something that got in, and it didn't kill her right here, it had probably carried her off to its lair, which meant it was a job for one man alone. Now I have my share of trophies, you might as well know back home I was an Eagle Scout and furthermore I am a paid-up member of the N.R.A. Plus which, this is not exactly the wilds. This is suburban living enhanced by proximity to the woods. If something carried off my wife I would stalk it to its lair and lie in wait. Then when it fell asleep or went off hunting, I would swarm in and carry her out.

All right, it did cross my mind that we might get an exclusive. Also it was marginally possible that if I rescued her we might lure the creature into the open. I could booby-trap the terrace and snare it on the hoof. Right, I had guessed what it was, imagine the publicity! The North American serial rights alone . . . After which we could take our sweet time deciding which publisher, holding the paperback auction, choosing between the major motion picture and an exclusive on TV. I personally would opt for the movie, we could sell backward to television and follow up with a series, pilot and spinoff, the possibilities are astronomical, and if we could get the thing to agree to star . . .

But my Sue is a sentimental girl and I couldn't spring this on her all at once. First I had to get her home and then I was going to have to walk her through it, one step at a time, how I was going to make it clear to the public that she was an unwilling prisoner, so nobody would think she was easy, or cheap. You know how girls are. I was going to have to promise not to take advantage of her privileged relationship with the Thing. But what if we could train it to do what we wanted? What if we taught it to talk! I was going to lay it out to her in terms of fitting recompense. I mean, there is no point being a victim when you can cash in on a slice of your life.

Lord, if that was all I had to worry about! But what did I know? That was in another country and besides . . . Right, T. S. Eliot. I don't want you to think of me as an uncultivated man.

I got up before dawn and dressed for the hunt: long-sleeved shirt and long trousers, against the insects; boots, against the snakes. I tied up my head for personal reasons and smeared insect repellent on my hands and face. Then I got the rest of my equipment: hunting knife, with sheath; a pint of rye, to lure it; tape recorder, don't ask; my rifle, in case. A coil of rope.

It took less time to track it than I thought. You might not even know there was anything in the woods because you're not attuned to these things, but I can tell you they left a trail a mile wide. Broken twigs, twisted leaves, that kind of thing. So I closed in on their arrangement while it was still light; I came over the last rise and down into a thicket and there it was. I had expected to have a hard time locating her once I got to the lair; the Thing would have tied her in a tree, say, or concealed her under a mass of brush or behind a pile of rocks.

This was not the case. She was right out in the open, sitting on a ledge in front of its lair just as nice as you please. Except for the one thing, you would think she was sunning in the park. Right. Except for the dirt and the flowers in her hair, she was *au naturel*. There was my wife Susie sitting with a pile of fruits in season, she was not tied up and she was not screaming, she wasn't even writing a note. She was—good Lord, she was combing her hair. I went to earth. I had to be careful in case the Thing was using her for bait. It could be in its cave lying in wait, or circling behind me, ready to attack. I lay still for an hour while she combed and hummed and nothing happened. There was nothing, not even a trace. I got up and showed myself.

I guess I startled her. She jumped three feet. I said, Don't be frightened, it's me.

Oh, it's you. Where did you come from?

Never mind that now. We have to hurry.

What are you doing?

Suze, I have come to take you home.

Imagine my surprise. All this way to rescue my darling helpmate, the equipment, precautions, and all she could find to say was: You can't do that.

What do you mean?

So she was trying to spare my feelings, but that would take me some time to figure out. You have to go for your own good, Thomas. He'll tear you limb from limb.

Just let him try. I shook my rifle.

Thomas, no!

I did not like the way this was going. Not only was she not thrilled to see me but she showed signs of wanting to stay put. I was not sure what we had here, whether she was playing a game I had not learned the rules to or whether she had been unhinged by the experience. You should only have to court a woman once. What I did at this point was assert my rights. Any husband would have done the same. I said, Enough is enough, honey, now let's get home before it gets dark. Listen, this is for your own good. Susie, what are you doing with that rock?

To make a long story short I had to bop her on the head and drag her out. I don't know how we made it back to the house. Halfway down the hill she woke up and started struggling so I had to throw her on the ground and tie her up, in addition to which the woods were filled with what I would have to call intimations of the creature. There was always your getting pounced upon from the shadows, or jumped out of a tree onto, to say nothing of your getting grabbed from behind and shaken, your neck snapped with one pop. I kept thinking I heard the Thing sneaking up behind me, I imagined its foul breath on my neck. As a matter of fact I never saw hide nor hair of it, and it crossed my mind that there might never have been a Thing, a thought I quickly banished. Of course there had. Then I figured out that it was afraid to run after what it believed in, which meant that it was craven indeed, to let her go without a fight.

As soon as we got inside I locked all the doors and windows and put Susie in the tub with a hooker of gin and a pint of bubble bath, after which, together, we washed all that stuff out of her hair, including the smell. I guess the gin opened the floodgates; she just sat there with the tears running down her cheeks while I picked the flowers out of her hair. Somehow I knew this was not the time to bring up the major motion picture. What we had here might turn out to be private and not interesting to anybody but us.

There there, Suze, I said. Don't feel bad.

She only cried louder.

Now we know who loves you the most.

She just kept on crying.

I tried to cheer her up by making a joke. Maybe it found a cheap date.

She howled and wouldn't speak to me.

So I looked at her naked, heaving shoulders and I thought: *Aren't you going to apologize?* I was afraid to ask but I had to say something; after all, she was my wife.

Don't be ashamed, Suze. We all get carried away at least once in our life.

When she would not stop crying I thought it must have been one of those one-night stands, if the thing cared about her at all it would be tearing the house down to get to her. She would get over it, I thought. But she would not be consoled. There there, I said, there there. When this blows over I'll buy you a car.

Fat lot I knew. It was a tactic. All the Thing had to do was lay back and wait for her to get loose. Which I discovered shortly before dawn when I woke to an unusual sound. I sat up and saw her moving among the bedroom curtains, trying to unlock the sliding door. Was the thing in the bushes, waiting? Would she run outside with cries of delight? I was afraid to find out. I sprang up and tackled her, after which I laid down the law. She didn't argue, she only wept and languished. It was terrible. I had tried to arm against the enemy outside and all the time I had this enemy within. I called us both in sick at work after which I marched her with me to the hardware store and surveilled her the whole time I was buying locks. Then I barred the doors and put extra locks on all the windows. The Thing was so smart it wasn't going to show itself. It was just going to sit tight and wait. Well two could play at that game, I thought. When it got tired of waiting and showed itself I would blow it apart.

I suppose I was counting too much on her. I thought sooner or later she would clean herself up and apologize and we could go back to our life. Not so. We went from vacation time into leave without pay and she was still a mess. She would not stop crying and she wouldn't speak to me. She just kept plastering herself to the windows with this awful look of hope. In addition to which, there was the smell. It would fill the room when I least expected it. My Susie would lift her head and sniff and grin and if I tried to lay a hand on her, look out! It was enough to make a grown man weep.

I had to act.

So what I did was put her in the cellar and lock her up, after which I put on my hunting clothes and located the equipment; rifle, knife, rope. The tape recorder, she had smashed. I didn't know how far I would have to stalk the Thing or what I would have to do to make it show itself but I was sick of the waiting game. Damn right I was scared. I took the double bar off the back door and went down the steps.

I tiptoed across the night garden, and over to the trees. I know you're in there, I said in a reasonable tone. If you don't come out I'm coming in after you.

There was nothing, only the smell. I thought I would pass out.

Homewrecker. Bastard, come on. Right, I was getting mad. I cocked the rifle. In another minute I was going to spray the trees. Then it showed itself. It just parted the maples like swinging doors and walked out.

Huge? Yes, and that fetor, wow! The hair that covered it, the teeth . . . You've heard tales brought back by hunters. You can imagine the rest. The Thing stood there in the moonlight with its yellow teeth bared while I kept my rifle trained on its chest. It just stood there snuffling. I was, all right, I was overconfident. I yelled: Are you going to leave Susie and me alone or what?

At which point it sprang. Before I could even squeeze the trigger this great big monstrous thing sprang right on top of me after which I don't remember much except the explosion of my rifle, the kick. So it must be wounded, at least, which I suppose means it has left a trail of blood, but Lieutenant, I don't want to press charges. The thing is, my Susie left me of her own free will and now that all is said and done I understand.

No I can't explain, not exactly, except it has to do with the Thing: the stench, the roar, the smack of its prodigious flesh. It must have squeezed the daylights out of me and thrown me into Malcolm's grape arbor, which is where I woke up. They were gone and he was calling the police. And I will never forget its wild embrace.

What am I saying?

I'm letting her go, Lieutenant, and with my blessings, because I learned something extraordinary in that terrible moment. There are things we don't *want* to want but that doesn't stop us wanting them, even as we beg forgiveness. Life lets us know there is more than the orderly lines we lay out, that these lines can flex so we catch glimpses of the rest, and if a thing like this can happen to my Susie, who am I to say what I would do if it happened to me?

—1984

132

THE HALL OF NEW FACES

Women save all their lives for the Hall of New Faces; all our lives we are running ahead of the knife. We look in the mirror and we know one day our time will come. Not me, we think. Not yet.

But even you are going to get up one day and look in the mirror and think: That isn't me.

"The Hall of New Faces." Preparing herself, Maria tells her daughter, "We all end up there."

Nineteen-year-old Molly thinks: Not me. This will never happen to me. Automatically, she gives the good daughter's speech. "You'll always look beautiful to me."

But angry Maria goes to work and reads it in their eyes—withdrawal, contempt; she looks in their eyes and sees herself getting old. Quickly she moves into her daughter's clumsy hug, holding fast so Molly won't see what the world knows: beginning ruin. "It won't be so bad."

"Oh Mom, promise me you won't go."

Maria will not promise anything. But the problems:

—You can sell everything you have and you still won't have enough to do the job. What must be done will not stay done. This is the worst.

—Knowing that, you will do this. Will do it anyway. Will do it in spite of children like Molly who love you and men who care.

—The truth now, who *hasn't* thought about it? Who among us has not looked into the mirror and thought: oh, smoother!/fewer wrinkles!/less nose/more chin? Who has failed to place her fingers at the temples and in one fluid motion, lift slightly to make the face smooth out?

Oh, God! Maria thinks wistfully, I want to be beautiful, am beautiful now, in certain lights.

—Who *wouldn't* want to be gorgeous all the time?

But the consequences are harsh.

—Amazements take place in the Hall of New Faces, but like life itself, the miracles are only temporary; some things refuse to stay done.

—You have one painful year, her friends report; your body needs time to recover from the assault, they say. They say that if fate is kind you may have two good years in the middle, and then in the fourth year the results of the surgeon's artistry begin to deteriorate.

"It's like watching a time-lapse film of the picture of Dorian Grey," her friend Margaret says, or coming upon a rose that's just about to blow. "Naturally in the fifth year you will need to see your doctor," her best friend adds.

—At the Hall of New Faces they prepare for your return. They initial your peach hospital gown and show you to your old room. The staff greets you warmly because over the years they will get to know you very well. "How nice to see you again."

"When you are on the cusp, you think it's silly," Margaret says, "Vanity, you say because you're too supple to be old but look, you're already too—what is it, drawn-looking? to be young.

"Dangerous," Margaret says because women collect horror stories—silicone or collagen injections that solidified or slipped down behind the victim's skin and settled in lumps in the cheeks or underneath the chin: tales brought back by sailors, but still . . .

Because we are women.

Angry, Maria rails. "Why should I have to do this anyway?"

"I personally earned the thanks of a grateful nation," Margaret tells her with a laugh. "Nobody wants to look at an old bag."

Maria broods. "I mean, who am I doing it for? Myself or them?"

"Nobody wants to be ugly," Margaret says, touching her own varnished face. Currently, the only traces of her reconstruction are three minuscule scars. "Nobody wants to get old." What she means is: *Nobody wants to die.*

Maria presses fingers to her temples and lifts. Am I running toward something, or or away?

With the idealism of unblemished youth, Molly tells her it shouldn't matter what people look like, as long as they're good and kind and productive, but it's getting harder and harder to face the face she meets in the mirror these mornings; Maria has to do makeup before she can bear to look.

She thinks: Dammit. They should take me as I am. As an intermediary step, she begins to color her hair.

Brown spots appear, that she can't get rid of. The boss gives the plum assignment to her assistant, who is ten years younger. It's getting harder to outrun the knife. But she has these fears.

—Go too late and the pain is hideous and it takes forever to recover; go too soon and you risk wrecking whatever looks you still have. If you don't go at all, society will throw you away.

Contrary to legend, Margaret tells her, beauty is not in the eye of the beholder. It is written on your face. "Listen," she says, and even wary Maria would have to admit the results of Margaret's third procedure are gorgeous, "Beauty may be only skin deep, but believe me, it's the first thing people see."

Enough. Maria makes an appointment.

Margaret says, "Watch out for the psychiatric evaluation. At the Hall of New Faces they refuse to do the Right Things to you if it turns out you want the Wrong Things."

"My God," Maria cries, "what do they want from me?"

"They have to make certain your motives are pure."

Maria says bitterly, "I don't have any motives. The clock is pushing me."

Margaret touches her newly smooth throat. "Then look me in the eye and tell me you don't care about being prettier."

A direct hit: Thock! Maria has to look away.

Then Margaret issues a caution. "Don't expect this to change your life. Looking *better* is going to have to be enough." She sighs. "But that isn't it either. It's another holding action, OK?" For a fraction of a second her new chin quivers. "All any of us wants is to go on looking the same."

As it turns out, Maria is to upset to go through with it.

Some days, in some lights, Maria thinks her excellent bony structure may see her through the catastrophe time is writing on her face; she may shrivel like The Mummy but she'll always have good lines. On other mornings she meets the Yale bulldog in her mirror—the dewlaps! The strings at the neck! Rubbing in Retin-A to burn wrinkles out of aging skin, Maria thinks bitterly that she's running out of alternatives.

Hearing her mother groan, Molly says, "I don't see what you're so upset about. You still look beautiful to me."

For the first time Maria snaps at her. "That's easy for you to say." Looking at Molly's flawless skin she sighs. "You probably don't believe I used to be nineteen."

Unfeeling girl can't hide her incredulity.

Maria is the same person inside, but the mirror forgets. "So I'm going to do it, understand?"

"It's such a *nice* face. It's." Molly gasps. For the first time she understands. "Oh, Mom!" She sees her own future written in her mother's face. Women do.

"Listen," Maria consoles her, "You're so pretty you'll never have the problem. Besides, this is only a business thing." It's partly true; they've just promoted her pretty assistant over her head. It's getting harder and harder to make a sale. Her new man is easily distracted, looking over her shoulder into the middle distance—for what? Somebody younger? Prettier? She thinks he loves her, but for how long?

It's almost time.

—The Hall of New Faces! Results are promised, but never guaranteed. There are atrocity stories, tales of failures, women turned out looking like Quasimodo, running away to plunge burning faces in the mud of the river bank, blundering through the fog to hide themselves in the marsh. The face is not like fabric, she knows. It *will not stay* where you put it. Once you start, you have to keep on taking tucks. She is angrier than she is afraid.

—Why do I have to get a new skin cut just to make it at the office?

—Why do I have to be the one who gets cut up and sewn back together just to keep our love alive?

—Why is it always us, and not the man?

—Why can't I just *be*?

She would like to go to an island where there are no mirrors. Where there are no ugly truths in other people's eyes.

—I'm too young, she thinks. Not yet. Not me. Damn you all. Her new man loves somebody else now. It's her former assistant, from the office.

It's time.

"Molly, don't look like that!" Maria has just broken the news.

"I'm not going to let you do it," Molly says. "You don't even need it," she says.

"You can't stop me," Maria says. Now that she has made up her mind she's like an astronaut at the launch. She won't let anything stop her now.

"Oh Mom, what if they hurt you? What if you die?"

"It's not life-threatening." I don't think.

If it can happen to you, it can happen to me. "What if they ruin you?"

"This isn't like that. Really." Maria parrots the surgeon. "A really simple procedure. Like liposuction," Maria says too loud. "Laser surgery, just a few tucks. You don't feel a thing."

Walleyed with anxiety, Molly sees the rest. She has inherited her mother's body. Their futures are linked. Damage Maria and you hurt Molly. "I don't want to have my face cut!"

"Sh-sh," Maria tells her daughter. "It isn't happening to you." Yet. Poor child! Between now and then, they may find a cure for aging. Pigs may fly. Oh listen, the world might change.

Molly is gnawing her knuckles. She cuts to the chase. "What if they make me look like somebody else?"

"Shh shh. It's not nearly your turn. Oh Molly," Maria says, sadly, giving it all away. "If only you had been born a boy."

Molly winces as if struck. "Oh, Mom!"

Maria knows all women have to kill their mothers in order to grow up, a fact she has managed to keep from Molly so far. Is Molly really protesting for her sake or is there something more complicated going on? Maria understands she's going to have to sneak away to do the job.

She pretends to let Molly talk her out of it. "OK, Molly," she lies.

Molly does not see her duplicity. "Oh Mom, I'm so glad."

"But I have to do *something*." Maria tells a partial truth. "After a while you get tired of yourself."

What she means is: *I am tired of my life* .

Marking time until she can escape Molly's scrutiny, she begins a holding action. She goes to a clinic for a chemical peel. The Egyptians used to burn the faces of their slaves to keep them beautiful. The chemicals burn her face just like the Egyptian slaves' faces; her face is painful, pink and slick as a newly healed wound and then she scabs; it is horrible. She hides out until the skin fades from red to white. The whole time sweet Molly says, "Why are you crying? You look beautiful to me."

Pain laces her tone with bitterness. "Oh, sure."

Maria has six good months in which to complete her plan. Boyfriend says she looks lovely, boss asks if she's lost weight. Then to her despair, the burned skin heals and quickly reassumes its old contours. Given a Magic Marker, she could easily chart what needs to be done to her face—and soon! But, God, like the face peel, it is only a holding action. Have to settle this for for good, Maria thinks. Settle it for good and all.

Molly watches her mother with increasing anxiety. Her mother consolidates her savings, sells off paintings and the weekend house. Molly knows she ought to try to prevent what is coming, but she doesn't know what to do. One morning the girl gets up to a silent apartment and fixes forever in her memory the way the kitchen *is*: sunlight coming in on undisturbed dusty surfaces; the untouched toaster and the silent coffee maker and in the living room, the note. *Don't worry. Back soon.* Molly crushes the note to her chest and weeps for her mother, but when she looks in the bathroom mirror she stops crying because tears leave her blotchy and all this rubbing is going to damage the delicate skin around the eyes.

Back soon, the note promised, but it's been three weeks now and Molly still hasn't heard anything.

When she calls the Hall of New Faces for information they turn her away because after all, she could be just anybody calling, a rival at the office or in love, and the business of this place is to be discreet. Some women lie to their friends when they come here; they go home radiant and the boss asks: have you lost weight?

Maria is incommunicado somewhere deep within the Hall of New Faces. She will emerge a changed woman, Molly is certain—but changed to what?

"Don't worry," good old Margaret says when Molly calls her in a panic. "Sometimes they have to take fat out of your thighs to pad your face and it takes weeks to heal. It's nothing. They may need to transplant a little bone to enhance the jaw, and sometimes . . ."

"Oh, stop!"

Molly is wild. She has to find out where her mother is. Has Maria been stashed in some cell at a thousand a night while they do the psychiatric evaluation or is she lying in the dark with damp gauze lightly resting on her face or have they locked her up forever because the job was hideously botched?

Margaret says women who emerge safely from surgery in the tall, glittering hospital building always recover in the small hotel across the street. They share the lounge and the dining room with out-of-towners who are waiting their turn. When Molly goes to the hotel to check they claim her mother isn't registered. Is this the truth?

At the Hall of New Faces, everyone is painfully discreet.

Molly decides to find out by working from inside. Security clearance at the hospital takes six months—too long—so although she's a law student with a promising career, she drops everything to wait tables in the hotel dining room.

The recovering women don't mix with the women waiting for their faces to be rearranged. There is a mystique to having your face done, more: they are in pain and covered with bruises, and waiting for the swelling to go down. Still the bruises look faint to Molly, the scars small, the swelling minimal, so that even from a distance the survivors are probably an inspiration to the women still waiting for the knife. The veterans are mysterious and slightly superior, like those who slough off the questions of anxious virgins: You'll know soon enough. Be cool.

Every once in a while a successful new face drops in to swoop down on the other women at the tables in an aura of furs and perfumes: See how wonderful I am! Without exception the others fuss and exclaim; it's the least they can do, and the returning beauty? Glowing as she is, she wears something designed to distract: photo-grey aviator glasses or a hat with a tiny polka-dotted veil.

Molly brings the alumna her Perrier with failing heart; when she finds Maria, is she going to be able to recognize her mom?

The aspirants chatter nervously because the wait for a bed in the hospital is long. It's depressing, listening to the list of reasons they are here.

- "The children have left home and he's gone all day at the office and I'm so alone."
- "I'm doing it because I came home and found my new man in bed with my teenager."
- "People are secretly making fun of me. They *condescend*."
- "It's a business thing. Nobody wants to buy insurance from an old broad."
- "I don't get wrinkles, but I've always hated my nose."
- "He says he loves me but he treats me like his mom."
- "It's simpler than divorce."

The women give all these reasons, but then there is always something more. Molly sees this written in their faces: *It isn't really my face I'm trying to change. It's my life* .

In the hotel kitchen, Molly discovers they are preparing food for twice as many people as she sees in the dining room. Where are these trays going, covered as they are and stacked on a rolling steam table? Is there another dining room somewhere? With the practiced air of someone who has counted every step on his appointed route, Louie the blind man rolls the table into the service elevator.

"Who are the trays for?"

"Don't ask," one of the waiters tells Molly, casting his eyes to the heavens.

The old cook scowls. "Believe me, you don't want to know." But as was bound to happen, blind Louie of the steam trays gets sick and stays home from work one day. The waiters aren't allowed upstairs—no men! and so it falls to Molly to go up in the elevator with the steam table. Her instructions are not to bother the recovering patients in the rooms on the fourth floor; she's supposed to leave trays outside each door. Cook says, "They know the food is coming so don't even bother to knock." Cook lowers his voice. "They don't want you to *see* them that way."

Excited, Molly thinks: *they won't mind me* .

"Dinner," she says cheerily outside the first closed door and before the woman inside can say Do Not Disturb she has opened it and carried the tray in. For the first time, she can get one of these women alone. She can ask about the hospital; maybe one of them has seen Maria and Molly can find out how her mother *is*.

"You had to find out sometime," the first patient says with enormous dignity. The second sees Molly looking at her and weeps. No wonder they told her not to open any doors. Except for nurses who change dressings and IV bottles for these victims of misbegotten operations, nobody is allowed to see the women on the fourth floor. The horror stories women tell: the victims are all here.

She supposes there are a few successful surgeries represented here, women who are only temporarily disfigured but in terrible pain, but she can't tell who will get better and who won't. Weeping with compassion, she opens every door. Going from worse to worse yet, trying to find a kind word to say to each of the women, she discovers the rest. In one, a severed facial nerve creates an ineradicable scowl; in another, one side of the mouth droops in a perpetual sneer.

"You look fine, you do; listen, you can still go home," Molly says with false cheer. She knows as well as these women do that even if they do get up enough nerve to go among the people, the fixed expressions forever doom their best efforts. No matter what they do or say, they will be misunderstood.

Starved for company, they seize on Molly, and every one of them has a story to tell.

—There's the woman whose skin has been drawn so tight so many times that she can no longer eat in public because her lips won't close and no matter how careful she is the food falls out of her mouth.

—She meets the woman who can't sleep because her skin's been drawn so tight that her eyes won't close.

—Molly talks to victims of silicone accidents, liposuction disasters in which the bottom halves of faces disappear as if decayed by leprosy, sees faces distorted by misplaced collagen and fat transplants, people whose wounds became infected and whose faces have been eaten away by the ravages of uncheckable staph, and the victims are women all. In spite of the claims of the magazines, which suggest that the nip and the tuck are common to rising executives, these things don't happen to men.

Molly is too distraught to dwell on the body catastrophes: the carved-away bellies with internal organs punctured in the process, oops; thighs liposuctioned to bony shanks. Body work goes on in the Hall of New Faces, but Molly cannot contemplate it now.

In the last room of all, weeping Molly leans close as the last patient whispers her request. Unpracticed as she is, she squirts artificial tears into the eyes of the woman whose eyes won't close. Gently, she inserts the glass straw into a mouth that has been reduced to the size of a buttonhole by escalating feats of corrective surgery. The woman who can't sleep also cannot close her mouth.

The cosmic horror story then, is not anything Molly saw at the movies. It's not about things that seep or ooze or axe-wielding corpses that pounce upon unwary teenagers copulating in summer camps. (She murmurs, "Oh, mom!")

It's about what women do to themselves.

Here is Molly, frantic with fear for her mother and teetering on the brink of the next discovery. Once she has dropped the last tray and turned to run she does not go back to the elevator; instead she rips off the hotel apron and the perky hat and stuffs them into a standing ashtray and heads for the emergency stairs. She has to get out of here. She has to break into the Hall of New Faces and pray to God she is in time to rescue her mom.

Getting in turns out to be easier than she'd thought. The pastel lobby is completely accessible, papered in silver and upholstered and carpeted in mauve. On the walls photographic blowups of successful operations make her think her mother may be all right. The outsized photos of cosmetic triumphs smile standard smiles and look at her out of standard eyes set just *so* in faces pared, trimmed and chiseled into classic, or is it standard shapes. Molly is pretending to admire the photos, trying to decide where to start, when she hears her own name. Astounded, she wheels.

Behind the boomerang-shaped Lucite reception desk, the receptionist has called her name. When Molly turns a blanched, expressionless face in helpless acknowledgement, the receptionist says, "Ah yes, I thought so. Your mother is waiting to see you on Five."

And Maria? She is not in much pain any more; the swelling is almost gone and the anger that's simmered in her ever since girlhood has bubbled to the surface, expressed itself and been assuaged. She is at peace.

Like a figure in an old Joan Crawford movie, Maria sits in her chair in partial shadow; although it is night she has half-turned to the window so Molly won't need to see everything that has happened all at once. When loyal Molly knocks on the door she cries, "Oh, sweetie, I'm so glad you came. It's OK, Molly. Don't worry, I'm fine." Conscious of the fact that her daughter is still lurking just beyond the sill, apprehensive and taking cover behind the open door, she says, "Listen, it's all done."

Molly can't bring herself to come in.

"Understand, I got what I wanted," her mother says.

When Molly does not respond, Maria says in a strong voice, "I did."

Still shaken by her experience in the small hotel across the street, Molly hangs back. Her mother knows her well enough to understand. She calls out in a staunch, hearty, good-old-mother tone, "Listen, darling. I've found a way to solve the problem. If we're all brave enough, we can solve the problem once for all." She gives an artificial little laugh. "Hey, it may even become chic."

Maria keeps talking as Molly advances; her daughter is peeking around the edge of the door; now she is advancing into the darkened room. "When I first got here, I did a lot of thinking. I researched the pressures and I researched the possibilities."

Good, smart tough lady, Molly thinks; she says, brokenly, "Oh Mom."

"You can't say I didn't fight the good fight," Maria says. She is remembering the unending morning workouts, the cold packs, the face peel, certain side effects of Retin-A. "But what we're up against here isn't nature, it's the society."

Right on, Mom, Molly thinks. Damn straight. From this distance, shadowed as she is, Maria seems like her old self, Molly thinks. She has to be. She says, with dawning relief, "So you changed your mind."

"Right." Maria cuts her off. She says, with force, "Up to a point."

If Maria is still in shadow, Molly thinks, it is for a reason. Frightened, she begins to back out.

Her mother's voice rivets her. "Wait!"

She does wait, but she *will not look*.

"We all hate what age does to our faces, but there are worse things," Maria says. She will not understand that even now when she is so close to being right, she has it wrong.

"That we do to ourselves."

"We hate ourselves when what we ought to hate is what people do to us."

"The surgeons," Molly says. *Yes!*

"No. Time. Age. *Everybody*." For the first time, pain creeps into Maria's voice. "Our rivals. Our men. What they make of us. What they expect."

Oh, Mom!

"Nobody cares what we do. All they see is how we look. Why should I have to feel guilty for getting old? Well I won't. Molly, listen. " Her voice is deep now, loving, strong. "I'll never feel guilty again."

Molly gasps in relief. "You've decided not to have the operation."

"No. I've solved everything." Maria goes on in a burst of beautifully skewed logic, "If you're going to something, you might as well do it right, and the beauty of this is, I only have to do it once."

"Mother, what . . ."

"You'll see." In this mood, in this light, she even sounds like Joan Crawford—a woman's face! What is Maria hiding? She won't be hiding it much longer. As Molly watches with a sense of inevitablility, Maria lifts her hand to turn on the stand lamp over the chair and in the same fluid motion she swivels so Molly will see precisely what she has done. "In my own way, I'm a pioneer. You can look now. Understand, I'm never getting old!" Her voice drops to a confidential rasp; it is gutty, sexy, final. "And if I do, nobody's ever going to know."

Molly stuffs her fist in her mouth and screams.

The face her mother turns to her is as bland and smooth as an egg's. There is nothing on it, no brow, no nose, nothing but slits for the eyes and a slit where the mouth used to be. There are no wrinkles. No features. Nothing at all.

She is gleeful, half-mad. "You see?"

Maria has had her face removed.

—1992

LIKE MY DRESS

Oh God, to have style and money in those days, to take my place up there on the stage with hot Stud Ridley, the magnetic emcee with the neon eyes, my love. Bliss to be in the studio—but to be a contestant! Who wouldn't kill for the thrill? Imagine starring in the global sensation, the absolutely only TV show that keeps dogs away from their dinners, kids home from the malls and lovers out of each other's arms, everybody too mesmerized to turn it off, and, yes! All eyes on me in my most death-dealing costume, now *that* is power.

Imagine being the all-time winner in the grand playoffs at the end of the season, taking the trophy in front of the biggest TV audience in the history of competition. Feel the drumroll, hear the shouts as Stud Ridley— *Stud Ridley* crowns you all-time universal winner on LIKE MY DRESS.

Listen. I almost made it. And if the show went down in flames right afterward so be it. Fine.

With a loss like that, the skies should weep.

There was another winner that season, but there was never another season. All the heart and fire had gone out. Am I sorry? There's a hole in my heart that pills won't reach. Glad? OK. Yes.

But if you want to blame somebody, blame Lola. Lola Garner did it, my putative best friend. Lola, that I trusted; we used to wear each other's clothes! It was Lola with the baby-blue sweetie pie stare and her raunchy little ass and all her treachery that brought me down. And I thought she was my friend.

If you want to know the truth I got into it because of her; I flew so high—before I fell. But I am getting ahead of myself.

We worked in the same office and I ran into her in Labels for Less one day at lunch. She was trying on an orange sequined catsuit that made her ass look like a pumpkin going away. She was preening in front of the three-way mirror as if it didn't even show the back of her, and I had to intervene.

"Hi, you may not know me, my name is Gaby, from the office?"

Well the smile she gave me was flattering, to say the least. "Everybody knows who you are. You're that terribly chic girl."

"Oh, do you really think so?"

"This is such an honor. Everybody wants to look like you."

She twirled in the jumpsuit. "What do you think?"

I did it without even hurting her feelings. "I've seen you in better colors."

"Oh, thank you." She took my word for it.

By the time we left I had talked her into a mauve number that was *very* slenderizing and looked good with my grey suede boots, and she thought I was God. We were bonded from then on.

Or she let me think we were. To think I trusted her! But that was before we even dreamed of LIKE MY DRESS

Now let me explain a few things to you about costume, so you can see what made that show take off and fly. Now I'm not just talking about us women in the work force, this holds for every guy I know. Just look at the ads for guy makeup and the eye tucks for men and the hair plugs and the fluorescent shirts, the ass-hugging trousers and natty ties and the two-toned shoes, you think that's for fun? It's for survival. When all about you are losing theirs at least you know you look good. Shopping is nature's way of telling you you're not dead.

Plus, the pressure is intense. Look at any magazine and you can see it. Look at TV. This world we live in could care less about what's going on inside a person; it's the wrappings that count. So everybody goes to work, we all do our jobs, and no matter how good we are at what we're doing the world is judging us according to something else.

And you wonder why the whole world fell for LIKE MY DRESS?

Maybe you're too young to remember the show in its heyday, the brocades and sequined jobs designed to stun, the ermine trim that could take out entire battallions, jewels that killed instantly.

And the great thing was, you didn't have to be rich. On the best nights the judges overlooked your elaborate hand-sewn one-of-a-kind evening gowns and your rich people's Issy Miyakes and Christian LaCroixes to give first prize to the Army Surplus coverall with the gold belt or the simple sack dress while a studio audience that numbered in the thousands rose as one person and cheered. It was about how you put things together, whether you had an eye.

In the world of LIKE MY DRESS, money wasn't everything; sometimes money wasn't *anything*. Style was. That imponderable: *chic*. You either have it or you don't. Which is what provided the suspense. There would be Ms. keypunch operator of Dallas, facing off with one of the crowned heads and some big star who'd dropped a bundle on Rodeo Drive. At the end of the evening she would parade, as good as anybody, and the applause meter would do the rest. She could win! The judges and the audience went for a certain totality of *look* that surpasseth understanding. How else could you account for the excitement, the surprise, the harmony of tension that made an international cult around a television show? I mean, the Golden Calf had nothing on LIKE MY DRESS. Those were the days. If you were old enough to shop, you could not help but hope.

And now I'm going to tell you something interesting, and if it splits the difference between men and women, fine. In the first thirteen weeks, there were also men contestants, but the producers dropped them for two reasons.

One, men's clothes are not nearly as good, so except for the one transvestite, in thirteen weeks there was not one male winner.

And, two, the bottom line. It was that when push came to shove with those guys, they were born losers. They. Did. Not. Know how to accessorize. Men don't know squat about style. They think they're competitive but when the going gets tough they just can't handle it. Give me a woman every time.

What had Lola said the first time we met? "You're that terribly chic girl." My heart rose up.

If only I could bring back that first night. We were on our way out to a Singles Fondue Party when Lola flipped on my set and Stud Ridley came up on the screen and I fell in love. He just sauntered into a pool of light, whistling the theme . . . the most hypnotically sexy man in the world, with the wavy hair and the sweet, sweet grin that made amazing promises. I died. Is it enough to say that since that night I've never wanted another man?

And this is what hummed along under the theme music, and radiated in his smile: If you won, Stud Ridley was part of the prize. Magnetic, gorgeous. Mine. Who wouldn't fall in love with him? Who wouldn't tune in week after week after week? Lola and I could barely tear ourselves away. There were women just like us wearing these beautiful clothes in front of all those people with the music playing; there was Stud Ridley with the neon eyes, there was the applause! The applause . . .

The show was broadcast live from Los Angeles and relayed by Telstar, so that in certain foreign capitols, even though it would be repeated later, people struggled out of bed at 3 A.M. just so they could see it live. Broadway producers buckled to the pressure and provided hour-long intermissions between acts of their new hits, with TV sets provided in the lobbies and the rest rooms. At the opera, everybody went to the special second-act TV lounge. In factories, management found the hour LIKE MY DRESS break increased productivity. Is it any wonder Lola and I refused dates and shuffled exercise classes to be home Wednesday nights?

Friends like to be with friends in times like that. Lola and I were close in those days. We used to do each other's hair!

We shopped together on lunch hours, and on Wednesday nights we went over to each other's house to see the show. At six we would sit down with our notebooks and tomato soup and brownies on TV trays, trying on clothes until show time. We made sketches of the winners, so we could sew copies for ourselves. I did the machine work and Lola put in the hems—the innocence! The joy! Would it be better to be forever the winner, or to be forever young?

I'll tell you what is worse. Not being either.

Ah, but at the time, I thought I was going to have it all. All right, all right, it was Lola's idea for one of us to go one the show. But I was the bankroll. Didn't that give me rights?

It was the second Wednesday in the first season, we were going to a party, but only after the end credits rolled on LIKE MY DRESS.

I saw Stud Ridley walking off through the circles of light and I wanted to melt into the TV and go after him.

This frumpy rock star won; her hair was a mess and the idea of her out on the town in the limo with my beautiful Stud was killing me. And then just like that, Lola turned to me and said innocently, "Listen, we could do better than that. You could."

"Right. Me and Lady Di."

She looked so *sincere*: "Listen, Gaby, you have style. You look better than that winner in what you have on right now."

It was my new black outfit, with the neat boots. I'll admit I blushed, but it made me walk a little taller. "Maybe you're right."

"By the way, can I borrow your lizard sandals?"

Longing like fire smouldered in my joints and went flickering along my bones. I even loaned her the matching shoulder bag. And when we went out that night we took large steps.

Lola led me along, "So, listen. We look as good as they do. We could win."

Do you wonder why the show was such a hit?

Lola and I spent the whole night talking about weight training and jazzercize, just in case. When push comes to shove a person has to look good in something tight. Not our fault that we got so far into it that our guys felt left out. We didn't say it right out, but even then Lola knew where this was heading, and I knew.

Still we didn't watch *every week*, or we tried not to. At least not that season. We still had lives. But in the second season we were pulled in tight. Lola was over at my house, we had two really sweet computer programmers from Mobil coming over, she was trying to bring in MTV so we would have dance music but she got the season premiere and there he was back in my living room: Stud. Oh yes I was in love.

Plus, there was a new feature. Listen. They showed movies of contestants in training. Including everyday people, just like us. LIKE MY DRESS sent a camera crew to follow you around for two weeks before the show. We saw this sweet woman getting breakfast for her family, knitting her own dressy tank tops, going out to shop . . . Then we saw this rich lady exec, she had staked her corporation and her reputation on winning, so most of the pictures were of this woman shopping, shopping, she was so rich the stores sent models over to her office! Then they showed us the girl from design school—at class, in the dorms gluing bottle-caps to the hem of her velvet evening dress so it would shine and clatter when she turned. Who wouldn't love her. Who wouldn't envy them!

And one of those women was going to be the first winner of the year. She would get the crown, the night with Stud Ridley. She would get the week in Acapulco, the evenings in London, Paris, Rome, the lifetime purchase card backed up by American Express and honored in every major store around the world. As it turned out, the lady exec won it that night, but it *could* have been one of the common people.

It could have been us. Lola looked at me. "TV," she said. Her lips were wet. "We could be on TV."

"On our bankroll?"

"If we pool our talents." Her eyelashes were like flocked velvet. She was wearing my little red thing. "With our chic."

I said, "We could," but even then a little bell was sounding somewhere inside. I would find out too late what it was jingling about: *One of us could.*

When the guys rang we were too hypnotized to buzz them in. That was the season my ficus died of neglect. It was the season Lola and I moonlighted at a Bagel Nosh to help support our wardrobes, working every night of the week except during the show. It was the year we bought the Polaroid to take pictures for the nationwide talent search and the camcorder to shoot videos of us in our pretty clothes, and the year we gave up men because there wasn't time for that and weight training too. When we won there would be plenty of new men and they would all be rich, and handsome, and elegantly dressed.

And I would have Stud.

If I could just win I knew I could make him mine for good. And Lola — when I confided, she was so generous. The bitch. "You want him? You should have him. All I care about is the glory." She was so cool; she made me think she didn't even care which one of us went first.

That year we sent three dozen sets of snapshots and videos and all we had was rejection slips. By that time the cheerleader from Temple, Texas, had been declared the winner for October and Lloyd's of London was covering wagers that put Lady Di out in front in the end-of-the-year finals, although sheik Ahmed Fouad's entire harem was considered the dark horse because their ensemble breakfast costumes stopped the show.

Lola said, "Maybe next week."

We had just gotten rejected again. I was so depressed I groaned. "Maybe not."

Was she looking at me sideways? Stupid, I never saw. Her eyes got all slitted — strange. "Maybe if we spent more on photographs . . ."

"Maybe if we had a million bucks."

"I'm not kidding, Gaby." God the woman was quick. She slipped it in like a needle full of Novocain. "If only we could afford to get Venuto to take our photographs."

Now that sounded innocent. Of course it turned out we could only afford one set of photographs, so on the way to Venuto's studio we had this heart-to-heart and Lola said, "Which one of us gets photographed first?"

"I don't know," I said.

"It doesn't matter who goes first," she said, "Whoever wins, we'll use the money to get the other one on the show." Then, boy, you should have heard her, that voice clear and empty as a glass of water, Lola beginning the lie of all lies: "Tell you what, why don't we let him choose?"

It sounded fine to me. Oh sure, I thought I was going to win, and why? Because all these months Lola had been telling me so.

So we went to his studio. I have spent two decades on the couch trying to get over this one . . .

This Venuto was an artist, right? Well he decided Lola's cheekbones (which I happen to know she'd sucked in her cheeks to get the effect) made her the one. Plus she had stuffed herself into my best white thing so she looked better than me. The bitch.

Those photos got her the show. OK, I tried to be glad for her. "Oh don't worry," she said, "when the DRESS crew comes to make the audition video, you can be on the video too. Stud can choose."

Sure.

All our money for the one set of photographs. But it got her the show. Not three weeks later, my best friend was coiled on my chaise like Cleopatra waiting for the asp, all dolled up in honor of the DRESS audition video crew. We were going to be on the show.

I mean, she was. I tried to be glad. I even promised to sew her a new dress. Gaby, the brave little tailor. Gaby, the tool.

I *tried* to be glad for her. She didn't make it easy. Once I had fallen into the sidekick role she started using me like toilet paper, you know? If I said maybe it wasn't fair, her going first, Lola would string me along with promises: "Oh, Gaby, just think of the two weeks in Acapulco, think of the perpetual charge account, think of the *shopping* we could do."

Lola, with her everlasting WE, when what she meant was I.

But I ended up letting her take the pick of my closet and after we pooled our savings for her wardrobe, I carried all the damn packages. I even altered her rotten evening clothes.

Well I showed her.

It was kind of an accident. I mean, she was trying on costumes at my place (which I had kindly agreed she could use for the audition shoot because her dump was not presentable and mine was, even with the sewing mess and the ficus dead) and she was still going: "prizewinner's date with Prince Albert" this and "year-end championship date with Prince Edward" that, worse and worse and then, "Imagine, Stud Ridley," the other thing.

I just couldn't help it, I said, "Listen, Lola, friends are friends and you can go first on the show and no hard feelings, but there is this one very important thing."

She was so busy looking in the hand mirror that she hardly heard. "Sure, Gabes, anything."

Can I help it if everything in me boiled up and popped? "Keep your damn hands off of Stud Ridley. He's mine."

Then she said as cool as cool, so offhand that I wanted to murder her, "Oh, him, I wouldn't touch him with a stick."

After which *my best friend* did this awful thing to me. The words just fell out, like garbage on the rug. "I bought something for you."

I was doing up her hem. I tried to smile. "Oh Lola, how nice." To think I was ashamed for what I was feeling right then.

She was all pink and big-hearted and smiling. "Here it is."

You can imagine my emotions as I opened the box—the *thud* when I saw what it was! "A maid's uniform!"

"Don't you like it? Now you can be with me on the show."

"In *this?* "

"Better that than nothing." She was wearing my best rhinestone clips on her shoes.

"Don't do me any favors, Lola. After you win the everlasting charge account, I will get on the show in my own right. After all,"—dumb thing to say, bad timing, "I am the one with chic."

She choked.

"Why are you looking at me like that?"

She was trying to swallow the words; she knew they were garbage. I yelled at her to speak up. She couldn't help herself. She said, "You'll never make it, you're too fat. Your clothes all look better on me."

"Fat!" So much for her flattery. All lies. All these years and the bitch had been using me so she could wear my clothes.

I lunged for her throat but she stopped me in mid-flight, squeaking, "Gaby, the doorbell. The camera crew! Gaby, my hair!"

"In hell."

So much for Lola. I bopped her and locked her in the closet. Right, my mistake. I should have murdered her. Little did I know.

The first thing was I couldn't get at my best shoes. Instead I had to wear her rotten narrow dressup pumps, but when the crew came they didn't seem to notice that I limped. She ruined my aqua sweater the last time she wore it so what if I did stretch her rotten shoes? After the crew knocked off for the day I went to the closet and revived Lola, but before I did, I took precautions. I got out my toenail scissors and cut off all her hair.

I will not describe the scene that ensued when she saw herself in the mirror, but I will say this for Lola. She is a practical girl. I reasoned with her. Since she couldn't do the show with no hair, it was only right for me to do it—after all, I had put up half the jack. Besides, they already had me on the video. Plus, after I promised to split the prize money and the everlasting charge account—in fact, everything except the night with Stud Ridley, which I swapped her for the date with Prince Edward—she agreed to go along. By the time she had access to the winner's credit cards, which I signed in blood that I would share, her hair would be back. After I promised to throw in a free sitting with Venuto, she was positively philosophical. Her time would come. She would get her chance to be on the show.

What I would never forgive her for was the garbage she had spewed

151

on the rug between us, that would not go away. All these years the two-faced bitch had been wearing my clothes when she secretly thought I was fat.

In the next weeks I was so happy I forgot. There was no way I was going to take Lola along to Hollywood as my maid or my secretary or any other thing. Not now that I knew she was a liar and a sneak. She wasn't about to be seen in public anyway, because of the hair. In fact she took a leave of absence from work to grow her hair back, so she was out of my hair. Sorry. Instead of her being the queen, I was going to be the queen.

Los Angeles!

You should have seen it. You should have seen me, going around in the studio car. Unfortunately, even the last pirate tapes have been destroyed. Nobody wants to remember because nobody cares. *Sic transit*. You know.

They got me there a whole week early, which I spent in hair salons and nail parlors and makeup clinics which the funny-looking short woman with the clipboard sent me to twice — I suppose because even though Lola and I bear a passing likeness, she couldn't make the Venuto photo match my face. But I was in heaven, stashed in the Beverly Wilshire. I didn't mind.

Before the show we waited in the Green Room, me and the Japanese manufacturer's wife who had taken anabolic steroids to make herself tall enough by American standards of beauty, along with the ex-wife of the chairman of the board at Lord and Taylor, who had divorced her husband so she could compete in spite of the conflict-of-interests clause. Nobody wanted us to rumple our opening-round costumes so we were leaning against tilted ironing boards. As we were in competition, it seemed best for us not to talk. Instead I eyed them, and they eyed me.

I know I looked fine. Even before Stud Ridley kissed me — *kissed me* in the winner's circle and gave me the crown for that night, I knew I looked fine. And that kiss. I have lived a lifetime on that kiss. You can have your Prince Edward *and* your Prince Albert of Monaco. Listen, Stud Ridley kissed me. Once.

I was leaning against my tilted ironing board with my simple cashmere spread out around me and the amazing find I'd made on Rodeo Drive carefully draped, touching my deceptively simple jewels. Then the music came up and I thought I would asphyxiate as the manufacturer's wife tottered out on her platform sandals into the light and the show began. The light! The applause was only a prelude to mine. I could tell you a thing or two about applause.

I can't tell you much about the rest because all I remember are the lights and the applause—the applause! The clapping whisper of the billions out there watching, via satellite relay.

What can I say about Stud Ridley in person, the eyes, that seductive touch? And the betrayal. Terrible.

How can I describe what he and Lola did to me? In the first round they show your clips—hard to watch because it brought it all back: the ugly scene with Lola, the closet, how I cut off all her hair. I couldn't nurse the guilt because I had to look happy for the second round, where the contestants reverence the all-time winners while dressed for afternoon. The Hall-of-Famers make little speeches about how hard it was for them, how great we look; I remember thinking: *every one of these women has been with my Stud.*

Then I looked into his very special eyes and jealousy disappeared. I triumphed in the third round. I had designed and made the evening dress. I'd only had to let it out in a couple of little places to make it fit me as well as it fitted Lola.

After the commercials we were called back to tell the studio audience, in our own words, where we got our clothes.

I was halting. I was eloquent. I was wonderful. I was so good I won. I could hear a little murmur that began way back in the enormous studio, gathered force and broke like surf over me, wave after wave of applause. Stud Ridley put the crown on me—I could feel his fingers trailing promises across my bare back—and then I got what I had always wanted— I got to show off in my party dress in front of everybody, I heading onto the Mylar runway to the music and the applause. Behind me was *my picture* on this giant monitor above the stage. It was wonderful. I will never forget the feeling as I started out . . . I never should have turned my back on that monitor.

But I am forgetting Lola. No. I had forgotten about Lola then, the bitch. What she might be up to that night. I don't know how she managed it, I don't know what she promised Stud Ridley or what they did to make it work.

All I do know is that at the beginning of the the prizewinner's promenade, just as I was heading down the runway and out over the heads of the audience, the runway lights went out. Like that. I was there but nobody saw.

Never mind, I thought, trying to make the best of it. They can see me on the monitor.

So I was on the runway, looking, I thought, double gorgeous in Lola's dress, and if only the people sitting nearest could see, no matter, because I was backed up by the giant monitor, I thought, Gaby Fayerweather in the prizewinning costume and thirty feet tall, beamed out to every TV screen all over the civilized world.

It was what I had been working for all these years. It was better than anything; it was better than sex, it was like being queen of the world.

And something was wrong.

I was lost in the wild blue waiting for applause. First there was nothing. Then this *awful sound* started somewhere down deep and ripped through the air, it was—it was this hideous rattle, a whip of scorn, followed by a guttural, angry rumble, followed by some thing I had never heard before, so final and terrible that I gave up the promenade and for the first time I looked at the giant television screen . . .

It was horrible.

It was me and it wasn't me.

There I was thirty feet tall in front of thousands and being beamed to the entire civilized world, and what did they see?

My golden dress was gone and the crown was gone and the cape was gone; the me that was up there on the screen was not me in my moment of triumph, being broadcast live.

It was me on tape. There I was smiling for Lola's camcorder on a sunny afternoon back home, absolutely not the way I planned for them to see me. I tried yelling *look everybody, I'm still here, and I'm still all dressed up*, REALLY, but nobody heard; they were all looking up there at the me on the screen. And they hated what they saw. You would think I was up there with my hair in rollers.

The bitch. Who did she sleep with to make this happen, who did she have to bribe?

Up there on the screen: Gaby Fayerweather in her shame, with a pink string of words trailing across the screen underneath: LIKE MY DRESS?

Then Stud Ridley, *Stud Ridley* said into the microphone: "OK, people, like her dress?"

It came from a hundred thousand throats in the studio and out there all over the globe, it was enormous: "Noooooooooooooo . . ."

I died.

Then it disappeared. TRANSMISSION INTERRUPTED TEMPORARILY, the screen said, DO NOT ADJUST YOUR SET. It was all over for me.

Then transmission resumed. There was a winner on the stage and on the giant screen but it wasn't me. Stud had put Lola in my place. Lola—in a wig, I suppose, since there wasn't time for her to grow her hair back after what I did to her; Lola was up there in a copy of my evening gown—I looked from her to Stud Ridley and back again and all I could see was treachery. That duplicitous heartbreaking lying bastard Stud Ridley wrapped his arm around her waist and said, "Look everybody, this is the real queen," and then my God he said, "After the finals we're going to be married, let's all greet Lola Garner, my winner and my fiancée." You know, it didn't matter how I waved my arms there at the end of the runway in the dark, Gaby Fayerweather in the prizewinning golden dress, poor Gaby shouting, *I'm still heeere*; nobody saw.

Instead they all looked at Lola and cheered.

And me? They threw me out. Just as *my best friend* accepted the prizewinning kiss from Stud Ridley, studio guards on orders from that same Stud Ridley lifted me like a log and carried me off.

If that had been all, I might have handled it, but I am ruined for life. No matter how I disguise myself people know me for a failure; they follow me in the street like dogs, laughing and pointing at poor Gaby the pretender, Gaby Fayerweather, who thought she was so cute.

See, in addition to cheating me of my triumph, Lola and Stud Ridley ruined my life. What they did was, they exposed me to the final unspeakable horror, the hell from which nobody returns and which nobody survives, which is why I firebombed the studio the following Wednesday, causing Stud Ridley extensive plastic surgery that took him off the air and effectively eviscerated the show.

What it was, was, that video that started them howling at me? It didn't look half bad. I mean, in that particular video, I had on my best purple thing, with my rhinestone earrings and my hair done special, with the pretty little poufs over the ears? I even had on my favorite orange shoes. That wasn't one of your embarrassing home videos, it was the real me, OK? And the rotten hateful final insult, that sent me over the edge in a barrel?

They hated me anyway.

So if I am not much to look at these days, if my teeth are long gone and my hair is going; if my figure went first, a casualty to despair, if dogs bark at me in the street and children cover their eyes and run there is a reason. Failure makes you ugly, and this was the worst.

I went on LIKE MY DRESS, all right? I had to lie and cheat to do it, I locked my best friend in the closet and I cut off all her hair and took her place, I went on LIKE MY DRESS and it was the end of everything.

They didn't like my dress.

—1993

LAST FRIDAYS

Margaret back-combs her hair with her fingers, hissing, "Look alive." She has to go down to the Bay Club again. Simple ladies' lunch that stops her heart. They aren't what you'd call intimidating—just early Americans, on the road to old. Stacked up against them, Margaret looks pretty good. So what is it about last Fridays that makes her skin shrivel, and why does her spit come in so sour that it poisons her smile?

They have so much in common, she and the others—Ted's mother and Johnny's and especially Jeff's mom, who's almost as new to this as Margaret. The shared vocabulary of experience. At these monthly luncheons the mothers have a chance to sit down at a pretty table, safe from outsiders' questions in a territory where they can put aside doubt and pain. Unfolding pink napkins, they smile—nice ladies, bonding over fruit cocktail and chicken à la king. Sweet: the long afternoons here at the club with Al's mother and Ed's and Richard's moms and the mother of the two Charlies, yet at the door to the bayfront dining room, Margaret seizes up.

It isn't just that she's going to hear today.

She hates going in. When this group meets the manager routes regular members to the grille or the trellis room, as if to spare them the spectacle, like it's *something we did*. This mothers' club is so exclusive that nobody wants to be in it.

But she is.

At least she's not alone in this. When Billy's dad left them he said, "Support him and you're alone in this." Fine. This is Billy, after all. She could travel to the end of the world and jump off and still never leave him behind. How could she not support him? She's his mom!

She plans not to blink this time but she always does. They stick the mothers at the round table in the bayfront window; she can't see them for the light. Sunlight strikes reflections off the water behind them and ricochets, hitting the ceiling and bouncing off all those white tablecloths, and Margaret is dazzled all over again.

The mothers are like cardboard outlines with the faces obscured, so

Margaret can't tell if they're glad to see her or only embarrassed because they're caught talking about her. When the afterimages halo out she will see them swiveling with fishbowl eyes, regarding her. No matter how early she starts out the others get here ahead of her, turning in their captain's chairs to watch her approach, and judge.

Why can't we just sit around on cracker barrels in some country store and brag?

She would like to go to live in early America, before TV and the Bomb—optimistic and easy, secure. A place where no bad things come. For Margaret, early America is like Oz. God she misses it, country roads, stagecoach, quilting bee, ice truck, lemonade, general store. Tales brought back by sailors from a land she's only read about. Why can't life be all soda fountain, drive-in, soft grey summer nights with kids calling in the dark and lovers on the porch swing and lightning bugs in jars the way it used to be, before she was around? Some mornings she pretends she's waking up in the Little House on the Prairie or just anywhere in the past when people were happy with the simple things—Sunday night suppers around the radio, two chickens in every garage, nickel ice cream and none of the grief and notoriety that come with life in late America, where you can do something bad in the morning and tune in at six and see it on TV.

When did life break in two? She doesn't know.

How did we—I mean he . . . No, she means the country. How did we slip so fast, from nostalgia into savagery? Poor Billy, born into this! she thinks, without knowing what *this* means. Is this what did it to him? TV. It was TV. Unless it was bad companions. Or the bomb. He was such a good boy . . . Now, *Oh, Billy*. He and I are in late America. Way late.

Fishhooks snag her soft places. Like the mermaid dancing on bloody feet Margaret licks her mouth and grins, advancing as the mothers look up from their fruit cocktails with those soft, ruinous smiles. "Here she is."

Like welcoming like. Into the same boat, with a certain vindicated look. *Welcome aboard.* "Margaret, so nice to see you."

"And you look so *well.* " Considering.

What is it about misery? Loves company.

Margaret's lips quiver. "Thank you."

Entrenched as she is, secure in her position, Jeffery's mother looks relieved because with Margaret here, she is no longer the new girl. Tears stand in her eyes. "So nice."

Even the oldest, plainest moms look sweet and brave today in their splashy earrings and gold neck chains, their pastel playsuits that hang badly and coordinated cork-soled wedgies that call attention to the slack skin on their legs. Stylish and lumpy alike, they are dressed in spunky resort clothes and tanned to the bone. At home in this nice, sunny city that is, essentially, retired. In a way, the mothers are retired.

While she wasn't looking, he just passed her by, rocketing into the unimaginable. Her boy traveled out of her reach. Can't call, doesn't write. No forwarding address to send those homemade cookies to. No buddies in uniform crowding around to watch him open the tin, even though she likes to imagine him turning to the others with that smile she's loved ever since he was six weeks old: "Fudge brownies, my favorite."

When he was little he was so easy, satisfied with a little toy.

He is far beyond her now.

But motherhood is a permanent position. The job is never over. Even when he's in the grave.

He is still and always her little boy.

And so on the last Friday of every month the mothers meet, and talk. In some cases, the stories she tells are all she has left of him.

"Hello, everybody," Margaret says to Ted's mom and Johnny's and Jeff's and Ed's and the mother of the two Charlies, and Al's and Richard's mothers, good women all. They greet her in the usual bland currency but it is the unspoken exchange that bonds the eight of them: *I did the best I could.*

Of course you did.

Only Ed's mother grumbles, "You're late."

Look, Margaret forgives her. She's just old. Nobody wants to hear about Ed—a reclusive late bloomer, Ed was old, and not what you'd call cute. Whereas good-looking Billy is barely twenty-three. She slides the glass fruit cup around on her plate. Spears a grape. "Sorry."

Jeff's mother murmurs, "No problem. You're entitled. Especially today."

They are watching her chew.

Since she can't swallow, Margaret talks. "I heard from Billy."

"How nice. A letter?"

"Not really."

"Phone call?"

"Sort of." Not hers to let them know it was only a call from the St. Petersburg *Times*, asking for a quote. "He's holding up," she says. "He's doing fine."

That doesn't cut it here.

She says, "They offered to send a car for me." Should she have gone? Should she be up there in the capitol, waiting with the rest? Posterity has not supplied her with the answers. One problem: what to wear, what to wear.

Ted's mother smiles. "But you had obligations."

"I did."

"Of course you did."

"They claimed he asked for me, but you know those people, always looking for good TV." She sighs because she'd do anything for Billy but she just can't be there. Not today. She swallows regret, saying falsely, "I said we'd be praying for him here." *Do we pray?* She isn't sure. In the lexicon of hope and the need to transcend guilt, every mother prays, but as a group? Has she made a faux pas?

But approving murmurs rise like filmic crowd noises: budda-budda-budda: *good answer.* Jeff's mom says, "You did the right thing."

The others are deep into affirmation. "You did."

"I hope so. They told me he understood."

Someone says, "Sweet boy."

"He is!" Because Margaret needs to be here as much as she hates being here, because she can't walk out or they'll start talking about her, she adds, "I asked the manager to bring in the Advent screen, in case they come in with it today." She gestures at the far corner. The arrangement is in place. "If it's today, we can all see." Margaret means, the old ones will be able to see: the two Charlies' mother, through her twinned cataracts; Al's mother, whose huge lenses turn her eyes into giant bugs; Ed's mom, who is functionally blind.

Ted's mother says, "I should think you'd want to be there with him." She draws herself up: a mother in history. "I was there." Her Ted's name is legend and she doesn't let them forget it.

Margaret says, "But not at the end."

"Not the very end. Not exactly," Ted's mother says. She withdraws inside herself for a second to mark what they all know and are not here to necessarily discuss. "You can't be. No."

There were banners and placards about Ted, cheers from the crowd. The vigil was huge. It was on TV.

Margaret is not ready to face this as a possibility. She says uncertainly, "I don't *think* this is the end."

"No way," Johnnie's mom says, "it's only first round."

Ted's mother reassures her, "Nothing finishes in the first round."

Johnnie's mom reaches across the table for Margaret's hand. "It isn't over until it's really over."

Jeff's mother says softly, "If then."

Al's mother's English is broken at best, but they all know what she means. It's never over.

Even Margaret, the new mother here, knows this is true. There is a little silence as the waitress clears the first course and brings chicken à la king.

The two Charlies' mother waits until she leaves and they're alone again. "You should have had two. When I lost my first Charlie, it like to kill me. But then my second Charlie come, and he was nothing like the first. So smart, and all power!"

Smart, Margaret thinks uneasily. Billy was smart. Maybe it's my fault for not sending him to private school.

The Charlies' mom is winding down. "My Charlie traveled wide and deep—great love story, them two . . . But she betrayed him at the end. Women. They always do." Time and pain have merged the two Charlies in her mind; she has them all mixed up. "So smart, he had them in his power! They blamed him, when he was really sitting home that night; he could *make things happen* without even being there!" She sighs. "A great love story. Charlie died for what they did, but, truth is, I think it was her."

From deep in her wheelchair, Ed's mother turns the conversation. If these women are going to be able to keep getting up in the mornings, if they're going to be able to dress in bright playsuits and put on a nice smile and keep on trucking, somebody has to raise the tone. "Did I tell you that by the time my Edward was six months old he had a full set of teeth?"

Jeff's mom sighs. "Jeffie too." Neither she nor Ed's mother will address the other element their sons have in common. It's not why they're here.

The Charlies' mom says, "Two is economical. The little one can wear the same clothes."

"Now, Johnnie," John's mother wants her chance. "By six months, he was walking. And so sweet with the other kids . . ."

Margaret ventures, "Billy was standing up at six months."

But John's mother overrides her. ". . . he just loved the younger kids . . ."

Yes they are bragging; isn't this a mothers' club?

So Ed's mom rewards them with a milky smile. They can forget everything, just nice mothers together here. "All his teeth."

". . . and such a clown."

Margaret hr-hms to clear the tears. "If Billy could only . . ." Out of sheer nervousness she takes out her handwork even though her puff pastry shell has turned to glue underneath the chicken à la king. Hockey hat she's knitting, as if it's winter where Billy is. Life is winter, she thinks, and can't stop herself, "He was so sweet when he was little."

But the mothers are launched like plastic boats in a bathtub, afloat on love. "Richard was a dreamy kid, I'd ask him, where were you just off to, little doctor, and he'd laugh . . ."

"The big laugh. My Johnnie always went for laughs," his mother says. "The kids thought he was so funny . . ."

"See, he always wanted to be a doctor," Richard's mother says. ". . . and he was. A regular clown."

Margaret cries, "Why couldn't they just stay little?"

Jeff's mom says defensively, poor woman, "What do you care, as long as they stay sweet?"

When she thinks of Jeffery, Margaret's teeth shake in their sockets. *Sweet.*

Ted's mother's voice is light. "Sooner or later, your little birds have to fly."

"Loved them," Margaret says hopelessly, "hugged them and handfed them, let them grab our finger and hang on until they learned how to walk, held him around his little waist and told him, 'Go to Daddy,' and he did. All that love, you think you have him standing up right, and he just lets go . . ."

Smiling, Ted's mother reminds her, "But he learned to walk on his own."

"And then he walked away from us. What happened to him then, my God. What did we do wrong?" Margaret claps her hand over her mouth. This kind of talk is not allowed.

"You did your best," Ted's mother reminds her firmly. It's the whole of their canon. "We all did."

"A full set of teeth," Ed's mother repeats, as if they haven't heard.

Ted's mom says softly, because Ed's mother is so old that history has forgotten Ed, "That's wonderful, Mrs. Gein. You should be proud." Ted's mother can, after all, afford to be generous. There've been books, TV miniseries about Ted. Without numbering them, she's bragging. "People won't forget."

Albert's mother groans, "Nobody forgets."

But they do. Until she met these women, Margaret had never heard of Ed. No matter who suffers, they forget.

The Charlies' mother smiles. TV is nothing. Both her Charlies have inspired major motion pictures plus the miniseries, one epic poem and a passle of insider books. She only says, "You kids know a legend when you see one?"

A legend. King Arthur is a legend, but this . . . Front page, TV, worldwide famous but it gets old fast, sad songs trickling into nothing because the world is easily bored and it's harder and harder to top the last outrage. Front page, TV, silence. Until the next nightmare explodes in blood. It is so sad! They forget. They all forget. Except the mourners. And us. Grief overturns her and she blurts, "Oh, God! Is it something I did?"

The others hiss, "Shh!" This is a subject they never discuss. "You did your best," Ted's mother says firmly. She makes a preemptive strike. "So, Margaret, what's your rights picture?"

Forcing her to recover. The next breath hurts but she says firmly, "Well, we do have one offer."

"You, or Billy?"

"Billy, actually." She tries to smile.

"There," Ted's mother says. With the moistened tip of her handkerchief she turns up the corner of Margaret's mouth. "That's better."

For each other: why they're here.

The Charlies' mother see her opening and goes for it. "Did you hear, my Charlie cut a record?" Starkweather? Manson? It's never clear.

Albert's mom starts jabbering in Italian, and Ted's mother is so used to this that she automatically interprets: "She's asking who besides her Albert is the star of a major motion picture?" Ted's mom inclines her head. "Alfred was the hero, dear. Tony Curtis was the star."

An old picture, Margaret thinks but does not say. So old you can't even get it on tape. She says, "Doesn't she mean, the hero?" She isn't sure. Nothing is certain here in late America, where people chase fame as if between now and the apocalypse they have exactly fifteen minutes to star in their own lives.

"Now, Charlie. Charlie is a hero," the Charlies' mom says. "In *Badlands.* For one, that is. And that's only for one. Plus miniseries, we've even got books . . ."

But Margaret knows Billy isn't about fame. He is altered, propelled by forces too hideous to contemplate. No film bios! No as-told-tos. Billy is her love and her shame. Like Jeff's father, she will handle this by writing her own damn book. If she can stand the pain, peeling back the layers, maybe she can flay the monster, addressing the question nobody's allowed to raise in this company. *Where did I go wrong?*

"Our offer is in six figures." She clears her throat to remind the mothers that she was working on recovery. "For Billy's diary."

One of the niceties of this gathering is that the mothers brag, but in the context of becoming modesty. Margaret has overstepped. Jeff's mother says sharply, "What could he possibly have to write about?"

So the others have come to the part of the meeting that keeps them coming back.

"Compared to Charlie and Charlie."

"Compared to Ted."

"You'd be surprised," Margaret says, surprised herself by the sick, sweet feeling that spreads in her loins and suffuses her belly. "He has a lot to say." And chokes. On her dessert.

But now that the plates have been cleared and the waitress won't be back, it's safe to begin. Before Margaret can regroup the mothers are launched on a little threnody of shame and pride that every mother feels, at least every mother whose son is famous for being bad. It's a hard ticket, but in the context of late America, killer or not, he is her boy. TV, bad companions, forget it. Forget the bomb. She made him. Genes and chromosomes, conditioning, blood and bone. After everything, she is his mother. Isn't it her job to be proud of him?

Because they're alone in the one company where its safe to brag, the mothers take turns numbering their sons' accomplishments: two kills-and-eats—poor Ed, those midwestern winters, not at all like Jeffery's forays in the easy city, all too easy, when they found him was he really gnawing on the . . . Among them the mothers number one strangler, one shooter, one who lured his quarry in a clown suit and buried them under the house; plus the escalating killer, so charming, started methodically and ended by pouncing and bludgeoning willy-nilly, *pam, splat, blam*! and none of their exploits surpass those of the two Charlies, the first a rampaging shooter and the second wily enough so he sent other people out to do the deed, and Margaret is quite new to this company with her smiling Billy, loved to take out convenience store clerks just before sunrise, leave the stock in good order and the register untouched, so maybe all those Sunday School classes and kneeling down with him at bedtime and the little blue booties she crocheted—maybe some of it did him some good after all, but. If there turns out to be an end and she is there with him just before the final moment, will her son take her by the two hands and thank her for the good parts or should he revile her? Oh, God!

One mother's son wrote on a mirror in lipstick, *Stop me before I kill again.*

What are they saying about society and the company we keep, is it Billy who did this or can we blame the world? Is there really a devil after all?

She does not realize that she is groaning out loud.

Not Margaret's fault the discussion escalates.

Liberated by recital, grasping what remains to them, the mothers of serial killers have begun matching murders, hacking for beheading for strangling for shotgun murder for murder by a third party inflamed to pillage and deface . . .

Until, satisfied, they slow the rhythm, making a space for Margaret to lay in the melody of her son Billy, who decapitated his victims and set the heads on the counters next to the hands and in uncertain shaving cream wrote on the nearest broad surface, HELP. She is supposed to gloss over the agony and number her steps to discovery: details on the front page that rang oddly familiar, the inexorable march from suspicion to illumination; the Greek recognition scene, no it can't be, but it is; that first infusion of shame with throbbing underneath it like a pinged nerve the knowledge that he is notorious. She is supposed to perfect her recital, drawing it over raw pain like a protective shell. But Margaret is blinded by photos of the victims, squares of black over the worst parts and she wails, "God!"

While the others mutter like nuns numbering their beads.

"God knows I did the best I could. Poor Billy, I wanted him so much, I waited so *long*." Margaret out-sings them all. "Who doesn't want a baby, and who isn't scared to hell of the moment when it comes?" Her low voice carries to the corners of the world.

So the others fall silent, aware that they are present at the birth of a new account, or threnody, that pours out of her in a dying fall. It is their business to turn it into a survival narrative: Margaret, saying through a mouth full of tears,

"God knows I wanted a baby. Nobody told me how hard, how *hard*. I was standing by the telephone, timing the pains. Trying to find the doctor's number when everything came out of me in this rush, the beginning, nobody said there would be blood; it isn't love and plastic rattles or cocktails and ginger ale after all, this is agony, ambulance, breech birth, spinal, forceps, my baby got trapped in the birth canal and when he was born he was born into terror and blood, my God, I felt like an animal, ready to gnaw my belly apart if it would stop the pain . . ."

They are watching her with their mouths fixed in tremulous Os.

"Understand. The first thing Billy tasted in his life was blood . . ." Margaret looks down into her hands and looks up at them: "The blood."

For the first time she comprehends their silence.

She asks, "What can we expect from them, really, when it all starts in blood??"

Intent on the hop, skip and the jump to the next thing, Margaret doesn't see the double doors opening. The manager sticks her head in, interrupting in a stage whisper, "Mrs. Abel, the jury is coming in."

Sobbing, Margaret gasps. "*So it is my fault. Ours. It's our fault after all.*"

"No it isn't."

"Mrs. Abel!"

The other mothers are on their feet now, clustering, murmuring, shhhshhh, there there.

"Shh, dear. It's nothing we did."

"If it isn't what we did . . ." Margaret screeches into the terminal with a sob, thudding into the end of the proposition. It makes her gasp. "Then it's who we are."

"No," Ted's mother says in a low voice. "We're who they are. And who they are . . ." She can't or won't finish. "Shh. The manager."

The Advent is in position. The CNN correspondent is on the steps of the courthouse, waiting for the spokesperson to come out. The jury's just come in with the verdict in Billy's case.

"Oh my God, who are we?" Margaret's belly shudders. "Or what?"

"Why, we're their *mothers*," one of the mothers says.

"Just—mothers?" Margaret sobs.

"Mothers, that's all."

"Sshhhh," they murmur, surrounding her. Reinforcing. "Mothers, no matter what."

"And we did the best we could."

"We did," somebody says. "We loved him."

"And he loves us."

"Yes," Margaret says, gasping. "He does."

Their soft hands make an armature to support her. "And that's enough."

"Oh, God." She wants to see him, she doesn't want to see him, God she loves him, she does! Her breath catches. "Maybe they'll let him come out on the steps and make a statement."

"If he doesn't now, he will later." Ted's mother does not say, From Death Row. "And they'll let you visit him."

"I can't."

Somebody says, "Take it from us, you will."

Comprehension shimmers just beyond her reach. "So at least I'll get to see him."

"One way or another."

"One way or another."

"I tried so hard." If Margaret is crying, will the victims' mothers understand? They can never put their own children's deaths away, but, Margaret! It isn't only Billy she's lost. She can never put any of his victims' deaths away. She cries for Billy, to all the dead and the mothers of the innocent dead, "I tried!"

"Shh, shh, dear. We know you did." the mothers say as the manager closes the door on them. "Everybody knows you did the best you could."

—1995

UNLIMITED

Not everybody knows it yet, but sooner or later everybody needs our services. That is, everybody who matters. Sooner or later they come to us.

We are the best at what we do. R****** Unlimited, a subsidiary of Velvet Martinet Enterprises. My company. But you know this, or you would not be here.

We take only A list clients and we get top dollar. You can read this in the hang of our cool suits—laid-back ensembles in pewter and silver, the walking year's wages that we go out in when we do business. Think relaxed cut, think designer items several notches up the food chain from Armani. Top of the line RayBans. The boots alone! Every hair shining. It doesn't matter what you're doing as long as you look drop-dead gorgeous doing it.

Take the lobby here in R****** Unlimited. Elegant. Gleaming. Testimony to our success. Success pays the rent and I can tell you, we have a one hundred percent success rate.

See the malachite reception desk and the glistening parquet of our outer lobby, the silk Persian rugs with a corner flipped back so you can count the thousand-knots-per-inch until one of our assistants bothers to come and take your history. Get a load of our carpeted walls and the tinted one-way glass that juts over Wilshire Boulevard and Little Santa Monica. The glass for obvious reasons, the carpeting to muffle the screaming, something we never discuss at these preliminary meetings. We are at the apex here! Note the Brancusi fountain and the malachite steps you mount to remind our receptionist that you are still waiting.

Once you have cleared the outer lobby, observe the lush kidskin sofa in the Gauguin room where you sit and stew, waiting for me to clear ten minutes for this interview.

Success? You bet. Our assistants alone! Quick and clever in their chic black dresses, the best they can manage on what we pay them. Phi Betes from the Ivies, these girls killed and died to get here and they're every one of them a size six, OK? And if the pay scale seems mean to you and fourteen-hour days excessive, remember that every one of them aims through craft and diligence to become one of us.

The upper echelon. Note that we are all women here. It's a policy decision. Tact and efficiency. Finesse.

Further signs: my office! Instead of a desk, we face each other over my bronze coffee table. Chinese, dug out of some tomb in the year one thousand, don't ask. Then there's the art: Naum Gabo, a treasure in plexi and monofilament. A tiny Rothko. A Bacon, and if the torn jaws gape as if the victim is being flayed alive and screaming as we sit here—well, we'll get to that. A Pollock. A Degas. Double-rubbed black lacquer on the walls and silver floors; see our logo inlaid in gold, which is why you are wearing complimentary terrycloth booties over your Guccis.

Yes I know you are a major player. If you were anything less, you couldn't afford me.

Now regard me. Velvet Martinet, the captain of our industry.

It's OK to look. You have, after all, been cleared by Security. After Accounting. We've accepted your nonrefundable deposit, Krugerrands as per the preliminary agreement. Naturally we had the items in question authenticated and the dollar amount pegged to the market value at the close of that day's trading. And your net worth and growth potential evaluated before our receptionist could even think about making an appointment for you. The balance? We know you're good for it.

Otherwise you would not be sitting here.

Meet my eyes! This is when I look deep into you and see whether I trust you. I am the last barrier. All that stands between you and the service you so badly want from us.

If I clamp your hands to the table hard enough to scare you, tough. When I take hold, there's no man strong enough to free himself. Don't look away! Not if you want this. I said, meet my eyes!

Do not be frightened by what you see. It's what you're paying for. Hold still! Quit hyperventilating. It'll be over in a minute.

This is essential. The moment in which I make sure. Sure you won't panic, sure you are good for it. Sure you won't back down or attack me, sure you're not from some agency bent on breaking me.

More. Rapport. We must establish rapport before we can even begin to talk about your problem.

Now.

You can speak. Be assured that if we proceed your down payment and today's billable hours will be credited to your balance, which as you know comes due immediately upon signing.

Time to lay your problem on the table. Don't worry. The room's been swept and secured. Our people have been over it twice since I met with the last client. It's safe for you to say it out loud.

It's even OK for you to call me Velvet.

Oh yes, and for client protection, our cameras are recording this transaction.

. . .

Um, Ah. The client sits with his head between his knees. This is so hard! The humiliation. The desire. Uh. Ah! Before we start, could I ask you a couple of questions?

. . .

Meanwhile, elsewhere: In deepest Brentwood just north of Sunset, producer/developer Whitney Ryder is waked by a phone bleating. He swims in his empty bed, groping for the damn thing. Got to stop that noise! It is late afternoon. Daphne's been gone since Sunday—no biggie—and he's snorted and popped a few things in the interim, not because he's bummed, exactly, just to ride the wave until he hears from Bobby that the big deal is completed.

It is not exactly nice to be awake right now. The larger circumstances of Ryder's life have begun sliding into place like massive stones on rollers moving in to seal some pharaoh's tomb.

Pawing through yellow satin sheets, he hits a lump. "*Gotcha!*" He snaps like a seal catching a fish and pops talk with his thumb, shouting, "Ryder!"

"It's me," Bobby says. "You don't have to yell."

It's Bobby. "I was asleep!"

"While Rome is fucking burning," Bobby says. Bobby finished U.C.L.A. before he moved up from the mail room to become Ryder's assistant. He's right in there with the classical allusions. It's one of the reasons Ryder keeps him around. "We've lost the deal."

"Fill me in."

"Drove my Chevy to the levee but the levee was dry." Never one to say a thing just once, Bobby says, "I called our money but our money isn't returning our calls."

"They—*what?*"

"I'm telling you, somebody got to them."

"Our money?" Betrayed, Ryder howls, "Somebody got to *our money?*"

"Somebody got to our money." Bobby rides on. "They backed off and Maxamar waltzed in and scooped up the property."

"Maxamar! Bastard, bastard!" Ryder growls. "Getchell!" "You don't know it was Getchell," Bobby says.

"My best friend! It's gotta be." Yes there is a rat loose in the infrastructure. Gnawing at his vitals. Ryder snaps, "Who the hell else could it be?"

"He wished you success," Bobby says like a good assistant.

"Yeah, right," Ryder says bitterly. "Right before he walked." He's pissed at Getchell; best buds since fourth grade in Ocala, coming up together under the Florida sun, two little kids with big ambitions. Move west, make it big in L.A. Together. Three days before the key meeting, his sandbox pally Duane Getchell takes his marbles and walks. "Eight bucks gets you 160 K it was Getchell."

"He sent flowers."

"Flowers," Ryder snorts. "Horseshoe or funeral wreath?" Dead is just as dead. He feels creditors gnawing away to that old grade-school refrain, "Oh heck, oh heck, it's up to my neck . . ."

Bobby strikes a note halfway between hard and gentle. "Look at it this way, he's not the only one out there . . ." who hates you.

"Whoever it is..." Ryder is wired by this time, wide-jawed and furious, wacked out on adrenalin and crosshatching the bedroom like a retriever bagging flies. "The bastard is going to pay."

"Who?"

Ryder says through clenched teeth, "Whoever's behind Maxamar."

"Don't be so sure."

"And pay bigtime—what did you say?"

Bobby mumbles something Ryder can't quite grasp.

"What did you say?"

". . . sure it's a bastard," Bobby mutters, frff, "um . . . Daphne."

"Daphne would never do a thing like that to me. I think she still loves me." Ryder shakes the flip-phone angrily. "I told you, *quit mumbling.*"

Bobby mumbles, marginally louder. "Egil Hoover."

"My *broker?*"

"Well," Bobby mumbles, "Daphne *is* still married to him."

"Oh, Egil. Egil's a bastard, but he isn't vindictive."

"That's what you think," Bobby says.

"Then think harder!"

Bobby is trying to find a way to break bad news. Out of his fuzzy silence comes the worst. "Could be our money screwing us."

"Just because our money isn't returning our calls, that doesn't mean we're being screwed by our money."

Bobby mumbles a little louder.

Some days Ryder hates Bobby. He growls, "I said, *what? What did you say?*"

Oh, desperate man, Bobby just keeps mumbling, but loud enough so Ryder either will or won't be able to catch what he is pitching.

"Fuck that shit," Ryder shouts, even though he's not exactly sure what Bobby's telling him. By this time Ryder has shouldered the phone in and out of the shower without getting it wet; he's combed his hair and he's shaving with his sweet little electric. In another minute he'll have to unglue his ear from Bobby long enough to wriggle into the Gap T-shirt and the Armani. Once he is armored, he has to go forth and slay multitudes. Reaching for his Calvin briefs, he starts with the day's instructions. Pickups. Folders to be pulled for the next meeting. Calls to be arranged so there may even *be* a next meeting.

Bobby says into the brief silence that falls as his boss ducks into the T-shirt, "Anything else?"

Ryder ticks off ten items for Bobby's phone list—the small private investors they have to squeeze just to keep going until their money kicks in—and right before he pops Bobby out of existence and clicks the phone shut he says, "Find out who's screwing us. Get on it!"

Which leaves Whitney Ryder alone and silent on a peak in Brentwood. In full armor, he stands in the darkened room with the round bed slippery with satin sheets and redolent of Daphne. And broods. The big project up in flames, Daphne gone. Ryder has thirty days to pay up on the house or get out and ten days to cover certain key investments. Stones rolling in to seal the pharaoh's tomb.

It is so fucking *inevitable*.

Doom creeping up, followed by ruin. And all he can fix on is finding out who gave the first stone a kick and started it moving.

Surprised by grief, Ryder belches words: what Bobby was trying to tell him that he didn't want to catch but knows he's going to have to deal with. Our money, he thinks.

We don't even know who our money is.

. . .

Questions. Questions! What gives you the right to ask questions?

. . .

I just thought maybe the deposit. Um. Ah. Entitled me to a further explanation. Miserable, the client shifts in the deep sofa. This is so hard!

171

Putting it in words. The rage. The humiliation. *I mean, before I tell you my problem.*

The need.

. . .

Woman like me, you think I don't know where you're coming from? Honey, this is *Velvet*. You're sitting here, and you think I don't already know your problem?

Your problem. Your problem. I know more than you do about your little problem. Where it comes from and who did it to you. What you're feeling. Who to get for this. How. I probably even know exactly what you want done to him. The perp that ruined your life. The exquisite torture you want prepared for him.

And count on it, we here at R****** Unlimited know precisely how to make our solution beautiful and specific. A work of art that you will treasure forever, preserved in memory. Tapes if you want, transcripts. Stills. Laminated front page of the L.A. *Times* with an account of it. The whole magilla. Which is, of course, what you are really paying for.

As described in the preliminary, this job's complex, but doable. You can count on our discretion.

But you have reservations, and since you're on our A list, I'll indulge you. Let you in on the A. B. and C. of a few of our major successes. Rest assured, when we do your job, nobody but the target knows who hit him. And, of course, our client, which is why you are paying top dollar. When our targets fall, believe me the world hears about it, but only our clients know how exquisitely it came about or that your victim—yes, let's just come out and say it—*your victim*—knows the why. And who to thank for this beautiful feat of ruination.

Take the studio chief, you know his name. His exec gets hell from the guy because he's quit the studio for something better. Exec quits, right; chief gives him his blessing, right, but all around the poor exec, new partners bail and sure deals start col lapsing. Right, the chief is out to get him. So the exec calls us.

You know what happened, it was in all the papers. Bingo-bango, studio's top bankable stars, *things start happening to them.* Car wreck, to say nothing of the fire. Forget reconstructive surgery, there goes half the chief's stable, and on the first day of principal photography. His biggest star goes schizzy, our work—now that you know, you've got to admit that one was especially creative. And untraceable. His three stars that bail to undergo sex change operations and five years of deep therapy, to say nothing of the mud slides that took out the hundred million's worth of stuff they'd built for Kostner's *Iliad plus Odyssey: Aeneid Days,* your complete Troy plus Crete plus various trinkets like the genuine life-sized sandstone face of Abu Simbal on the back lot annex: director *says:* "accept no substitutes, spare no expense," you can imagine. You think it's easy to take out Troy with a mudslide in the dry season?

So that was one.

And that fat presidential wannabe—white hair, bestseller, holier than us until, *sprong,* he goes bats on TV and *in one speech* alienates and loses the votes of the entire moral majority. That was our work. Can't give you any more details because we are pledged to protect the identity of our clients, but you begin to get the scope of our operation?

Not to mention the recent demise of a head of state who shall remain nameless for reasons which I can't share with you even though your own peculiar situation here guarantees your perpetual silence in this sensitive matter.

And you will note that this isn't a punishment-fits-the-crime situation, it is bigger than that. And subtler.

We *take large steps.*

So. The thing. What you want from us?

You will get from us. It's guaranteed.

· · ·

That's kind of what I'm afraid of. This isn't a big thing, it's a little thing. At least I think it is.

· · ·

Big thing? Little thing? Rest assured, we tailor our services to fit the client. I myself originated the program, I and my friend Serena. You think we started big? No way. We started small. All the best things in this town start small, that's the beauty of L.A., you can come in on the rails and ride out in a white stretch with built-in swimming pool.

We weren't always what you see before you. Plush Velvet Martinet Enterprises. Not by a long stretch. Just two nice girls fresh from Fall River, move west to make it in the biz; Serena's an actress, and I . . . I thought I was writing the script that would kill the world, mega-budget, mega-stars, pickup in ten figures. But for the time being we were only clerks in Bullocks' at the Beverly Center. Serena made buyer, on her way to the top as a manager, and I was selling fucking bras while I worked on my idea—the one I developed with this cute guy I actually thought was really in love with me.

173

Then things happened. Little things. Like a clerk in Serena's department gets jumped to department chief, and doesn't she feel shitty. So we deal with the problem. After the accident, Serena's promoted to section manager. Then a friend has a knockdown dragout with a customer and you know how things are, word gets around, and she comes to us. Serena and I deal with the problem, but by that time we are both bored of Bullock's and we set up a small office on Third Street, right next to the bridal shop? You know the corner. And one thing leads to another. Woman standing by the parking meter outside Celine's, fighting with a suit in wraparound RayBans until the guy's car pulls up, the suit gets in the back and zooms off and his girl is left standing there crying. Serena sidles out and next thing she knows, bingo-bango, she's in our office. As it turns out she's a Mafia princess. We were brilliant.

Because let me tell you, OK, the guy in the suit is a lying, two-timing bastard, and if there's one thing we here at R****** Unlimited know, it's how to deal with slimy, scum-sucking, two-timing bottom feeders that lie and take your . . .

But we were talking about you.

·   ·   ·

Meanwhile, elsewhere: Whitney Ryder has flipped his plastic onto the waiter's tray at Spago. He and his foreign business contacts have just finished dinner—the early seating. It's so early that nobody who *is* anybody has even thought of arriving, but for the first time in the decade he's been eating here, Ryder has failed to get a window seat. Their table is behind the stairs and entirely too close to the kitchen. Instead of admiring twilight exhaust fumes above Sunset, his Danish guests are gaping like gummy fish in a Jello aquarium.

It is testimony to Ryder's precarious position that the only contacts he has left right now are from countries so far away that the news of his imminent demise has not reached them. Annoyingly, the waiter returns and after a murmured exchange leaves with Ryder's other plastic. Across from Ryder, his Danish investors sit, regarding him with unblinking eyes that seem to crack and dry as they wait and go on waiting. Would they please, just *please* excuse themselves and go upstairs to the bathroom? The waiter returns from the register, embarrassed. He grimaces at Ryder. There is a long silence. A looong silence. Finally one of the Danes reaches across the table, slipping something into Ryder's hand. Five crisp hundreds. It is humiliating!

It is both logical and terrible that when he goes to the ATM for valet parking money the LCD tells Ryder that in both savings and checking departments, he is functionally a dead man.

.   .   .

We've been sitting here for a long time. A very long time. Do you realize that you've exceeded your deposit in billable hours and we haven't broached the matter of your problem?

.   .   .

No, we haven't. I'd like to tell you everything, but I'm just not quite comfortable.

.   .   .

Oh, don't get all shy on me. We're supposed to be doing business here, and every minute we sit here not laying our cards on the table is costing you another hundred. That's six K an hour, which at the rate we're going is going to be a lot of K if you decide not to go through with the operation. In for a penny, in for the whole deal, so you might as well cut to the chase and let it all hang out for me so we can get started.

You're lucky I cleared my calendar tonight. Otherwise I'd be on my way out the door right now for drinks with my colleagues at the Peninsula before dinner at a place so exclusive that even you have never heard of it. Snuff show at the interval, living party favors, yes it is hot—this week, at least. If I were you I'd get on with this, because every minute we sit here not laying open the spine of this critter is costing you, so I'll tell you a couple of things and then you'd better get ready to tell me a couple of things.

I know how it feels to get stuck sitting on an embarrassing problem. Slide this way, slide that, you're still stuck on a ridge and the damn thing is cutting into you. And don't by any stretch think you're the first person to walk in here with an embarrassing problem.

Or the only person sitting here who's ever had one. I could tell you things . . .

OK, OK, I could tell you. Serena? Right, she isn't on the masthead, you noticed, so that's one story. There we were in our little shop on Third, me and my first partner; we could barely pay the rent but we were beginning to, you know, get a leg up on the business? A world of people out there, and most of them are hurting. Serena and I did pretty well nickel-and-diming, but no way was I going to spend the rest of my life nickel-and-diming. Remember I was developing this script with my boyfriend, he was going to get us a meeting and *if we could only get a meeting* we could sell it on the basis of the pitch alone, or that's what he told me.

But I forgot to mention the best job that ever came out of R****** Unlimited. We're all too young to remember *The Godfather*, but it's on TV a lot and there is this scene in *The Godfather*? Guy crosses the Don. Wakes up with blood in the bed, reaches down by his feet and there is this severed head, his prize racehorse! And they *slipped it in there so quiet and smooth* that he slept through the night without even knowing that they put this thing in his bed or even feeling it.

Compared to those guys, we here on Wilshire at Little Santa Monica work like ice cream on velvet. If Saddam Hussein has that *funny walk* and keeps his elbows tight to his sides today, if every time he sees a rose or hears somebody humming a certain tune his breath stops, it's because of a little job we did. No no, I can't name the client. I can't even give you the details. I can only tell you if Velvet Martinet Enterprises tops the pops in the Fortune Five Hundred, we have earned it.

Serena? I told you! Gone. Left the company. Right, Serena.

I'm sorry, I can't tell you that. What I can tell you, I can only say that by the time I was done with her, Serena wasn't going to be poaching on anybody else's boyfriend, not then, not ever, and she knew what had happened to her and where it was coming from and there's not one damn thing she can do about it, shit, the bitch can't even prove it. *My boyfriend.* And if I . . .

Sit down! Am I scaring you? Man, that's what you're paying for! You better believe you're lucky to be sitting here. You'd better thank your damn stars that you're knee to knee with a professional with enough guts and fire to scare the crap out of you. And that you can afford it.

·   ·   ·

All right, all right, I know! But would you please lighten up a little?

·   ·   ·

Meanwhile, elsewhere: It's odd. Now that he's alone in the house again, now that he's downloading the contents of his bulging Filofax on the Biedermeier table, now that he's moving scraps of paper from pile to pile, Whitney Ryder is, not depressed exactly, but thoughtful. On the road to enlightenment. At the moment his train of thought is stalled at a stop midway between suspicion and certainty.

His hands crosshatch the burled wood surface. Whole fucking desk stops being his as of the first. Without having to be told he's finished, Ryder knows he is finished in this town. Still he can't stop moving piles of things to other piles. Sorting. Discarding. This, from Getchell. Nothing, or nothing much.

This from Egil Hoover, forget it.

This, from his money, but he still doesn't know who in hell his money is, much less where were they when his operation went into overcall. All he's got is this phone number printed on a featureless card, that's all, and forget about trying it, they've stopped returning his calls.

When all is said and done, he is left with three items.

This, from Maxamar. Note: *find out tmw. who bought Maxamar.*

And, crumpled almost to extinction, a note scrawled on the back of a grocery receipt. Bobby's hand. And on the back of a Visa receipt, Ryder company plastic, this other note. Daphne. Daphne's illegible smudge crosshatched with the handwriting he knows by heart, Daphne and . . .

They've cleaned him out.

Son of a bitch! Cleaned him out and scared off his money and now he knows that the two of them are sitting there, wherever *there* is, sitting there laughing at him, the fucking, fucking . . .

"I gave you the keys to the store. I took you fucking shopping at fucking Armani and now . . ." He stands up and howls. "Bobby!"

Everything in him solidifies: Whitney Ryder goes cold and hard. He is resolved. *Son of a bitch.*

Fixed on what he will do to them.

. . .

Ms. Martinet, you've been extremely patient. You've told me everything except how you do what you do. But you haven't given me a clue as to how you do it. You . . .

. . .

That's the beauty of our operation. Until you state your problem, that remains to be seen. Our madness always fits the method. Sorry, I don't mean to make light of this.

But I was telling you about me. Remember, this is my business and I am the master of my business. Serena, you know about, but the boyfriend, the man I was writing the picture with—OK, you saw it. My baby, my picture! Big budget, major studio, big-time gross exceeding the net and my name nowhere on it, not in the credits, not in the ads, me nowhere near the bank when the fucker that stole my fucking script waltzed in and took the front money and the pickup plus points, believe it! My boyfriend! And me on the outside, like fucking Lazarus. He and Serena pulled my beautiful, make-me-famous property out from under me and sold it like a Persian rug and I . . .

What?

Oh, I took care of Serena.

My old boyfriend, my betrayer? You don't want to know. Suffice it to say that I've been biding my time. Wait. My light's blinking. Call I'm expecting.

Oh, Stephanie. Yes. Put him through to my assistant. Get him here and when you get him here . . .

Make him wait.

But I was telling you about me. I bide my time. I am the master of this game and all related operations, and you will note that in spite of my own concerns you have my complete attention.

Nothing that happens here happens accidentally. My betrayer. My scheme—now you will see precisely how good I am at what I do.

My old boyfriend will be here—wait a minute, the display on this Itchy and Scratchy watch is hard to read—in about three minutes.

Oh, Stephanie. He is? Fine. He can wait until I'm finished with this client. Then he can wait a little longer. When he looks fit to deconstruct, you can buzz him in.

So he's coming in here, he'll be walking in that door some time after I finish taking your particulars and we have the complimentary champagne to seal our arrangement. He'll come in that door well after I open this one and you leave by the Privileged exit. Right, as a preferred customer, you get primo treatment.

Oh, him? Listen, if he's here tonight it's in spite of the fact that he's got zero deposit and no hope of a downpayment. All he's got is the hunger. But I assure you, I will see him.

Pissed, he's going to be, desperate and begging for our services; hooked on his own story and so choked up that he'll sob it out before he even focuses on me. Panting for revenge, you dig? Hung up on the unanswered question.

Not the why, OK. *The who.* Who was his money, that drew him out on that limb and then pulled it out from under him. And me?

I'm going to look him in the eye and in the second that falls between eye contact and resignation, he will see everything.

He goes, *You.* And I go:

If you have to ask, you can't afford me.

—1996

THE MOTHERS OF SHARK ISLAND

On Shark Island the prisoners are free to roam the courtyard in the day-time; the walls are high and the cliffs precipitous. Nobody escapes the Chateau D'If. The few mothers who try are never seen again—devoured by the schools of sharks running in the channel or dashed to bits on the rocks at the bottom of the cliff.

By night guards stalk the parapets, but from moment to moment the faces of our captors change. Are we them? Are they us? Sometimes it is we who march in yellow arm bands—slit-eyed trusties, collaborating in our own imprisonment; we patrol with leather billy clubs, grimly keeping the other women in line. Unless we are the prisoners here, watching the guards from the high windows of our cells.

Who are the kept and which are the keepers among us here?

Who decided we had to be interned? When did we start being in the way?

Was it our randy, eager sons who sent us up the river—no remaining witnesses to prove that they are not self-invented?—*Mom, you look tired.* Or was it our images, the new improved version—our daughters with their sweet, judgmental smiles?—*Mom, let me do that.*

Is it in our stars that we are jailed, or is it something we did? Oh God, is it something we said that they can't forgive? This is the terror and the mystery. Why they put us here after everything we did for them.

Years of snowboots and school clothes and lopsided cakes and guitar lessons and tuition and trying not to pressure them—all that effort and now our young run free and use up the earth while we are here.

By day we pace and ponder. By night we tap out messages on the pipes. *Cour—age—Syl—vi—a. Per—se—ver—ence—Maud. Rev-o-lution is near. New—prisoner—in—Block—Nine.*

Unlike pneumonia, motherhood is an irreversible condition.

Like Edmund Dante I am close to the woman in the cell next to mine al-

though I've never seen her face. We whisper through the crevice I have made over months—no. Over years, gouging the stone with my fingernails, swallowing the dust and moving the bed in front of the hole to hide any trace. The unknown mother and I keep each other afloat, although like our guards she is not always the same person.

How many women have come and gone in the cell next to mine? We do not exchange names. But at night we spin stories for comfort and number the details; what we did for them on our way to the Chateau D'If. How cruel it is that we are here.

But our work lives are over. What else would they do with us? The nights are colder than the stones we sleep on and we are lonely here and sad, and if we could go back and change the past so that our children still needed us, we would not do it.

We wouldn't know how. We had to let them grow up. Now they intern us for war crimes.

Friends! We were never the color our children have painted us. We are innocent, I tell you. Innocent !

The prisoners speak.

REBA: I am the Mother Goddess, dammit. What I says goes.

I was a prisoner in my own house, trampled flat by the three of them—Gerard, who made me a mother in the first place. Demanding little Gerry. Whiny June. All day on the road, you know the story, practice, lessons, car pool, late nights folding wash and when I finally crawled into bed big Gerard's hands on me, yeah fine, but spring up at dawn to unload that dishwasher, drop kids at school on the way to work, where the men in my law firm—men with *wives* at home to do these things for them leapfrogged my spent body on their way to the top.

And Gerard! He said, "Starched shirts wouldn't be such a problem if you'd only quit your job." Said, "This house is a mess!"

After a while you just get tired. Too wasted ever to make partner. I quit my job. At first it was almost nice. Plenty of time to clean and wash and fold and cook and make the house nice and drop the kids at school, art lessons, team practice, plenty of time to lie down with Gerard who said, "That's more like it, you smell so *good*." I liked having his nose in my neck.

But when I got up again I was the one who had to change the bed and iron the sheets and drive the children everywhere while their hair got glossy and their teeth white and strong and they? What did they think of me? They said, "What do you know? You're just a Mom."

Life conceived as endless stovepipe, or is it Mobius strip. He wants less starch in his shirts, more in the collars; kids say cut my sandwiches cut this way, cut them *that way*. All that and when you walk down the street your children hang back so people will think they're walking with somebody else; he puts his nose in your hair and says, "I can't understand it, we used to have so much to talk about."

Crying makes you ugly so you drop a hundred bucks on Victoria's Secret but he isn't interested in yours; instead of punching your shoulder and climbing on he rolls away and goes to sleep, smelling of somebody else.

Right, I got depressed, I did Pillsbury Ice Box Cookie rolls straight from the fridge, gnawing while I ironed in front of the soaps. Gerard complained—kids squabbling, trash piling up because the more you do around the house the more there is to do, try perpetual mess machine and here's the man who made you a mother in the first place going, "Is that all you have to do with your time?"

Talk about couldn't go on like that. Talk about couldn't stand another day. Oh I did everything they wanted OK, fixed this, bought the kids clothes for that, but I schemed. A few purchases and I was ready.

One day I was miserable, reviled.

They came down the next morning and I was wearing the cape. "I am the mother goddess, dammit, and you are going to do what I say."

June snarled, "I didn't want cereal, I wanted Pop Tarts."

I pointed my finger and lightning came out.

Gerry whined, "Where's my Exo-skeleton T shirt?"

Zot! He never whined again.

Gerard came in and sat down in front of his plate without even looking up from the paper. "What's to eat?"

I bopped him with my staff. He was sniveling. "Reba, I love you. What did I ever do to you?"

"Not enough!" I rose up and rumbled down on him like thunder. I gnashed my teeth and lightning struck. My family looked at me and they trembled. "I am the mother goddess, dammit. This is my kingdom now."

They fell down and worshiped me.

Didn't they pay tribute then? Presents for me, sweets; sniveling Gerard begged for my smile. I ran a taut ship: hot breakfast, wash and ironing before Gerard could leave for work, the kids vacuumed and scoured the tub; KP at night, "Nothing thawed or nuked, Gerard, something French." We ate well. When he balked I banished him to the dungeon. He tried to kite out a message to the Battered Men's shelter. I called the cops. Who'd believe a little thing like me could do things like that to a big guy like Gerard? He got ten years.

After that it was peaceable in the kingdom: sweet, smooth, with me in silks and jewels my kids worked two jobs to buy. Sympathy from Gerard's colleagues, "He made your life a living hell."

But where's the joy in ruling when your most abject subject is in jail? I retired to my chamber in a cloud of thought.

When I came out my remaining subjects were all grown up. June, working as a supermarket checker, Gerry at State U. She blamed me for not being around to fix her SATs. He barked, "Get out of the manger, Mom. I'm in love."

They made their lives, I think. They think I did.

While I was sleeping, my grown daughter Junie— my little Junie — picked up my staff and

—ZOT, I am here.

See your mother come in the door in the green quilted coat that means she's staying well into the winter, see her smile that lovably tentative, tender smile and wonder why when we do love her, we do LOVE *her, these encounters are always so hard. Psychic space. A mother who is also a mother-in-law takes up so much psychic space!*

Nuclear families are built on privacy. If a nucleus can shatter, our mother's has fragmented, leaving her lost in the stars. We form our own. We are the new family here.

Is it her fault these encounters are so difficult? Ours?

She keeps coming back. We think every time: This time we'll make it different, *and discover that in spite of all our best efforts, it never is. Mothers, daughters. What are these patterns that determine our mutual future? When and how were they set? Is this loving estrangement really her fault? Mine? In spite of our best efforts she and I bring all the old freight to these meetings. What she said to us when we were little, what we failed to say to her.*

And spoil ourselves wondering about the old patterns that it's too late to change. Why it was always so hard.

Is it in our stars that it is this way, or is it in our genetic encoding? Do our daughters see their own futures coming in the door with the same loving, fearful eyes?

I whisper these questions to the woman in the cell next to mine but she is sick now, too sick to really answer.

When she speaks, it is to the eternal chain of mothers and daughters, leading from forever into eternity. I lay my ear flat against the chink in the wall, holding my breath so I can hear.

—All we can do is love them, she says.

The prisoners speak.

MARILYN: You think I asked for this? Dingy cell with flaking stone walls and no comfort at night but the message that come in on toxic pipes? Lead pipes bring water and carry waste out of our cells—lead, when we had all the old paint stripped from our houses just to keep our babies safe. Morse code. H-E-L-L-.

I gave my children everything. Vitamins to keep them strong and lessons to make them accomplished and flash cards to get them smart, and if I brooded over their progress, who wouldn't? Who wouldn't be enchanted by the genetic miracle: raw material to perfect. Pliable small people, look a lot like me. Speak the same language, members of the same club. We are them, yes? No.

My fault, for failing to understand the truth.

Mothers, do not be deluded. They may be cute when they're little, follow you anywhere, do anything to please you, laugh at your jokes. You work hard to shape them, to do the right thing, but be aware. No. Be warned.

They are nothing like you.

Your children's adult lives devolve into a litany of reproaches, a dizzying transport of blame.

"You used to make me wear terrible clothes. That green T-shirt. Those hideous pink shoes."

"You asked too many questions. Always getting in my face."

Or is it: "You never listened to me."

"You made me eat mixed-up food."

We used to talk about it when we lived in the world, we daughters who were mothers of small children of our own. We talked about our mothers. We talked about it a lot. We conspired. —Not going to get like that, we vowed. We colluded with our own daughters. —Promise to tell us if we start getting like that. And they vowed, —We will, we will.

On her mother's seventieth birthday CSB accidentally washed the cake.

Contemplating her mother, EBM said: —There ought to be an island somewhere, *surrounded by sharks.*

Before our eyes, the Chateau D'If sprang into existence. We looked at it and marveled.

Remember, she was still in the world with us; the Chateau D'If was designed with her in mind, not us.

As long as she lived, we could maintain our position.

Now she is gone.

Now we are in the front ranks. And the Chateau D'If? Admit it. It was only ever a matter of time .

The prisoners speak.

ANNE: They're yours, but only for a minute.

They grow up.

You get old. Maybe the worst crime is not the atrocities you committed in the kitchen—the pudding disaster. The casserole nobody would eat.

It's not the wardrobe errors: "The other moms all wear jeans." Nor is it the social gaffe: "Why did you have to tell them that, Mom?"

I think the unforgivable sin is getting old.

Sooner or later you are the outsider, begging your daughter to suffer your presence in her house. Slip in gratefully and try to be unobtrusive. Hope to earn your keep by doing little things around the place. Pat the sofa pillows and put them *just so.* Scour the sink and while you're at it throw out that dead plant. Do little favors and try not to make too much noise coming into a room.

"Mother, did you move my notebook? I can't find anything!"

"Nobody asked you to straighten my dresser drawers, Mom."

Don't reason with them. Don't argue. "But they're a mess!" And if she and her husband are having a fight, go sit at the top of the cellar stairs.

You become aware that they stop talking when you come into a room. One afternoon you find them waiting for you. "We've loved having you with us, Mother, but it's time to make some plans."

They tried to erase me, but I have left traces. Signs so the world will know what happened here. A hairpin in her stocking drawer. A gift painting she will be afraid to take down. When they took me I put long claw-marks in one of their walnut doors.

On Shark Island there is no time off for good behavior. There are only lifers here.

The woman in the cell next to mine has died. In the night I hear feeble tapping on the pipes and I move the cot and put my mouth close to the crevice in the wall. I murmur, —What is it? Are you all right in there? The sound of her harsh breathing tells me she will never be all right. She dies with her mouth pressed to the opening in the wall. Only I hear her last lament.

—All I did was love them too much.

AT THE TOMB OF THE UNKNOWN MOTHER

In the Chateau D'If the management declares a day of mourning. Matched pairs of trusties lower the coffin into the fresh place prepared for it while the mothers grieve. We never knew her name but it is clear to the women marshaled here that in her own way, she stands for all of us. She is the past, present and future generations of mothers exiled here.

The unknown mother died without betraying her origins; she died without recanting; *I did the best I could!* She died without regrets and without repenting. She died in a state of invincible ignorance, innocent of the nature of her unknown sin.

The prisoners lament.
Oh.
Oh how.
Oh how much we love her.
Oh how hard we try to keep from going where she has gone
    and oh, how we conspire with our own sweet daughters.
How delicately we tread the line!

Your daughter asks, "Is it being a mother that makes you crazy?"

You have spent your life proving that you have always been the same person. Therefore you dissemble. "If I'm crazy, I was born this way."

When you are in a less vulnerable mode you usually say, "You'll be a mother some day. Then you'll see."

The prisoners speak.

SUSANNAH: One tough babe, I am, and she could reduce me to a jelly. *Not going to be like that, never going to be like that.*

Tales brought back by sailors: my daughter has a daughter of her own. In the gift packet allowed prisoners on high holidays, my daughter includes snapshots of her son and her new baby girl. They are beautiful together—my daughter and this small, new woman, her daughter, who bears my name. I look at the children's faces and I see hers. Tears come too fast to swallow. We look alike.

Shark Island is for lifers. So is motherhood.

The prisoners speak.

MELANIE: This place is rough. The stones are cold and I don't like it here. On my cot at night I try to figure out what I did that was so terrible, numbering my crimes.

OK, I nagged them about their homework, for one. I bought them clothes they hated, which they told me later, and in spades. I made too much mixed-up food. Mushrooms. Onions. Yeugh! I gave them until the big hand reached the six to clean their plates or else.

I always said, "Why don't you go outside and play?"

I loved them, God I loved them, I still do.

I've been saving stuff. Sharp things. One of these nights, I'm going to gouge out the cement from around the bars and pull them loose and I am getting out of here. The going will be slow; I'll climb down the outside wall with bleeding toes and shredded fingertips. When I reach a point where I can swing out and avoid the rocks, I'll jump.

And if I can elude the sharks . . .

SARAH: Not me. I know a better way out. A friend who *never had children* is waiting just beyond the barrier reef. She has a skiff. If I make it, I'm going to find the people who put me here. I'm going to grab my children by the shoulders and look into their eyes . . .

REBA: And I, I am going to feign death. When the guard comes in to hold the mirror to my mouth I'll overpower her . . .

ANNE: And put on her uniform?

186

MARILYN: Or get work in the laundry room and hide myself in the bottom of a laundry cart!

Sunrise and moonrise race past in quick succession, a brilliant parade of time passing outside our cell windows. I look up and see new stars. I see novas burst and expire.

The future is written in their faces — the pictures my daughter sends on birthdays and holidays. Her daughter grows.

How quickly these things happen. How long our sentence here. How little time we had outside! Past and future, birthdays, Christmases, times of joy — we were only ever here.

The prisoners speak.

VAL: Since we're all, er. Getting down here, I might as well tell you, some of us have been working on a tunnel. At the signal tonight we're going out.

The devil's advocate, I say to her, —You may make it because right now you are a trusty, but the rest of us can't. At night we're locked down in the cells.

VAL: No problem. While the screws were sleeping Peggy stole the keys. She kept them long enough to get impressions; she's made duplicates. My cell. Sarah's. Reba's. Yours. Are you with me?

MELANIE/MARILYN: You bet.

ANNE: Count me in . . . I think.

REBA: Would you believe I'm standing guard tonight?

VAL: Then you can help us!

REBA: I can't help you, but I promise to look the other way.

VAL: OK, then. Everybody. Are you with us?

God knows I am tempted, but my blood is drumming with the recurring story. There is something I know without knowing how I know.

My heart stutters and my belly trembles. I can't.

VAL: Amazing free offer and you *can't*?

Someone I care about is coming. I know it. How can I explain this without explaining it? The grief and the terror. The sense of the inevitable that gives me such hope? I am polite, but evasive . —I can't afford to leave here now.

REBA: What do you mean, you can't afford to leave? You can't afford to stay!

I tell them, —Message I got. Tapped in on the pipes.

MARILYN: What do you mean, message you got?

New—prisoner—in—the—holding—pen.

I tell them because I am afraid not to tell them.

Unless I mark this with words it may disappear. —I heard it tapped out on the pipes. It's the new prisoner.

She was allowed one phone call. Instead she took the silver dollar the children provide the internees for that single phone call, and gave it to the guard, who brought the news to me.

VALERIE: —Twelve hours and we're free women! What's one new prisoner more or less?

ANNE: Twelve hours and we're out of here. What's the matter with you anyway?

MARILYN: Free women! What's the matter with you?

The mothers of Shark Island are offering me freedom that I can't afford to grasp. I explain as best I can: —She's waiting down there, alone and scared because she's new. *They're moving her upstairs tomorrow night. A few favors and I may be able to get her into the Unknown Mother's cell.*

My heart overflows. —We can whisper at night.

REBA: All that for somebody you never met?

I do not exactly lie but I am evasive. —I only said she was a new prisoner. New in a place she vowed never to come. But even with the best of intentions—you know. *I tell them,* —I never said we'd never met.

I do not add: —She looks like me.

Tonight the mothers of Shark Island make their break. At least they'll try. They may even make it if the island is less secure than we think. If the escaping mothers survive the jump into the deep, treacherous channel . . .

And if they can outswim the voracious sharks . . .

Even if they do make it, nothing much will change.

Motherhood isn't a job description, it's a life sentence.

Let the others dodge the sweeping searchlights and the spray of machine gun fire. Let them struggle through the icy waves and drag themselves up on the shore and let them fan out in the nation like a legion of avengers, intent on . . .

Intent on . . .

*She's coming. They know it. She's at the door. Soon she'll ring the bell.
Arrested by something they don't know yet, our children quicken.*

    —Lover, did you hear something?

    —No, I didn't hear anything.

*She goes to the door anyway/he shrugs on his bathrobe and goes to the
door.* Try not to let their voices sink. —Oh, it's you.

*See her come in the front door in the green quilted coat that means she's
here for another extended visit; see her smile that tentative, tender, heart-
breakingly lovely smile and wonder why when we do love her, we do* LOVE
her, these encounters are always so hard.

Listen, my darlings, my colleagues, mes sembables, *past and future:*

*These visits are hard, but they're all we have of each other, me and you.
And as for the future?*

The future was only ever us.

    Therefore I let the other escapees go, in hopes of a happy outcome, but
as for me? I will spin out my story here.

    Listen, there's a new prisoner in the holding chamber, and I have sent
down word that there's an empty cell on the other side of mine and yes I
can already hear her speak:

    "Mom, for the time being can you pretend like you, like, don't know
me?"

    "Oh love my daughter, my past and my future."

    Anything for you. I can hardly wait to see her.

—1996

MOMMY NEAREST

"Don't hit my hand away!"

"Mo-o-m!" She is tying a fucking ribbon in my hair.

"Tammy, dammit, smile!" In spite of the bonding, Mom's teeth are turning yellow. After all, she's eighty-nine which sucks, because I'm only sixteen. But hey, she looks all buff in the string bikini, tan as a Moroccan camel saddle, your aggressive size four, check out the Universal Trainer biceps and oiled six pack abs. The woman is oiled like a piece of antique furniture, which is what she is, while I bob along the beach in pink like a captive balloon.

Smile? "No way!"

She keeps running at me with the bow ribbon. "Shh, they're watching. Hold still!" Welcome to my mom. Regard the tummy tucks, butt lifts, herbal body wraps, hair weave, botulism shots to chill the wrinkles, laser peels, the woman is a miracle of technology. Older than the Aztec gods and she hits the beach like Baywatch is in its first season and she is the new star. You know those prom corsages you smoosh into books and a hundred years later they're still there but they're all shriveled and flat? Well that's my mom. It is obscene.

I hiss back at her. "I don't care." I am yet another miracle of technology, about which more when I am feeling stronger. Right now I'm battling the hair ribbon. She keeps coming at me, moving her mouth like you do when you're trying to get a baby to swallow something it doesn't want. "Leave me *alone!*"

She wails, "After everything I've done for you!"

"You mean fucking done *to* me!" These *clothes*! Pink jellies and this fucking ruffled playsuit, way gross, and she is all, it's *slenderizing*, whatever that's supposed to mean. What it means is, I'm supposed to look twelve, which in pink candy stripes, I do. You know, one more magic appliance, like the lipo and implants and collagen. She's all, Accessorize. Like, check out your look—sequined headband, Mylar bikini, fat kid . . . The woman looks like Barbie on Ultra Slim Fast in the bikini, while I could be Mr.

Poppin' Fresh on steroids. Or Mrs. Poppin' Fresh, if there is a Mrs. Poppin' Fresh, one more part of her total look. "I hate these clothes!"

Her Sicilian Sunset mouth begins to tremble. "You look lovely."

"I look fat."

"Pleasingly plump."

"Fat!" I look like an albino watermelon, and she knows it too. I am clawing at the ruffles on my front. The ugly truth is Evelyn locks me in my room a lot, along with my old buddies Mrs. Fields and Ben&Jerry's and SaraLee to keep me fat, like if you don't have a waist you'll never grow up. See, if I do grow up, she has to get old. "I feel like fucking Gretel." I do not have to add that she looks like the witch.

"Shh," she says, because we are going by the Caribe Zanzibar Resort and there is a party going on, you know, audience. She wants them all pointing at us and smiling. *Oh look, young mama, doesn't she dress the little girl nice.* She is hissing, "They'll hear."

I get louder. "This is a sick playsuit. Only a sick mother would make a daughter wear a sick playsuit like this." I thwap the back of her thong bikini; any fool could see she is wearing Shape Shifters taped to her butt.

"Don't use that tone with me, not after . . ."

"Everything you did." I cut her off at the pass. "Don't start."

She starts anyway. "Doctors, clinics, pain. Everything I went through . . ." Well, what she went through was . . . Look, you know. It was in all the papers. On TV. M.O.W. "A Mother's Pride." These days geriatric moms are no big deal. Some babe my mother's age just popped triplets, but it was a very big deal at the time. I have the clipping laminated in my bedroom, to keep me straight.

SEVENTY-THREE YEAR OLD WOMAN BECOMES OLDEST FIRST-TIME MOM

No wonder she's always tired. *Don't bother me Tammy, I'm tired.* Say you're bored and she goes, *Shh Tammy, I'm lying down.* Or she sighs. *Tammy, why don't you go out and play?* By this she does not mean go out and ride around in cars plus I'm maybe too weird for guys to want to ride me around in cars, I mean, nobody else dresses like this. Nobody else's mom is, like, a hundred years old. Kids go "Are you adopted?" When I'm like, "No," they back off fast, like, the light bulb goes on. *"Oh, you're that Tammy."* Like it's creepy, which is what it is. *"Test tube Tammy. Ohhhhh."* Can you guess what they call me at school? "Turkey Baster Tammy" is another one. Oh right, ironic. The Sexy Sixties name. God, we haven't even had the Sixties in History. Our books don't go back that far.

The newspapers said my mom made a million on the rights to our story, which she did. The papers also said this scary thing. That these old bags had other motives, like, birthing a nurse for The Final Days? Like when they've fallen and their beeper doesn't beep us kids are screwed: *Help, I've fallen, and tag. You're it*!

No way! My mom isn't like that. She's the picture of fucking health!

You bet she is. Look, while we're standing here Evelyn has gone down the bill of complaints in full voice and she is winding up, "I did everything for you, and look!"

Something inside me snaps and I go, "No, you look. And then you can fucking go to hell." I start unbuttoning the playsuit. It's time she found out this is only padding and I'm skinny underneath. If I drop the playsuit the whole world will know which of us is young and sexy here, and which is the rack of chicken bones. But her face crumples up and I don't have the heart.

"Oh, Tammy." I expect her usual, but instead she sighs like she'll never take another breath. "I didn't ask for this."

"Well I sure as hell didn't ask for you!" Like a high school junior needs a mom with orthotics plus Odor Eaters overflowing her beach shoes and Ensure folded up in the Depends Adult Undergarments in her beach bag and a secret aluminum walker that she keeps stashed by her bed? I mean, having a baby at her age has gotta be disgusting. Like a thousand-year-old mummy having sex. Right out here in the open I go, "What were you *thinking*?"

"Shh," she says. "They'll hear." We are stalled in front of the Caribe Zanzibar. There are a zillion people on the deck. I am *not* smiling. Instead I hit her where she lives. Not to put too fine a point on it, she had me to stay young. The LaMaze classes must have been a hoot. She says, for the audience, "Oh honey, I *wanted* you!"

I snap, "Yeah, like you want a face lift that sticks."

"Don't!" She pulls down the RayBans so I will see that she is glaring. But it isn't quite the same. Things in her face are fighting with other things so the parts don't match. It is too weird.

I am afraid to ask, *Are you OK?* so I growl fondly, to buck her up. "You think you're so fucking cool." Which Evelyn isn't, you know? Especially not now. I am beginning to itch all over. It's like having one of those things festering underneath a band-aid that you're scared to peel it off and take a look at?

But I do. I step back. I study my too-tired go-out-and-play don't-bother-me-I'm-resting mother. Except for the ankle bracelet, which does *not* go with the antique jeweled Judith Leiber cockroach handbag or the retro

Rave rocket shoes with the toes cut out, she looks all right to me. I snarl, "Go on, say you wish you'd never had me. Go ahead."

This is phase one of the ritual fight, where we get down and duke it out. Then we can make up and go home and she will buy me things. First I have to get her so pissed that she snarls, "I've failed."

Here's how it's supposed to go. She starts with, "On top of everything, you ruined my figure. *Breast feeding*, it made me flat!" Not! Truth is, you can forget the silicone implants and the Breastalizers glued inside the top of the bikini. My mom will always look like a transsexual in the middle of the change. Then I yell and she goes, "You murdered your father, you ungrateful bitch." Which is not exactly true. He was a hundred when he died but she blames me ("You were too heavy for him"). I personally think it was the shock. Her pooping out a baby at her age. Besides, who says that was my real dad in the test tube anyway? The egg, she got from a surrogate baby ranch. *Darling, I got knocked up.* No wonder he died.

Evelyn is supposed to be yelling these things and I'm supposed to be snapping off witty rejoinders so we can finish and get home. Instead we're out here in the sand and it isn't happening. "Mom?"

She is just standing there.

I yell, "Are we fighting, or what?"

Moms, I will never understand them. Evelyn starts blinking like a bird that just ran into a power mower. Her mouth is going mwah. Mwah. Mway.

"I wasn't your baby," I tell her, trying to bring her back to planet earth. "I was just your second career."

It is definitely her turn. Her line is, "And I'm doing a damn good job!" Then she's supposed to finish me: "You're acting like a child!"

What in God's name did she expect? It sure as hell wasn't me. Like, she thought she would miraculously be forty, like the other moms in the tenth grade? We have Civil War statues in front of our high school that are younger than her. But she is distracted. I hiss, "This is when you say, *You're acting like a child* . . . Mom?"

Nothing. No way. Me and Evelyn are in stasis here. In front of the Caribe Zanzibar and I can't get her going, not even with pumped old men watching from the Tiki deck. I give her a little prod. You know, like, when you're in the middle of the last act of a play and the star has lost their place? I go, "And I made your life a living hell, right, Mom? Well, I'll tell you whose life is a living hell."

Then Evelyn whirls with this bizarre little kiss-me mouth that the collagen injections have plumped it up so you can hardly see the witch-wrinkles except where the lipstick bleeds up into the grooves and she spreads her hands like a child. "I know. Oh Mommy, I was bad."

You bet I am scared. "Mom!"

She sounds younger than me. "Mommy says it's against God." She is definitely getting weird. If we're going to survive here, we need to keep this fight on track. I go into attack mode. "You never had a mother, you were too old."

But instead of hitting me or throwing herself down on the redwood chaise with the black mattress emblazoned with *Caribe Zanzibar* in silver letters and going "I've failed" so we can quit and go home, Evelyn just sort of sinks down on her Shape Shifters(™) there in the sand and pulls her knees up under her chin and pats the sand and keeps patting the sand until I give in to something a lot scarier than gravity and sit down next to her. For a long time she doesn't speak. She has gone back inside herself like the witch on the weather house and what comes back out in the next revolution is somebody I don't know. She says, "Mama."

I try not to let her see that I am staring. Her face is sinking in to her skull in spite of the lipo and the laser touchups, dermabrasion, chemical peel. Her legs look like naked chicken skin and her knees are jittering. I say, "What's the matter?"

Then my mother scares me shit. She gives this silly little-girl giggle. "I lost my place."

My belly is bunching up in the horrible playsuit, or I think it is. Truth to tell, I'm a size eight under all this padding, but given the way things are going with my mom in this week before her 90th birthday, it seems safer to let her dream. I try, "So do you want to have our fight here, or go home or what?"

"Oh," she says. "Mother?"

Should I grab somebody's flip phone and dial 911 or what? "I'm not your mother!"

But she just goes, "Mama, have I been out in the sun too long? I know it's bad for my head. Should we go home now and can I have a lolly after my bath?"

Oh fuck, I think. She is having an attack of Alzheimer's. What am I going to do? "Wuow, Mom, you're sorry you ever had me. Remember?" Look, we can't go on like this. We are miles from the car. "Mother-daughter conflict, RIGHT?"

"I know you're scared I'll fall in love and go All the Way with some terrible boy." Her eyes are silvered over, burnt-out lightbulbs in some other continuum. She grabs my hand. "I promise, he won't touch me. I promise I'll be home by ten."

"Whoa," I say, but I am already wondering how I would look in her bikini, in case we keep regressing like this. Is this going to end up with us changing clothes and my mother going home in the ruffles, with me leading her by the hand? I bark, "Shape up! I am definitely not your mother. Evelyn! Do you know who I am?"

"Mama," she says in that girly voice, "I promise not to Do It until I'm married. And we won't have babies until after graduate school."

My God, I think. We're going through the Seven Ages of Mom. "Graduate school! You're a fucking full professor." Which she is. Retired.

"No, you're right, we should wait until I get tenure."

"Mom, you got the gold watch twenty years ago!"

"Tick," she says. "Tock. There goes the biological clock. Forget about Men with Paws, I'm having menopause!" She folds up and starts to cry.

"Oh, Mom!" I give her a little buck-up poke in the rib. "Hey look, you really showed them. You never had menopause, you had a kid!"

"My tubes are all twisted and dried."

"Baby? Remember?" I wiggle my fingers in front of her face but she won't focus. "Evelyn, you're a phenom! Name in all the papers, right? Natural childbirth, play group. You wrote a book!" I was so worried that I start to sing, "Tammy, Tammy, Tammy my lo-ho-hove"

Evelyn mumbles, "Medical breakthrough or medical mess?" I don't know if her head is back there in *then* or here in *now*. Are we in some odd transitional phase? Should I give into this and wipe her mouth, or smack her face to bring her back to now? She quavers. "Oh yes mother is embarrassed, my poor Mama is soooo mad at me!" Sand is getting in the Maalox circle inside those collagen lips.

"Would you please just quit regressing please? Mom?"

But she is sliding a different way. All of a sudden she turns into her mom. "Pregnant, Evelyn. At your age. It is disgusting."

Then she morphs back into the little girl. "Oh Mama, I made a big mistake!"

If she keeps on this way I'll never get her back. I've got to think fast. I roar: "*You* made a mistake. What about me? You think I wanted a hundred year old mom?" I rattle her shoulders, gotta try. I have to get her good and mad or she will sink into the sand here and fucking die. People have drifted over from other beach hotels to watch. "Mom. *Mom.*"

She just goes on in her mother's voice. "A baby, and at your age! You should be ashamed." Then she steps back into Evelyn, all girlish and embarrassed. "Oh Mommy, it was an accident."

"I'm not your mom!" Yes I am getting desperate. I shake her harder. I turn her so she'll see that there is an audience, "You're the fucking mother here, so *chill*."

Then she blinks a little and comes back to herself. Thank God. "Don't you dare use that tone with me," she says. "*Shh, they're watching*. After everything I've done for you."

Right on. I've got her going now. "Damn straight."

Her eyes flash, but only a little bit. She tries to get up, and can't. "They said I was crazy, wanting a baby."

That's more like it. Fine, Mom. Stay mad. "And they were right!" But she isn't moving so I rasp, "Now you're supposed to say you're sorry you had me, right? Right mom, right?"

"What? Sorry? Oh no!" Oh my gosh she looks at me and her eyes have cleared but I would swear to you that the middles have started spinning around. Then, it is so sweet and so scary, instead of going into the old I've-failed routine she says, "I went ahead and had you and I'm glad."

And something inside me goes, *squish*. This woman's present is my future and it is huge and terrifying. Mother. Daughter. God.

"Oh, honey." She is fixing to collapse into my arms. If I lose her now, this far from the car, I will never get her home. Adrenaline. We are going to do this on adrenaline. So I hiss, "Stand *up*. Don't faint or they'll think you're old."

That gets her, you bet. "Who, me? Old? I'm not old!"

"Shh. They're watching."

She whips her head around. They are. The clientele of the Caribe Zanzibar plus the Hilton and Fluorescent Gulls. Audience! "Oh," she says like a girl. "Oh. Oh!" She touches her hair.

Bingo. They are watching and she knows. I play her very carefully, like a fish you're scared to land. I bang on my ruffled front as if we have been arguing like normal. "Plus, I hate my fucking clothes!"

"Don't use that tone with me." She is getting mad.

I goad her a little bit more. "Why?"

"Because I said so." Spoken like a true mother. Cool.

"Because you *said* so?" I give her a push. "Like *you're* God?"

"No!" she says, and it does my heart good. She gets to her feet and she will stay on her feet as long as I can keep her fighting with me. "Like I'm the mother, and you're only a little girl!"

Way to go, Mom. "Like hell I am," I yell at her. Relief makes me incoherent. "This outfit sucks and you can go to hell!"

"OK, missy, I'm warning you." Evelyn grabs my arm. It hurts. I go, "Mom!" She is marching now, thump thump in the rocket shoes. Rage is making her loud. The whole beach has come out to see. She throws back her shoulders and shouts, for the audience. "OK, Missy. Watch out." Louder. Spotlight, music. *I'm ready for my closeup, Mr. DeMille.* Applause. Applause! Her wig bobs in the sunlight and striding along like that in the bikini with the Breastalizer inserts and Shape Shifters(™) bobbing every whichway, she is magnificent. "Or I'll unplug you from the Internet. And no dessert!"

I squint at her, to be sure the cure takes. Yup, she's up and running. Fine, I think, but I slip in the needle once more, in case. "Your dessert. You know what you can do with your dessert!"

"Shut up," she hisses because she knows what is coming. "They're watching."

Cool! I give her the finger and lay on one last infusion like rocket fuel. "You can take your dessert and shove it up your ass!"

So we are cool. On the strength of this one fight, we're good for at least a year. When we get home I'll let Evelyn spank me. After that we'll both cry and she'll make me sit on her lap. *My little girl.* Then she'll send me to bed. And I can go down the garage roof with my backpack and hitchhike over to the mall. By this time I've boosted enough cool clothes that I can just segue in and, like, mingle, I look so different that even the cute guys don't know it's me and if I slip up with one of these guys when we're rolling around in his car in the parking lot and I end up pregnant, hey, what'll we do? Evelyn won't even be mad. I'll have it but we'll say she did it and it will get her in all the papers, and hey, what retired professor about to be retired as a mom wouldn't want to start a third career?

—1997

WHOEVER

1.

No way could this Doris and Sam McDaniel be my real parents. I mean, look at me with the skinny wrists and ankles, coffee skin and fine black hair. Look at them.

No way. No way could I come from *this*.

Poor Sam and Doris are all, like, dead pink, like those pink plastic babies you get by the hundred down at K-Mart? Grey hair, legs like boiled hot dogs; soft, humongous butts. Mrs. QVC-queen-size-shopping queen says she's my mother, but how? She, like, waddles like Daffy in her Delta Burke crepe sole wedgies, and dumb? Doris thinks your electronic bulletin board is cork in a frame, that you stick messages on it with colored tacks. Don't-talk-like-that-to-your-father is smarter, *but*. Mr. Show-me-some-Respect goes out in short-sleeved white polyester shirts with the pocket protector?

Like the Mont Blanc ballpoint Sam got for 25 years of service in the software department at Digital is going to color his pocket black, or accidentally stab him in the chest.

They are like refrigerators. Big and white and square.

There's got to be some mistake. For I am *special*, whereas Sam and Doris are terminally *old* and way gross, just two more cogs on the treadmill to oblivion, that mysteriously got control of me. Treadmill to oblivion, that's cool, did I make it up?

Two, like, cogs? Or they were until the trial happened and we all got in the news.

Honor your father and mother, right?

Right. As soon as I find out who they really are.

I figure my real parents are, like, the last emperors of India? Bad guys conquer the palace. The queen bops over to Middletown, U.S.A. and hides her baby with this nice old peasant couple, right?

Ahah. Our enemies will never think to look for her here.

Unless my real folks are, like, deposed from some exploded planet like, Krypton? And I am, like, the long-lost daughter of somebody major, like, you know, Jorel and Ka-lel?

I am faster than a speeding bullet, I can leap you in a single bound.

When you don't belong, you're the first to know you don't belong. When my real mom and dad come back for me, everything will change.

I don't want you to think I'm not out there looking for them. Days I break into fat Sam's home computer and zap off on the Infobahn. I am all over with notes and clues, like: My real name isn't Susie McDaniel, you're looking at Electra/Cassandra/Layla you-name-it. Ring a bell? I describe the birthmark and the special baby bracelet? Like the emperors of India had to dump me here to save my life but they marked me so when I grew up I would know?

I zing around the noosphere like Hansel and Gretel, except instead of breadcrumbs I drop my secret electronic address, two symbols. Even you can reach me if you know.

Sam could die of old age before he finds my secret mailbox encoded on his system, it's hidden so deep that I and only I have the technology to log in. Forget Doris. She's scared of the computer. Like radiation will leak out and mutate your genes, as if she had any left. Sneaks in and sprays the IBM with Raid to get rid of bugs in the system, like they'll crawl up your legs and get in the food.

She's all, "I don't want you playing in there."

No problem. I have other ways of getting in touch. Nights I hang in on the back porch roof and throw my whole soul out into space. *Sending,* OK?

If you're out there and you hear me, YOU KNOW WHO YOU ARE.

No way do I belong on the planet Maple Shade Road in the Middletown system, stuffed in the units' idea of a cute sleeping capsule, beating up on Blue Teddy and sobbing my guts out on the ruffles while everybody I care about is hanging out at the mall.

I am stuck in here because of the fight.

It started because Sam and Doris are shitty to me, like, "Grounded, bla bla." "Can't go to the mall because you charge too much." "Clean up your room and stay away from that Duane guy, you're seeing him too much." *"Did you do that to your hair?"*

Doris's screaming like I am this axe murderer when all I did was charge a jacket at Companie Express.

I am pissed and yelling back when Sam comes in. He is, like, "What do you think you are, special?"

"Damn straight I'm special."

"Well I'll special you, miss Princess of the earth and air." For a fat guy too old to be a father, he can really yell. He is just starting, wuow. It is get-down ugly, all about how I never take off my Discman phones except to ask for money, and how I treat this Doris you-never-call-me-mommy like the maid. Plus I'm never nice to Grandma Horton, which is true. Grandma is definitely where all of Doris's fat genes came from. She hates me for I am skinny and therefore special, plus instead of kicking Doris into Weight Watchers Grandma Horton just sucks in her own stomach and buys my putative mom the flowered smocks in Godzilla plus. Grandma thinks keeping Doris fat makes her look smaller, which it does not, so I say so and Sam gets really pissed.

OK, one thing leads to another and I say something really shitty, never mind what, and Sam lets me have it with his belt.

No way am I going to let the peasants see me cry. I push them out and while they are banging on my door and going "We didn't mean it," I snake out on the porch roof.

Then I spin out into the dark and silence, and SEND. If I concentrate, if I can just locate the chosen blank spot between stars and *throw*, I feel like I can astrally project. So if my real mom and dad the deposed emperors of everywhere are out there, AND I KNOW YOU'RE OUT THERE, they'll get my signal and home in.

This is what I am beaming: Mmmmmmmaaaaaaamaaaaa.

You want to know what's weird? I think I hear something back. I am totally into it, but then Stephanie and Patty and Gert and Tiffany come by on the way to the mall in these cool Dayglo vests. I'm like, hanging over the edge. "Where'd you get those?"

"Peepers."

I want one too. But I am on the roof.

They're like: "What are you up there, Tom Sawyer or something?"

I'm all, "What do you, think Tom Sawyer whitewashes roofs?" Then Tiffany goes, "I saw Duane and them heading for Victoria's Secretions."

Duane. He looks just like Dylan, OK? I jump down. "Let's go."

Why should I get all bent waiting on the mom from nowhere when I might run into cute Billy or sexy Duane down at the mall?

Which is how I get caught crunching the hedge on my way out and why-can't-you-be-like-other-girls-and-call-me-Daddy nails a grate over the bedroom window and shuts me in. "No supper for you."

Like I want their rotten supper?

"You eat it," I growl. It will be rutabaga. "Serve you right."

Then Doris comes into my room, bad cop, good cop, she's supposed to play best friend. "Oh Susie, why can't you be like other girls?"

And I'm all, "Fuck you, mother, I am not like all other girls." I spare her the rest. *For I am better.* I know it, deep in the fine bones in my slender ankles. I am the queen.

Her fat face crumples. "At least you could try."

"I don't want to be like other girls." I kite a CD at her like a ninja throwing blade.

She ducks. "At least you could be nice to me." It lodges in the wall behind her head.

"Name one reason." I zing another.

Zap. "Because you're our *daughter.*"

So I let her have it. "Oh no I'm not."

Surprise. This doesn't nail her like I expect. She doesn't cry. Instead fat Mrs. Call-me-mother takes three heavy steps backward like stops on the train to a place you don't want to get to.

Then my God, her voice comes hurtling out of a tunnel, all black wind. "How did you find out?"

This squeezes me dry. "Say *what?*"

But she doesn't hear my silence. She's too wound up. "Your dad and me, we worked so hard to get you and now . . ." She is driven to distraction. Mrs. claims-she's-my-mother is shuffling through my candy wrapper collection like it contains secret letters that if she can just put them together this will make sense. Tears glubble up. "Now you won't even speak to me."

Now, when it is too late, she cries. I am focused on what she has just dropped, like By the Way. I speak to her all right, I am all over her. "*What do you mean you worked so hard to get me?*"

"We wanted kids so *much.*" She sounds so ashamed. "When we got around to it we were too old." Doris's voice squeezes out. "Everything was all dried up."

"So. What? Am I a black market baby or what?" Right, I am really a Brazilian princess, S. and E. embezzled many hundreds of K off Digital to buy me from the palace maid.

Doris just buries her chins in the stripes she thinks are slenderizing and won't face me. She squeaks. "You know."

I don't, really.

By this time she can hardly get the words out. "Sperm bank." *Gasp.* "Surrogate mom." *Glub glub choke struggle.* But she sounds happy, happy! *Gulp strangle.* At last she produces it. "You."

I am coming at this carefully, and slow. "What?"

She's all: *gack*. "It cost a fortune, but . . ."

"Gross!"

"I wasn't going to tell you, all the books say not to, but now . . ." Oh boy she is taking in so much air that she is getting bigger. In a minute the Ivana Trump pearls are going to pop right off her neck and Doris will start to float. "The. Ah. Woman said she was only doing it because she loves to help people but now . . ."

I am shouting. "WHAT WOMAN?"

"Your. Ah. Surrogate mom." She just lofts this grenade without looking to see where it hits.

What do you mean, *mom*? The grenade rolls into a corner of my heart.

"She's gone to court." Deep sob. "She wants . . ."

Ka-BLAM. "I have a *mother*?" I lose it altogether. I grab her and dig in with all ten fingers. "What? She wants *what*?"

Finally the words fall out of her. "She wants you back."

So I drop her. "Wuoow." This is big. It is like an invitation, right? Doris lays where I put her, looking up at me with those big old milky mother-eyes, so totally by accident I'm like, "Oh, Mom."

Mistake. She bobs up like an inflatable clown with this awful, eager smile. "You called me mom!"

"Yeah but I didn't mean it," I say.

2.

It turns out one reason Sam and Doris hated me going malling is Duane but the other is money. They're are paying so many lawyers that they're broke. See this surrogate mom figured out that I'm the only kid she'll ever have now that her biological clock has struck midnight. She says I'm hers and she's hired lawyers to get me back.

Until *Inside Edition* kicks in with a payoff and *Current Affair* comes up with a counter offer, which is as soon as I get on Oprah, we are practically on food stamps. Forget *Hard Copy*, the surrogate mom has them sewed up, she and her new man Burt are the top of the show all week, "Mother love laughs at lawyers," you know. I'd love to watch her on TV but to protect the innocent they call her Mrs. X and moosh her face behind an electronic grid.

Like, do I have her eyes?

I get the units together for a conference in the living room. I am ready to tear them up in little pieces and feed them to the Dispos-al. They have this William Wurbelow present. Esquire. Sam is like, "After all sweetheart, he is your lawyer."

"Speak for yourself, white man." Then I let them have it. "I've got a real mother and you didn't tell me?"

But they're all, "We thought we were protecting you."

"A real mother and you're *protecting* me?"

"Birth mother."

"And you keep it secret that she wants me back?"

"It's for the best," the lawyer says.

"We're your parents now."

"Really," Sam says. "Clean break. It's the only way. It says so in all the parenting books."

"You learned how to do this from a book!"

Doris's eyes fill up. "They came in the basket when we adopted you. You're legally ours."

"Yours!" I look at these two and what I feel is, I feel relieved. Like I could possibly come out of these *lumpy people*. Old and slow and heavy, like a retard could of made them, out of flour and mud? I go, "No way!"

Doris sobs.

I grab this Wurbelow esquire by his Save the Whales tie. I start twisting and I growl, "What's her name?"

He just kind of strangles and won't answer.

I twist the tie some more. "I said, what is her name?"

I think he gurgles, "Loretta."

Truth? I don't believe him. No way has my mom the empress got a hick name like Loretta. Something's wrong here, OK? I give his tie another twist.

I have a real mother somewhere; I always knew it. We need to meet. I have to look her in the face.

He is turning a funny color. One more twist and he will be all out of breath. Sam grabs my elbow, hard. "Don't," he says.

"Out of my face, I am Princess Leia."

Sam goes, "You're too young."

Doris groans. "Oh God."

The lawyer is gagging. I wrench the tie some more.

Sam jerks my hands off. "I said, don't."

If I hurt the lawyer he may walk out on us so I stop. Old Sam uses spit to rub the smudges off his pocket protector and even though he isn't sure he has my attention he says something that I am too weirded out to take in completely at the time. "This Loretta Huggins isn't the real mother, believe us. She's only the host."

I am filing the name for future reference. I say, "The *host!*" Not-my-mother looks at me and blushes. That terrible shame! Doris's voice drops to a whisper. "We wanted a baby so much. We were desperate."

"Oh shit." I look at Sam. I look at her and I think about ugly things like petri dishes and turkey basters, I think about kids growing up in jars and I think it is pretty disgusting. It's like finding out your parents got you by having sex and they might still be having it. No. It's like finding out your parents got you by having sex and they even *liked* it, way grotesque.

I've got whitewater crazies crashing behind my eyes.

The whole thing is so revolting that I run upstairs. I'm ready to york them into the toilet. Sam. Doris. William Wurbelow Esquire.

They yell after me, "Don't worry, we're going to fight this."

"Don't bother," I yell.

Asshole Doris is going, "Don't worry, she's just upset."

And me? I pry off the grate and roll out on the roof. I am in such an altered state that if I astrally project I might just astrally get there. Except the Action News van is in our driveway and News Eight is trying to look inconspicuous in the Otto the Orkin Man truck parked across the street. So I sneak into Sam's computer and hurl myself on the Infobahn, but my e-mail is junked up with flames, plus nasty questions from every hacker in the infosphere because while I wasn't looking we got on the news.

We are pretty much on worldwide TV. This surrogate mom Loretta is on a lot, but all I see is electronic squares. All I know is what I read in the papers, and what I read is this. Poor little Susie/Melissa is being deprived of her natural birth mother, which is a violation of mothers' rights everywhere, on account of Sam and Doris gave Loretta not much money to play cow and now that poor, exploited Loretta is married to a nice man, she wants her baby back.

Melissa! Cool name. But wait. Sam and Doris claim I am being ripped out of my chosen family that gives me everything by a paid brood mare who could care less. Like, this fine upscale Route 128 split-level couple has given up the world for me, and now . . .

Like I chose them?

Who asked *me* who I wanted to be? Plus something about the whole thing is *not right*; what can I say? Stuff they aren't saying. Stuff Doris at her most desperate won't tell.

So I go out on the roof at midnight and in spite of the floods trained on the house in case of late-breaking news, I start, and, weird! It's dark out there and dense, like a zillion black holes all linked and shifting like the nap on velvet. I am sending into a silence so deep that even you can feel it, and you know what?

MMmm. Maybe I am getting something back.

Then, the last night before we go to court?

I am out there, I've been out there for hours. The news guys have wrung the last word out of us and packed up and gone home. Wurbelow is leaving. Sam and Doris have run out of tears, and me? I am wired to the eyeballs and the fingernails, vibrating in every synapse and all visible and invisible connections, I am on the verge and I could swear to you that something or somebody out there is receiving.

I feel particles of the universe dislodging and reassembling. Something large is stirring out there and I could swear to you that light years removed as it is, whatever it is, it's waking, huge and ponderous, and. Say *what*? It's starting out.

But there's this racket in the yard below, giggling and disruption and then I hear, like, "So, are you coming or what?"

"I'm busy." *Something moving.* Excited and scared. Should I wait for it to reach me or should I call Geraldo or e-mail NASA or what?

"Like, are you too good for us?" It's Stephanie and Gert, Patty and Tiffany. They have on cool earrings and incredible boots and I have not been shopping for days. I've been so tied up with being on TV and all that I am out of touch.

Homing in on me.

"So what are we, supposed to tell Duane that you don't want to sit with him?"

Wuoow. I'm like, "Duane!"

Tiffany goes, "If you don't want him, I do." Some friends. Like they care if I'm famous, they don't even care if I belong to Sam and Doris or the empress. Like Tiffany cares if I love Duane.

Stephanie is a real friend, she goes, "Come on. It's ROCKY HORROR retronight."

"No way!"

"Way."

Think about it. Stephanie and Tiffany and all, plus *sexy* Duane plus Billy, you name it, us in black and white makeup and loaded with toast and rice, girls, boys, everybody jumbled in the dark until you can't tell whose hands are whose, or where. "Wait up."

As I skid down the stairs and bomb out into the cool world I hear the lawyer going, "Don't worry, tomorrow we go before the judge." You would think he was cheering old Sam and Doris up instead of signing their death knell. "Wherein I've earned my money. Judge Murtaugh has agreed to let your daughter choose."

3.

So. What. This Loretta doesn't look like the empress, but at least she isn't way old like Doris, and our shapes match? She's, like, taller, plus the not fat. In the courtroom Sam and Doris are crying and I'm like: should I, shouldn't I, but hey, Loretta promised never to ground me, plus I get a free ride to wherever because the Birth Mother and her cute new husband that's so *way* younger love Burger Chef and line dancing and hanging out at the mall.

I don't know, at the time Loretta and Burt Huggins looked OK, like cool in the tight jeans and concha belts and the genuine python boots with matching shanks, my kind of people, right? With a good eye for merchandise, like way judicious, catalogs *plus* malls. Burt is way nice to me and Loretta has great hair. It's cool to have a mom that you don't have to put a bag over her head to keep your cool friends from thinking you're a dweeb.

But, hey. A., they are not on line. Burt doesn't even know where that is, that's two. So I, like, have to get back on the Infobahn, but if I turn up at Sam's and try to log in now, he and Doris will catch me and start slobbering and beg me to come back after I had to lie and everything to get away.

They came to the McDaniels' to bring me and my things to their neat condo with the swimming pool? They came in the copper flake van with western sunsets in the back windows and the horseshoe motif, and the wire wheels were cool. The new Watchman was cool and the way this Loretta fitted her hip against mine in the studded jeans like we were kid friends at the mall instead of mother-daughter, that was cool, but on the sidewalk behind us Doris and Sam, they just bummed me out. They brought me home from the hospital fourteen years ago and cleaned up the vomit and bought me frilly bedspreads and there they were waving and trying to be brave and I felt shitty, plus as the strobes flashed and we rode away I felt this faint, like, sound way back somewhere inside of me? Ka-*ping*.

And this is what flashed across the front of my mind like an LCD display as I rode out of Sam and Doris's life forever except for alternate weekends and every other Christmas and two weeks every summer to be negotiated on a situational basis:

How are they ever going to find you now?

And *Duane*. My gosh he's running along and jumping up to see in the van window plus Stephanie and Billy and them are bobbing behind so I'm. I'm yelling, loud, "Scooby's!" so I won't get lost from them. Which isn't what I'm really scared of getting lost from. It's whatever I felt stirring out there in the big black universe, last night on the roof. It is sad when we drive away.

But Burt is winking at me and Loretta is half-strangling me, mooshing my face close to show the cameras we are happy, *happy* together and Judge Murtaugh and *Hard Copy* were right, and all my teeth itch because at the back of my heart I hear: ka-*ping*.

I have to get to the condo roof so I can *send*.

Plus, I need to find the sperm bank? Like, I have to find out what Kryptonites and Nobel prizewinners made deposits there on a certain date because I did not come from cheesy Loretta, no way.

It's twelve o'clock. Do you know where your mother is?

So I'm still waiting on them. My real mom and dad, Obi Wan or Jor-el and the empress of India or queen of the stars, but meanwhile me and the Hugginses are rolling away from Maple Shade forever and I'm like, WAIT!

And this Loretta is going, "Cool! We meet with the TV producers about me playing *me* in our life story right after Burger King, so how about you call me Mommy for now?" So it turns out she wanted me back just to wedge her into show business. It sucks.

I am already thinking, At least nice old Sam and nice dumb Doris, they really wanted me for me.

So it turns out that B. is, where you get to doesn't always turn out to be where you really wanted to go?

4.

Here's weird. It isn't just old Sam and Doris calling me on the Totalphone, we talk late at night while Burt and Loretta are out bopping at Fuddruckers, Sam and Doris fight over the receiver and take turns asking me how am I really and sometimes we cry on the phone. But that isn't the weird part.

I am hearing from somebody else.

Late at night after they come in and way early, while they're still snoring in their purple sleep masks and matching satin briefs, I hear these odd noises in the, like, purple bathroom? I was in there scoping all the drug names on the bottles in their medicine chest, looking for stuff that you snort or lick to make you feel good, but all I found was goldflake nail polish and Grecian formula in his color so even though he's cute and he flirts as good as Duane, Burt is older than you think.

And then. This is so weird! At first I thought it was bad plumbing. Sit on the lavender shag puffy seat on the purple toilet and you hear a voice like, spiraling? Like it is seeping out of somewhere near the purple bathmat under the purple sink. I can't make out it but it makes my individual hairs crawl.

Whatever, or whoever, going, *MMMMMmmm. MMMmm*, naming all the best things you can dream of or hope for or imagine, but is it fixing to come out or asking me in?

I can't be in there with it another second but I can't stay away either, because the voice or transmission—whatever! It's just about to come clear, like in the second after next I am going to make out what it says.

Who knows how it found me, since I haven't been sending at all. I've been too distracted. It's enough already, trying to keep up with my old friends when I'm stuck in a tough new school where I'm scared to go to the bathroom until I get home. Plus this Loretta threw away my cool clothes, I have to wear these Laura Ashley flowers because she is the babe here, whereas I, the true and beautiful Princess call-me-Leia, She-ra, Red Sonya, am only a little girl. She says I'm already too old play me in the TV version of my life story which we will get paid for as soon as her people OK the deal memo and we get the commitment from Home Box.

Plus she's like, "Susie, I don't want this Duane around."

"Hey wait. You said my real name is Melissa."

"Oh, that." Loretta snorts a line. "I made that up for the judge. And listen. No boyfriends. It makes me look old." Plus, Laura Ashley and patent leather shoes! Plus I'm not allowed to go out. So I'm like, oh shit, you go all the way to court to change moms and end up worse than Sam and Doris. Like, this mom totally sucks.

Like I don't have enough problems, Burt comes on to me under the condo pool lights and Loretta gets pissed. After all, he did call me Melissa, plus promising me red glitter boots.

So Loretta and me tangle in the purple bathroom, where I am heading in case, not knowing they had words and Burt took off and left Loretta behind. She's in there sobbing out her guts.

"Oh shit."

She looks daggers at me from the toilet where she is sitting on the lavender puff but she's cool. All she says is, "Go away."

So I try to be nice. I am all There there. Like Doris when Duane was mean to me. "Don't feel bad. Even the best guys need a little space sometimes."

"What are you, trying to make me feel good?"

What am I? Trying to get her out of the bathroom so I can listen for the voice underneath the sink. I give the speech that Sam and Doris bought from the marriage counselor. A thousand bucks and it's all they got. "You have to grab the day and live your life."

Don't ask why this freaks her. Loretta is like, "That's fine for you to say, you're only a kid, whereas I am on the sunset trail." Then she lets me have it. "Homewrecker!"

So I'm, "Fuck you, I'm only fourteen years old."

"Going on thirty."

"That's a cliché." Then I really piss her off. "Be nice or I'll go back to my real mother."

Then boy does she burn me past the fingertips and right on down to the second knuckles. "Mother. Fuck that shit. You don't even know who your real mother is."

"Doris, at this point. Like, she brought me up. She took care of me." My head is kind of clicking in one direction. Soon it will make a full circle on my neck. "All you did was pop the egg."

"Boy," she says, "boy are you dumb." Behind her there are faint noises rising: *MMMMMMmmmm* and getting louder. *MMMMMMMMmmmmm*. The words surge up from deep memory: "*She's only the host.*"

MMMMMMMMMMM.

I'm like, Say *what?*

But she is yelling. "You think they waste bankable sperm on old bags like me? Not when they've got your rock stars and Nobel prize guys to sell rich clients. Brain surgeons. Poet laureates." She pats her pelvis. "Good stuff like that, they pay to get it shoved in on top of solid gold."

The quarter drops. The news rolls out like a buy out of a ball gum machine. "You're not even my . . ."

"Surrogate mom. I did the deed, I didn't pop the egg."

Wuoow. I don't know how this makes me feel.

"Truth is, I'd be ashamed to pop an egg that turned out a rotten kid like you." She pushes me down on the lavender puff. "Now you sit here and think about that for a while." She slams out and locks me in. Through the door I hear her going, "If you knew where the egg came from you would puke. Think about it." She kicks the door: Wham! She kicks it so hard I know the life story deal isn't working out. "You think about it good." Then she yells for good and all, "And keep your sticky hands off Burt."

And all the time the noises are surrounding me like angels trying to scoop me up and fly me off to someplace better; the buzz is getting louder and I don't know why it makes my nose itch and all the back hairs on my neck crawl. *MMMMMMMMMMMMMMMM*.

So. What. I speculate. Space shuttle disaster descendent, look, I could be. Or pilfered off one of the Kennedy women or even Lady Di. Or. What. *MMMMMMMMmmmmmmmmmm*. The daughter of the empress for real. It comes to me that I have been thinking too small.

MMMMmmmm. I ammmmmmm. . . .

The daughter of something grand out there.

She may be the queen of space.

The *mmmmmmmmmm* keeps rising until I can't hear anything else and then I understand that all this time, ever since I first started *sending*, she's been hurtling my way. All this time I've been trapped in here with Burt and Loretta she has been shimmering outside, waiting for me to crunch through the last barrier.

"Mommy!" I cry and close my eyes against her huge beauty. I sink to the floor underneath the toilet, fully expecting what I most want to come flooding in. Across town Doris sits up in the night and goes: *You called?*

Outside the door, Loretta goes, "You called?"

I yell at her. "Not you, asshole."

"What's going on in there?"

Then this huge, sweet voice kind of wraps me up in itself. *I've been here the whole time, sweetheart.* It isn't exactly speech.

Loretta is like, "Kid, Kid!"

So I off her. "Shut up, you're only the host."

MMMMMMMMmmmmmmm . . . Wraps around me and curls tight and is all, *I thought you'd never call.*

I open one eye. Mmmmm . . . om? She's there but she isn't there. Like, I know she's there but I can't see her? *Mommy.* I'm like, "I don't suppose you'd get rid of this Loretta for me."

She goes, *Not like you want.*

Loretta's broken the key off in the lock and is wrenching the door handle. So I'm, "If you love me you'll get rid of her."

But she's like, *No way. I have retained a lawyer.*

So *weird!* —I hear her but no way can I see. "Your voice!" It is so *beautiful.*
We'll settle this the right way. In court.

I can feel it. She's about to lift and go.

"And you'll love me and take me to the mall and everything?" But she is lifting out of my presence. *After all, I am your mother.* I either do or don't hear a *whoosh.* It doesn't matter. She's just as gone.

5.

Which as much as anything is how me and raunchy Burt and old Loretta and lumpy Sam and Doris and the new mom with the beautiful voice that I think of as The Mother from Space — how all of us contenders plus Patty and Stephanie and all, like Tiffany, who is fucking holding hands with Duane, all end up in a shootout in the federal courtroom back in front of Judge Murtaugh, who keeps scratching his head and squinting at me because like me, he thought he was right but now he's wrong and if he isn't right, he can't for the life of him figure out what the right thing is.

The judge may not know, but I do. When you are a, like, totally *special* person like me, there's got to be an explanation, e.g., God came down and went: *Voila.*

Except if this is going to be so good why do I feel so bad?

The space mother is here but I can't see her is one thing. She's testifying via closed-circuit TV and instead of electronic squares covering her face to protect the innocent, they are filling the entire screen. Mostly purple squares, CNN can't explain it, and you want to know what weird is? Weird is, nobody knows where's she's transmitting from, only that she is being beamed in. And another batch of weird? Even when she isn't talking I can hear her voice inside, vibrating all the way down to where my soul hides, song without any words that I know, and there's noplace I can hide from her or blot it out, the Mother from Space going *MMMMMmmmmmmmm.*

William Wurbelow, Esquire is there for Sam and Doris, and for Loretta, *Hard Copy* has sprung for Vincent Bugliosi *and* Alan Dershowitz, who's already on Chapter Two of his book about us. The Mother from Space has the entire law office of Deveboise, Plimpton and somebody, and you want to know what else is weird? They've never seen her either, she communicates by fax and e-mail, cool!

It turns out there is nobody here for me.

I can't even sit with Patty and them, you know, my friends? Tiffany and Duane with his sweet eyes and that dirty grin.

We are like stuck listening to the lawyers talk lawyer, bla tort bla, while my friends giggle safe in the back and I am stuck up front freaking because

Tiffany is all over Duane. It is revolting, she's got her tongue in his ear. Like I don't see? I could die up here in the Laura Ashley dress except every once in a while I catch Duane looking at me over Tiffany's shoulder with this grin.

After a while the contenders get to testify and I'm listening to nice old Sam go on and on and on while Doris sniffles and I want to reach out and touch someone but I am totally bored, plus in the heat of the fight Loretta said this *amazing thing* to me about shoveling the Nobel prizewinner in on top of pure gold.

Pure gold! So the whole time she's testifying about natural law and property rights I'm like hey, I am not your pedigreed rottweiler, I am a *princess*. And the queen has come to take me back. If Loretta's the host, I want to hear from the guest. Except that even though the Mother from Space is shimmering behind the electronic grid up there on the screen, the lawyers do all the talking. "Plant a garden," Mr. Deveboise or Mr. Plimpton says, asserting her rights, "and the crop is yours."

Here they are chasing each other around the block about nature versus nurture when I don't even know what nurture is.

So partly I am bored but I'm also frustrated listening to all this N. vs. N. this, divine right of mothers that; after a while even though eight lawyers are begging me to chill I raise my hand.

So, cool! Judge Murtaugh calls on me.

I'm like, "Don't you guys care what I think?"

The judge is all, "We heard what you think six months ago and here we are back again in the same old story in the same old place."

"I didn't know what I was doing, OK?" I'm looking at Sam and Doris with their big hands and soft mouths and their wet eyes, oh wow they are so totally in love with me. I can see them going, *Way* and I am thinking, They would never let me go out with Duane, they don't approve of Duane. So I have to go: Sigh. No way. Then I look at Burt and Loretta and I'm all, boy, copper flake vans and purple everything totally a prison make, plus even though The Mother from Space is not present I can hear her: MMMMM-MMMMMmmmmmmmm, that fills me up with promises of love and everything I ever want.

It is like, an inspiration.

The words come into my mind. "I didn't know what I was doing when I asked to go with Loretta, but now I really know, OK?"

The judge is like, "Are you sure?"

"Here's how sure I am. I totally swear that whatever I say this time, until the end of the world, *that's it*."

The judge gives me this look. "For good and all?"

So maybe it's a mistake but I'm getting this *MMMMMmmmmmMM-MMM* louder and louder *MMM* it's so loud now that I know this is what I've got to do. Besides, the judge has pushed me to it. Like, he thinks I'm too young and stupid to know? "Whatever it takes!"

"You swear?"

I shout so loud that the space mother can definitely hear me. Wherever she is. "I swear. I'll sign a paper. I make up my mind for good and all and everybody promises to be OK with it. Right here on worldwide TV." I yell at Judge Murtaugh. "Are you OK with that?"

He's like, "If that's what you want." He is trying to sound judicious but I see his sad eyes. What he's really like is, he's like: *It's your funeral.*

"Well, it's what I want."

Every square in the electronic grid wriggles in a different color purple. *MMMM mmm.*

I'm thinking the space mother has got to be beautiful. I'm thinking she'll take me out and buy me things and she'll really really love Duane, and in the back of my mind somewhere I am listening and what I think I hear is her going, *I will reallyreally love Duane* so I go on quick, before the judge can change his mind.

"It's what I really, really want." I grin straight into the cameras. I yell. "This is it, OK? It's, like, my final vow."

Loretta is way pissed. Sam and Doris are crying like lost causes and all I can hear inside my head is *MMMMMMMMMMMMMMMM* so right there in front of the world I do it, I give myself over to my real mother the empress of Everything and it feels right, inside I am all squashy like, Knock me Over and wham, crash, they get it typed and rubber stamped and in front of everybody I sign the thing.

You'd be amazed at how fast a court can get out a decree.

And just as I am making a circle over the I in my new name which I have decided is going to be *She-Leia*, I hear Don Pardoe, who doesn't work for E.T., going, "And now by special arrangement, live, *Entertainment Tonight* brings you the *long-awaited reunion* between long-lost space mother and natural child . . ."

And the door behind the judge's bench flies open and she comes out.

A lot of people scream.

So there she is, and gag me, she is purple, and wuoow, there are tentacles, if you thought Doris was fat, next to this Doris is Princess Slenderella, big fluorescent green belly, freak me out!

But *Inside Edition* and *Hard Copy* are watching, plus *C-Span* and *Current Affair* to say nothing of the program that brought about this meeting, like, I have obligations to *Entertainment Tonight*. Plus I have sworn to the court that this time it's forever, and *MMMMMMmmm* she is yearning at me with all those tentacles and if I have a problem with this I am way late saying it so I go: "Wuow."

And the space mother goes, "Hey." Then she goes: "Where did you get that awful flowered dress?"

So the deed is done for good right there in front of all of you and I don't know what's next or even if the space mother is going to let me stay in Middletown where my friends are and you can still get to the mall? But for a start she really wants me and at least she likes Duane, and like it or not she and I are now legally bonded and if Doris runs out of the courtroom crying because she can't bear this and poor old Sam runs after her because he can't bear to see the last of me which has already been negotiated and stamped and sealed in the new court papers, it's way sad.

But not as sad as the part of me that nobody can see that goes running out after them?

All this trouble and all this, like, *looking* for her and this is me smoothing my hair and trying to smile and twitching because I am kind of moving into the space mother's creepy tentacles because it is expected while Sam and Doris are running out.

OK, my heart is running right out the door after them going, *Mommy, Daddy, wait!*

—1996

UNIVERSITY PRESS OF NEW ENGLAND

published books under its own imprint and is the publisher for Brandeis University Press, Dartmouth College, Middlebury College Press, University of New Hampshire, Tufts University, and Wesleyan University Press.

ABOUT THE AUTHOR

Kit Reed is an Adjunct Professor of English at Wesleyan University. Her twelve novels include *Captain Grownup, Catholic Girls, Little Sisters of the Apocalypse,* and her newest *J. Eden.* She is a Guggenheim fellow and the first American recipient of a five-year literary grant from the Abraham Woursell Foundation. In SF, she has published three short story collections and the novels *Armed Camps, Magic Time, Fort Privilege,* and *Little Sisters of the Apocalypse,* a finalist for the Tiptree prize. "Whoever," the next-to-last short story she read in the New York Review of Science Fiction's series at Dixon Place this year, appeared recently in *Asimov's SF,* and "Mommy Nearest," which she read at Dixon Place this year, is forthcoming in *The Magazine of Fantasy and Science Fiction.* "The Singing Marine" was a short story nominee at the 1996 World Fantasy Convention.

LIBRARY OF CONGRESS CATALOGING-IN-PUBLICATION DATA

Reed, Kit.
Weird women, wired women / by Kit Reed.
p. cm.
ISBN 0–8195–2254–6 (cl : alk. paper). — ISBN 0–8195–2255–4 (pa : alk. paper)
I. Title.
PS3568.E367W45 1998
813'.54—dc21   97–43287